1943

Bliss Turner— An English civilian. Young, attractive and very vulnerable. She fell in love the night she met Paul Carmichael. Her life was never the same again.

Paul Carmichael— An American pilot. Blond, blue-eyed and cocky. He found the love of his life in Cornwall, but had to leave her behind. He regretted it until the day he died.

1995

Simon Flynn— Paul Carmichael's grandson. He's come to England to uncover the truth behind his grandfather's past. The last thing he expects is to follow in Paul's footsteps.

Rebecca Penberthy— Bliss Turner's granddaughter. She's curious about the blue-eyed American who's come to Penmorten asking about her grandmother. And attracted to him. Until she finds out they *might* be related....

Dear Reader,

I've always been fascinated by wartime romances. The knowledge that something terrible might happen, the inevitable partings, the constant stress add intensity and urgency to any relationship.

I experienced some of this when I met the man who was to become my husband, though our meeting took place many years after World War II. Jim was in the American Air Force, based in England for only three months, and I was an English working girl. We could see each other only on weekends. As if that didn't create enough stress, Jim was on his way to Japan for two years and as we didn't want to rush into marriage, we decided to wait. "It won't work," all my friends told me. "He'll find someone else." But he didn't. And we were married and lived happily ever after.

Exactly how did we meet? I'm glad you asked. For the answer, read *As Years Go By*. Paul Carmichael's meeting with Bliss Turner is *our* meeting—even down to the dialogue. I had just returned from Cornwall, there was a birthday party, I was tanned, Jim asked me where I'd found the sun and we fell in love almost immediately. To research *As Years Go By*, we went together to Cornwall a couple of years ago. Some of the experiences we had on this trip also found their way into the story.

I hope you'll enjoy reading this book as much as Jim and I enjoyed living parts of it.

Margaret Chittenden

Margaret Chittenden

AS YEARS GO BY

Harlequin Books

TORONTO • NEW YORK • LONDON
AMSTERDAM • PARIS • SYDNEY • HAMBURG
STOCKHOLM • ATHENS • TOKYO • MILAN
MADRID • WARSAW • BUDAPEST • AUCKLAND

ISBN 0-373-70666-9

AS YEARS GO BY

Copyright © 1995 Margaret Chittenden.

This edition published by arrangement with Harlequin Books S.A.

® and TM are trademarks of the publisher. Trademarks indicated with
® are registered in the United States Patent and Trademark Office, the
Canadian Trade Marks Office and in other countries.

Printed in U.S.A.

ABOUT THE AUTHOR

Margaret Chittenden has been writing nine to five, five days a week, for twenty-four years. During that time, she has published various short stories and articles, three children's books and twenty-three novels. This prolific author has won several awards, including the Pacific Northwest Writers Achievement Award, and was nominated for The Romance Writers of America's Lifetime Achievement Award. Originally from England, Margaret now lives in Ocean Shores, Washington, where she spends her time writing not only fiction but books and articles about the craft of writing. She's also a popular speaker at writers' conferences all over the country.

For all the "Yanks" who went "over there"
and for the women who came back with them.

CHAPTER ONE

STARTLED, SIMON LOOKED UP from the newspaper article he was reading. "Grandfather Paul had a *what?*"

His mother, Elizabeth Carmichael Flynn, known to everyone as Libby, was stretched out on his father's favorite, formerly despised recliner, an ice pack clutched to her injured rib cage. With her fair hair and skin and athletic, slender body, she didn't look at all her fifty-three years, Simon thought distractedly. And her blue eyes were a lot like Paul's had been—only much warmer.

Simon had inherited Paul's vivid blue eyes, too, but his craggy face, tough-looking physique and unruly black hair were due to his father's Irish genes.

"Your grandfather Paul had an affair with an Englishwoman during World War II," Libby repeated patiently.

She was sitting with Simon in the master bedroom suite of the huge old Colonial house she shared with her husband, Brandon, in Seattle's Queen Anne Hill district. As usual, Brandon was absent. A hard-driving, dedicated, one might say obsessed, professional golfer, Simon's father had recently flown off to Augusta, Georgia, to compete in the Masters tournament. It was generally agreed that he was a shoo-in to win the coveted green jacket.

Brandon had met Libby while she was watching her mother take part in a women's golf tournament. He'd thought a female golfer's daughter would make a tolerant wife for a golfing-obsessed male. He'd been right.

Setting the newspaper down on a nearby drum table, Simon shifted and extended his long legs out in front of him. He was sitting in a French Provincial chair that was too low to be comfortable. "Grandfather had an affair," he repeated. "You'll be telling me next that the world is flat."

His mother's father, Paul Carmichael, an admirable man in many ways, had died recently of pneumonia— as gruff and uncommunicative in his final days as he'd been in life. Trying to picture that tall, distant, somber figure in the throes of passion was too big a stretch for Simon.

An image teased at his memory—Grandfather Paul coming toward him, right hand held forward tentatively. Yes. It was when Simon had returned to Seattle after graduating from college thirteen years ago. He'd become aware at college of how much his grandfather had taught him about land use and ecology-preserving development and was committed to learning more, and so when the older man came forward to greet him, Simon had experienced a burst of affection. Ignoring Paul's hand, he'd attempted to hug him, but had felt only stiff resistance. The deliberate rebuff had chilled him to the bone.

Libby eased herself to a different position, wincing at even that slight movement. "Just before he died, my father asked me to bring him an envelope from a drawer in his desk."

Simon looked at the desk in question. Contemporary, sleekly surfaced, it no more matched the decor of this daintily decorated room than did his father's recliner, but Libby had insisted she wanted it when her widowed mother decided to sell her house and all its contents and buy a condo on a golf course in Phoenix.

"The envelope contained a photograph and a postcard," Libby went on. "Dad studied them for a long time. Finally he handed them to me, then lay back against his pillows and closed his eyes. As I was looking at the photograph, he said in this anguished voice I'd never heard come out of him before, 'If I hadn't been so stupid, if I hadn't left bliss behind in Penmorton, I might have been a happy man. I loved her. I just didn't know how important love was.'

"To my astonishment, there were tears rolling down his face. 'Bliss?' I asked. 'What do you mean, you left bliss behind?' Then light dawned. 'Is that the woman's name—the woman in the photograph?' I asked, and Dad said very softly, 'Yes, her name was Bliss. Tell her, Libby. Tell her I loved her.'"

Libby shifted again and groaned. "Could you push me a little higher?" she asked.

Simon got up and gently raised the back of the recliner to a forty-five-degree angle. "Don't stop now," he said.

Libby sighed. "That's all there is. Dad didn't say another word. I thought he'd gone to sleep, but Mom and I discovered later that he'd slipped into a coma. He never spoke again." She glanced up at Simon. "The envelope's on my dressing table."

Opening the envelope, Simon took out a picture postcard and a black-and-white photograph of a long-legged, healthy-looking young woman with excellent posture and a glowing smile. Her hair was rolled up and pinned in a forties' style. She was wearing jodhpurs and

a short-sleeved shirt open at the throat. In her left hand
she held a round hat with a wide brim.

"Take a look at the postcard," Libby said.

The street in the postcard's sepia-tinted photograph
curved attractively. It was lined on both sides by handsome stone buildings: shops, a pub with a sign hanging
from a wrought-iron bracket—The Cock and Fox—
a bay-windowed restaurant. "Penmorton, Cornwall,
High Street," read the legend in the upper right corner.

Both postcard and photo were faded, worn and
slightly bowed. It seemed likely they'd spent the past
five decades in the breast pocket of one of Paul Carmichael's beautifully tailored jackets.

Simon frowned at his mother. "This is why you
booked a trip to England? You're going to see what you
can dig up on the old man's past?"

"I *intended* to," Libby corrected. "I'm supposed to
leave in a couple of weeks—April the twenty-eighth. But
Dr. Rassner says I may not be completely mobile for
four or five months."

Libby had spent the previous weekend at Crystal
Mountain, skiing in her usual flamboyant manner,
thrilled by unexpected new powder. Turning her head to
yell a comment to a friend, she'd collided with a tree.
She'd not only fractured six ribs, but damaged the
costo-chondral cartilage that held them together.

"I guess you'll have to postpone the trip," Simon
said.

"Mmm-hmm," his mother murmured.

Her casual tone alerted him to trouble ahead. Normally his mother didn't readily accept disappointment.
Walking over to the fireplace, he repositioned a couple
of things that were out of line on the mantel—a gilt-
framed picture of exotic tropical fish and a beautifully

detailed model of a cable car, which his grandmother had brought back from a golfing trip to the San Francisco area.

"After my father's funeral," Libby continued, "I asked my mother why Dad was never demonstrative. You know how he was. It seemed as if somewhere along the way he'd lost some essential part of himself and hadn't been able to find it again."

She paused for dramatic effect. "Mom told me a surprising thing. She said when they were first married, Dad was quite happy-go-lucky. Can you imagine that?"

Simon couldn't, and said so.

"They were married in Los Angeles right after Pearl Harbor was bombed," Libby said, then frowned. "According to Mom they never really loved each other. It was more a marriage of convenience. My grandfather Malcolm thought it would be neat if his partner's daughter, Jane, married his son, Paul. Evidently Malcolm was a strong-minded nineteenth-century sort of father—Paul was in awe of him, Mom says. In any case, a lot of their friends were getting married, the men going off to war, and it all seemed very glamorous and exciting, so they did it too. Everything was fine up to and including my birth in 1942. Then Paul went off to England. That was in 1943. According to Mom, when he came back a year later, he was different—morose, silent, gloomy. Gradually he got gloomier."

She paused again, thinking back. "The three of us moved up here to Seattle after the war. Mom hoped the change would be good for their marriage, but it never did recover. Dad just grew more and more distant. He devoted all his time to his work, coming home only to eat and sleep." She sighed. "Mom said such a sad thing.

She said Dad never did catch on to what family life was supposed to be.''

Her glance at Simon was loaded with meaning. He got the message immediately. He had followed in his grandfather's footsteps. Like Paul, he'd become an extremely successful land developer, which left him little free time. But surely his mother must realize that no one could be truly successful without being single-minded. Would she have preferred him to spend his life playing golf like his father? His father hadn't caught on to what family life was supposed to be, either.

Perhaps that was part of the message.

"Grandmother knows about this supposed affair?" he asked, to get himself off the hook.

His mother's laugh was without real mirth. "Heavens, no, Simon. And we're certainly not going to tell her." She looked thoughtful. "It seems possible, considering that my father said he might've been happy if he hadn't left Bliss behind, that he and this woman must've had something pretty hot going. Wouldn't you agree?"

Without committing himself, Simon said, "I take it you plan on playing Sherlock Holmes? Or should I say Jessica Fletcher?"

Libby sighed heavily. "That was the general idea, yes, but of course it's not possible now. Not for me personally, at least. Injured as I am. Poor old thing."

Simon was even more alert now. During his thirty-four years, his mother had learned exactly how to manipulate him. Narrow-eyed, he stared at her. She smiled winningly back at him.

It was always difficult for Simon to refuse his mother anything. Though she'd been born to wealth and privilege, life had not been easy for Libby Carmichael

Flynn. First of all, she was the child of a loveless marriage and, considering Paul's penchant for overwork, virtually fatherless. Then she'd gotten married right out of high school—to a man who, though always charming, had rarely been around since their wedding day. But she had lovingly made life as pleasant as possible for Simon, her only child. She was the one who'd cheered him on at Little League games, applauded when he played trumpet in the high-school marching band. She was the one who'd helped him with science projects, English assignments, Halloween costumes.

"No, Mom, I can't do it," Simon said firmly. He made a show of checking his wristwatch. It was obviously time to call his mother's devoted housekeeper/ acting nurse to the rescue and go home to his condo in downtown Seattle.

Libby gazed up at him, managing to look as fragile as a wounded bird. "You're not even curious about your grandfather's past?"

"Well, sure, it's intriguing, especially when you remember what the old man was like, such a cold—" He broke off abruptly, shaking his head at Libby's hopeful expression. "It's absolutely impossible for me just to drop everything and rush off to Cornwall on some wild—"

"You always said you wanted to visit English towns and villages," she reminded him, adding without a pause for breath, "Pass me that travel guide from the dresser, will you, dear?"

Still marshaling arguments, he did as she asked.

"Listen to this," she said, opening the book from her semiprone position. " 'To experience true charm, visit the ancient town of Penmorton, Cornwall, where stone houses and cottages cling to terraced hills as though they'd tumbled out of the sky. Walk the narrow, winding streets, photograph the old harbor, the guildhall and the secret sheltered coves where smuggling was once rampant.'"

She fixed him with her innocent blue gaze. "Didn't you tell me recently that you have a hiatus right now?"

"I did. I do. I'm waiting for an ecological-impact statement on the Bramwell Point project, but that doesn't mean I have nothing—"

"And isn't it true that you have two very hardworking, honest partners who are perfectly capable of running things in your absence, just as you did when they went off on that Caribbean cruise with their wives and children last year?"

"Well, yes, but—"

Libby fired her next shot before he could finish. "How long has it been since you took a vacation?"

"I went to Chicago last year," he said defensively.

"Chicago was *two* years ago," Libby said with a triumphant smile. "Anyway, that wasn't a vacation, it was a conference."

She let her voice sink to a doleful murmur. "You don't even have a woman in your life."

"Sure I do." He was on safe ground here.

"A serious-minded woman?"

"Well, you know, Mom, it's not that easy to get involved with a serious-minded woman. Bar cruising turns up very few. I could take a personal ad out, I suppose, but I'd just as soon not. As for dating agencies, I'm not sure how good I'd look on a video, and you know how important first impressions—"

"Simon!"

Unrepentant, he grinned at her. "I date all the time, Mom. Ask anybody."

"I shouldn't have to ask anybody, Simon. You never bring your dates here." She narrowed her eyes. "Sometimes I wonder if you even like women."

"I adore women," Simon assured her. "I was raised by one of the best." He raised his eyebrows as her expression softened into a smile. "Which doesn't mean I understand women. I am constantly befuddled, perplexed and confounded by them. The reason I haven't brought my dates home is that women get nervous if they think things are getting serious."

"*Women* get nervous?"

Judging by his mother's indignant expression, his safe ground had developed a number of cracks. He summoned up a little indignation of his own. "Women aren't what they used to be, Mom. Liberated women don't *want* to be tied down. Take Georgia Grenham. Just as I was beginning to feel settled and thinking of asking her to move in with me—she's a great cook, her mushroom polenta is fit for the gods—what did she do? She bought a small airplane and went off to start a crop-dusting business on the other side of the mountains. Then there was Laurie Bergstrom. She wanted to spend weekends skydiving or white-water rafting or bungee-jumping. It seemed to me just getting around in Seattle traffic was hazardous enough. Anyway, I brought Beth Chaplin over . . ."

"To Thanksgiving dinner."

Had it really been that long ago? He'd liked Beth. Quite a lot. They'd talked about going to a New Year's Eve party. What had happened to that idea?

"Time flies," he said lamely. "You may be right, Mom. It's time I stopped behaving like a social butterfly. Found myself a steady girl."

"I didn't know you *were* behaving like a social butterfly," she said sternly. "And you should be finding yourself a woman, not a girl."

Simon managed not to roll his eyes. "Okay, Mom, have it your way. Maybe I'll call Beth up and suggest dinner, the theater, something..."

"Beth Chaplin got married in February, Simon," his mother said, sounding exasperated.

"She did?"

"I understand she popped the question herself. After hanging out with you she probably figured no one was ever going to ask her. It's quite obvious, Simon, that you're afraid of commitment."

"Hey now, I wouldn't say afraid, exactly. Wary, maybe, mildly antagonistic to—"

"Scared to death," Libby said.

"You may be right, Mom," he said soothingly. "It's probably some kind of phobia. It may even have a name."

"It has a name all right. It's called the Paul Carmichael syndrome. If you don't look out, you're going to turn out just like your grandfather. He got married, yes, but he never acted married. So how did he end up? Lonely. Sad. Detached from life."

Simon searched his mind for an argument, but couldn't find one. Libby had hit a raw nerve. Recently, coming home late from the office, he'd begun noticing how empty his condo seemed. He'd become aware of a nagging feeling that perhaps hard work, no matter how interesting, how fulfilling, wasn't enough, even when you took time out to play hard, too. There were empty spaces inside him. Spaces work and play couldn't seem to fill. He had a recurring dream, seeing himself as a cardboard cutout with a large hole in the center.

He shook his head as his mother opened her mouth to speak again. "No, Mom. I'm sorry. I'm sure it'd be interesting to find out what happened to Grandfather in England, but I can't possibly take the time to do it. You'll have to wait until you recover, then go yourself."

"But, Simon, darling, I just have this feeling that time is of the essence. If the woman is alive, she has to be in her seventies. Dad was seventy-seven, remember." She flapped a dismissive hand, although Simon hadn't said anything. "I know, I know. It's possible she could live another ten or even twenty years, but what if she died just before I got there? I'd never forgive myself. This is the only thing my father ever asked of me— or anybody, as far as I know—to tell this woman he loved her. I don't know her last name—I went through all his papers and I couldn't find a single mention of her. I can't just write a letter to 'Whom It May Concern, Penmorton.' And I've already booked the flight, arranged to rent a car—"

"Flights can be postponed," Simon pointed out. "Rental cars can be canceled."

Libby opened her mouth again.

"No way," he said. "Forget it, Mom. I'm not going to England for you and that's final."

"But, Simon—"

"Final," he said again. Forcefully.

"'OH, TO BE IN ENGLAND, now that April's there,'" Simon recited aloud as he drove by plowed fields and green meadows divided by ancient stone walls from which wildflowers sprouted. Robert Browning, William Wordsworth and his dancing daffodils, William Blake talking about England's green and pleasant land had all been popping up in his mind since he'd driven across the River Tamar into Cornwall.

Although he was part Irish and proud of it, Simon was not normally a man who quoted or even thought about poetry. Never mind that he couldn't say no to his mother and make it stick, especially when she was in pain, he was still a practical, down-to-earth, hard-working, hardheaded, if occasionally fun-loving, man who normally drove on busy freeways from where he was to where he had to be without particularly noticing the scenery.

By rights he should be too dog-tired to notice it now. After the long flight from Seattle had arrived at Heathrow, he'd had to sprint for a bus to take him clear across the huge airport so that he could catch a small plane to Plymouth. Then he'd discovered that the rental-car agency had set aside a tiny car he couldn't even begin to fit his legs into, and he'd had to wait an hour for the agency to come up with something larger.

Besides all that, he had to get used to driving on the left on narrow, winding roads barely wide enough for the Peugeot Clarion he'd finally been issued.

Yet instead of being pooped, here he was, declaiming poetry, feeling enchanted by daisy-starred meadows dotted with sheep.

He wasn't normally a man who was enchanted by things, either.

Now, as he entered Penmorton, his senses responded to the small stone houses that flanked the narrow road. Looking as though they'd stood there a century or more, which they undoubtedly had, the cottages had multiple chimney pots, slate-tile roofs, casement windows. Spring flowers bloomed riotously in tiny plots at either side of solid stone doorsteps.

To his left, steep lanes offered occasional shining glimpses of a fair-size harbor and the English Channel beyond. In the bright midafternoon light, the trees arching over the streets seemed...cleaner than any he'd ever seen. It was as if each leaf and needle had been washed and brushed up in anticipation of his visit. No industry, he presumed. Hence no pollution.

It seemed entirely possible that the seaside village of Penmorton had changed little, if at all, since his grandfather had visited it during World War II. Maybe it was a mythical place, like Brigadoon, except that it showed up every fifty years, instead of a hundred. Maybe it had appeared especially for him this time.

Then again, maybe jet lag had scrambled his brain cells. He'd better find a place to stay before he became so addled he wrapped himself and the Peugeot around one of those clean trees.

He had discovered the day before he left Seattle that his mother hadn't booked a hotel room of any kind. She'd thought it would be more romantic to stay at bed-and-breakfast places, moving around as whim seized her, depending on what she found out about the woman named Bliss.

Penmorton wasn't a large place, but it turned out that almost every block yielded a bed-and-breakfast sign. Simon didn't begin to worry seriously until he'd worked his way down the steep hill to the harbor, crisscrossing almost all the streets in between. Everywhere the answer was the same. Sorry. Full.

Catching sight of a pub called the Smugglers' Inn, he pulled into the parking lot, remembering that the travel guide his mother had given on him had mentioned that public houses sometimes rented out rooms.

In Seattle, a tavern named the Smugglers' Inn would have struck him as terminally cute, but here in Cornwall, it was an obvious reference to the area's colorful past. At times during the last couple of centuries it probably *had* been frequented by smugglers.

At first glance the pub interior appeared properly traditional, similar to several he'd visited in the States— horse brasses all over the place, blue-willow plates, oak paneling, a dartboard. There were a couple of large bow windows, low wooden beams carved with clusters of grapes, a sign that said the premises were protected by the government as a place of historic interest. A middle-aged woman with an old-fashioned upswept hairdo was playing a big-band standard on an upright piano.

A second glance showed him a couple of video games in an alcove, some high-tech equipment at the back of the tiny dance floor and the bartender, who was female and young and black, her wildly frizzy bangs striped yellow and magenta. She was wearing a flowing, multicolored garment that looked decidedly African.

"Clytie Belyar," she said as Simon straddled a bar stool. It was a moment before he realized she was telling him her name, rather than greeting him in a foreign language. "I'm the owner, I am. This pub's a free 'ouse."

He blinked as much at her cockney accent as with confusion.

"The pub doesn't belong to a brewery. It belongs to me," she explained.

"Proud of this place, Clytie is." This unnecessary comment came from a little old man perched on a high stool farther along the bar. He spoke out of the corner of his mouth without even turning his head to look at Simon. The man's flat tweed cap was pulled so low over his forehead Simon wasn't sure he could see. He was irresistibly reminded of the comic strip character Andy Capp.

A German Shepherd slept on the floor beside the stool. Simon would have taken him for a seeing-eye dog if he hadn't noticed the sign beside the outer door that said dogs were welcome, but only on leads.

He turned to Clytie. "I'm Simon Flynn," he said. "I just arrived in Penmorton."

"Pleased to make your acquaintance, love. It's always a pleasure to 'ave a good-looking bloke come in. Bit of all right you are, mate, if you don't mind me sayin' so."

She batted extremely unlikely-looking eyelashes at him. "I'm a pushover for blue eyes," she added cheerfully. "Specially when they're combined with curly black 'air and big shoulders. What d'you do when you're at 'ome, ducks? Chop down trees? Wrestle bears? Leap tall buildin's in a single bound?"

Simon laughed, liking her. Her voice was warm, her good humor contagious.

"You'll be wanting lager, I suppose?" she said with a dramatic sigh. "Yanks usually want lager. *Chilled* lager. I might even 'ave some in the fridge."

He leaned forward over the bar. "I'd prefer a Guinness," he whispered.

Clytie gave him an approving grin.

"I'm looking for a place to stay," he said as Clytie set a tall glass in front of him, the wooden bracelets on her arm clattering.

"Yer out of luck, my darlin'. I only 'ave two rooms above and they're both occupied." She clucked her tongue pensively, her dark eyes glinting at him. "I suppose I could toss out the old couple in number two.

Wouldn't 'ardly 'urt them to go 'ome early. They do look a bit tiredlike.''

Simon laughed. "I'd just as soon not be responsible for anyone's eviction. I didn't think I'd have a problem getting a room this time of year. Kids are still in school, aren't they?''

"Sure they are, ducks. But the town is filled up with retired people. Grannies and granddads don't stay 'ome in their rocking chairs like they used to.''

"They don't in the States, either, but many of them take a motor home along.''

"Well, let's put me thinking cap on, love." Picking up a checkered cloth, Clytie wiped down the already spotless bar, her brow furrowed with thought.

"How about the Ancient Mariner?" asked the older man with the dog. "They had a sign out this morning.''

"I checked there," Simon told him. "Nothing." He grinned at Clytie. "Don't worry about it, I'll find something." He picked up his glass of stout, which had a perfect creamy head on it. Giving Clytie an appreciative nod, he took a thirsty swallow, then set the glass down. He was in Penmorton for a reason, and since the bartender was friendly, maybe she could help. The sooner he finished his quest, the sooner he could get back to work.

"Do you know of a woman in the area named Bliss?" he asked.

"There's an unusual name," Clytie said, evidently not recognizing that her own was a little out of the ordinary. She shook her head. "I'd remember that name if I'd ever 'eard it. Nice, that is. Bliss. That her surname or her Christian name?''

"I expect it's her first name. I don't know her last, I'm afraid. She'd be an older woman. Mid-to late seventies maybe."

"Bliss Penberthy," the man at the end of the bar volunteered, still without turning his head.

"Well, blow me down!" Clytie exclaimed, staring at him. "Mrs. Penberthy's Christian name is Bliss? Fancy that! I only ever 'eard 'er called by 'er nickname or Mrs. Penberthy." The bartender arched plucked-thin eyebrows at Simon. "The Duchess, they call 'er mostly. She's a bit prissylike."

"Bliss Penberthy," the man said firmly. "That'll be the woman you're wanting, I'll be bound. Never did hear of another Bliss hereabouts or any other place. Bliss Turner, she was. Father was John Edward Turner, the rector. Mother's name was Lizzie—Elizabeth when she had her hat on. Bliss Turner married Foster Penberthy. Their son, Travis, and his wife, Nell, used to help her in the shop—until their car ran into a wall. Lovely couple they were. Their daughter took over, last I heard. Bliss Penberthy's granddaughter, that would be. Rebecca Penberthy."

Simon was impressed. Every town should have an oral historian. He imagined the woman who would go with the name Rebecca Penberthy—someone round and jolly with berry black eyes.

"Amazing lass, Rebecca Penberthy," a middle-aged woman at a nearby table said. She had a tooth missing right in front, which distracted Simon enough that he missed part of what she went on to say—something about somebody's skin going red on one side of his face. "Skin got so tight it pulled his lower eyelid down," the woman said, then paused for a sip of her beer.

"Went to a dozen so-called specialists, George did,"
she went on. "Used ten kinds of cream. Nothing did a
bit of good. You go see Rebecca Penberthy, I said to
him. And so he did. She sold him a tiny little bottle full
of tiny little pills, not one of 'em bigger than the head
of one of them fancy dressmaker pins. Told him to
swallow it all down in one go, she did, right there in her
shop."

"Did it do any good?" Simon asked when it became
apparent the woman was waiting for him to comment.

"Well, certainly," she said, as though there could not
possibly have been any doubt. "Never had a bit of
trouble since, our George. Turned out it was sulfur she
gave him, plain, ordinary sulfur. Homeopathic treatment, she called it. George swears by her."

"The Penberthys 'ave a 'ealth shop," Clytie explained to Simon. "It used to belong to Mrs. Penberthy's mother, Mrs. Turner."

"It was called Lowther's then," the man in the cap
volunteered. "Lizzie Turner was a Lowther before her
marriage to the rector. It was a grocery shop at one
time, but then the supermarket came along on the edge
of town."

He paused for a swig of beer and Clytie took back
control of the story. "So now Penberthy's sells vitamins and 'omeopathic remedies and organically grown
yeast and flour and things like that," she said. "Better
than people relying on drugs. That's to be encouraged,
that is. Don't you think?"

A flurry of activity at the door signaled the arrival of
a group of young people. The dog raised his head and
looked at them suspiciously for a moment, then
stretched his nose along his front paws again, apparently deciding they didn't mean any harm. He kept his

eyes open, though. The newcomers arranged themselves noisily around a large table in one of the bow windows. Clytie went off to serve them, leaving Simon to wonder at his good luck in finding the woman named Bliss so soon.

"Another Guinness, love?" Clytie asked when she returned.

Simon shook his head and raised his glass to drain it.

Clytie cocked her head to one side. "You 'ave some business with old Mrs. Penberthy then?"

"I'm not sure," Simon said ambiguously, recognizing that whatever he might say in here would flash around the village in less time than it would take him to find the Penberthys' residence. "I'll have to talk to her first."

Clytie winked at him, obviously amused by his evasive tactics. "Closes at six, Penberthy's does," she informed him. "Better look sharp." Accompanying him to the door, she gave him voluble directions, along with graceful but indecipherable hand movements, then suggested that when he got through with his business, he might find a place to stay in Polperro, a few miles on. "Be sure to come back now," she said.

He crossed to the Peugeot, climbed in and sat there without moving for a few minutes, wondering, not for the first time in the past few days, if he was completely out of his mind. Why on earth had he let his mother talk him into trying to track down some minor little mystery in his grandfather's life?

Not so minor, he reminded himself. Libby had regarded Paul's request to tell Bliss he loved her as a sacred trust, which should, if possible, be carried out without delay. Apparently, whatever had taken place in this small town had affected his grandfather for the rest of his life, and by extension, his family, including Simon himself.

Besides, it wasn't just curiosity about his grandfather or even his mother's insistence that had brought Simon to England; he'd come to realize that he needed this journey, this quest, for his own sake. Here in Penmorton, Paul had lost some essential part of himself. A part that had something to do with bonding with other people. It seemed to Simon it was a part he himself had never found.

CHAPTER TWO

THE HEALTH STORE occupied the lower half of a two-story house built of sturdy stone. Plump tassels of purple wisteria dangled from a trellis around the front door. The only clue to the house's function was an Open sign in the window and a discreet brass plaque on one side of the door engraved with the name Penberthy and the hours of operation.

Before entering, Simon peered through a tall wrought-iron gate in the high adjoining wall. A bricked courtyard was hidden away in there. Bright-colored spring flowers bloomed in a miscellany of containers ranging from clay pots and wooden tubs to fancy jardinieres. A cluster of half-barrels held small green clumps that looked newly planted.

On the other side of the courtyard stood a small cottage. At first glance it appeared quite charming, but a more thorough study showed that the whole place was slightly askew, the lintel sagged over the French doors, and several tiles were missing from the roof. One small windowpane had been replaced with a piece of plywood.

Simon turned back to the shop door. Opening it activated a melodic bell. Inside, he ducked to avoid racks of copper pans and utensils that were suspended from the ceiling, along with fragrant bunches of herbs and twisted braids of garlic. He sniffed appreciatively, then moved past an old wooden counter, barrels containing various kinds of grains and flour and beans, and shelves loaded with vitamins, lotions and jars of loose tea with exotic labels—Nilgiri, Lapsang Souchong, Formosa Oolong.

Somewhere nearby he could hear the murmur of voices.

Rounding the end of the bank of shelves, he came upon a tall, dark-haired young woman in a crisp white cotton shirt and slim black skirt that reached her calves. She was wearing glasses with narrow metal frames and small oval lenses. Glancing at Simon, she gave him a nod of welcome, then continued reading a package label to a middle-aged man with a ruddy face and prominent ears.

"Don't 'ee be giving me nothing that's going to get me addicted," the man said with a teasing lift of his bushy eyebrows.

"Camomile's just a herb with little daisylike flowers," the young woman assured him.

"Opium do come off poppies, Rebecca," the man pointed out, straight-faced.

"There's nothing harmful in camomile tea," the young woman said with a brief smile to acknowledge his joke. "It's ever so good for the digestion. It will also calm your nerves and make it easier for you to get to sleep."

Her speech had a soft, country sound to it that Simon found very soothing. He looked at the young woman with interest. If this was Rebecca Penberthy, she was nothing like the round and jolly woman her name had conjured up in his mind. Probably in her late twenties, she had a slim, boyish figure and long, black hair pulled severely back and tied at the nape with a black, elasticized rosette of ribbon. The no-nonsense type evidently. Businesslike. Liberated.

"Don't 'ee never have trouble sleeping?" the man asked her.

Rebecca shook her head. "I have too much to do to lie awake nights."

A crafty expression spread over the man's broad face. "Maybe 'ee needs a man to keep company with, keep 'ee from working so hard."

Rebecca laughed, which caused all kinds of good things to happen to her face, especially her eyes. "I believe Eliza Doolittle had the right answer for that, Mr. Bridges. When someone asked her to walk across the park, she said, 'Not bloody likely.'"

Definitely liberated.

"That's a good 'un, Rebecca," the man said with an easy grin. "Put me properly in my place, that did."

"So now do you feel obliged to buy the camomile tea?" Rebecca asked.

"I do." Following the young woman to the counter at the front of the store, he paid for his tea and started for the door. "That's what 'ee needs to be saying, m'dear—I do," he said with one hand on the doorknob. "Not getting any younger, you. Must be getting close to thirty. I remember when you were born—same year as my Catherine. Three children she has now."

The door swung shut behind him and Simon approached the counter. Rebecca had taken off her glasses and was rubbing them with a paper tissue, shaking her head over her customer's remarks. How defenseless, how *vulnerable*, people who wore glasses looked when they took them off, Simon thought, as she gave him a quizzical, slightly out-of-focus glance.

Rebecca Penberthy might not be a beauty, but she was a good advertisement for her business. She wore no makeup, and her lightly tanned skin hadn't a flaw that Simon could see. Her eyelashes and brows were naturally dark, her lips and high, almost Slavic cheekbones tinged with the pink of good health.

"How may I help you?" she asked as she put the glasses back on.

It took him a minute to decide where to start. If he addressed her by her full name, she'd wonder where he got it. And he wasn't at all sure of the etiquette involved in explaining that he'd come here looking for a woman named Bliss who might have had an affair with his grandfather fifty years ago.

While he fumbled for words, Rebecca plugged a cord attached to a square steel tank into an electric outlet on the counter. The tank contained a big block of hard white stuff. Paraffin? Did she make candles?

"My name's Simon Flynn," he said finally. "And you are?"

She hesitated a moment, then gave him her name. Encouraged, he said, "I just arrived in Penmorton and haven't been able to find a place to stay. I noticed in passing that you had a small cottage at the back."

She raised a questioning eyebrow. As well she might. Hidden as it was on the other side of that walled courtyard, there was no way anyone could see the cottage in passing. Might as well plunge on, Simon decided. "I wondered if I might rent it for a couple of weeks."

Her expression had turned negative before the last words were out of his mouth. "I'm sorry, Mr. Flynn, but that cottage is in a very disreputable condition. I couldn't possibly let it to anyone."

"Even though I'm desperate?"

Desperate? Rebecca looked at the American more carefully. He had a strong, lived-in face, with a deep groove between his eyebrows that indicated he might be a bit intense, probably impatient at times. He had a smiley sort of mouth, though, and his face went well with his generally outdoorsy appearance. There was more than a hint of muscle under the black sweatshirt he was wearing with his snug blue jeans. His shaggy hair was as black as her own, his eyes as steady and clear as a child's, and as blue as a summer sky.

"I've driven all over Penmorton," he said. "Nobody has a vacancy."

"You might try Looe or Polperro," she told him without allowing any sympathy to enter her voice.

He hesitated as though thinking up an argument to convince her. "Penmorton's such a great-looking town," he said at last. "I'd really like to hang around for a while, use it as a base camp." He smiled wistfully at her, which made him look boyish and extremely attractive. She thought it entirely possible that he knew that.

"I'm sorry—" she began, but he interrupted.

"Have you always lived here?"

It was no business of his where she'd always lived, of course, but it might get rid of him more quickly if she answered him. "I've never lived anywhere but Penmorton," she said. "I've never been out of Cornwall, except for brief trips to Plymouth. I've had neither the occasion nor the desire to travel, Mr. Flynn."

She was amazed at herself. Why on earth had she trotted all that out? Anyone would think he'd asked her to run away with him. Besides which, the whole statement was a lie. She'd always wanted to travel, and she'd love to live somewhere else for a change. She'd just never had a chance to see the world and probably never would. Was that why she'd babbled on so? Was she covering up her frustration with denial? Something to ponder when she had a minute to spare.

"You live here alone?" he asked before she'd finished gathering her wits.

That question made her a little nervous. He might appear to be a respectable sort of person, but he was also a big man and fairly tough-looking, and a stranger, besides.

"I don't see a need to tell you who I live with," she started, but before the sentence was all the way out of her mouth, a door at the back of the shop opened and her grandmother entered.

The minute she caught sight of Simon Flynn, Bliss's tall, elegantly bony figure stiffened, and she gave him the look that had accorded her the nickname the Duchess. It involved narrowing her eyes, lifting her nose and pursing her mouth as if she'd just swallowed some vinegar. Had she already guessed that he was an American?

Better distract her, Rebecca thought. "Have you come for your paraffin treatment, Gran? It's just about ready."

Her grandmother nodded. "I barely got the herbs planted before my fingers seized up." She held up her gnarled hands and shook her head at them. "Horrid old things. But I managed to plant basil, coriander, hyssop, bay and woolly thyme, in spite of them. Oh, yes, and some tarragon and tansy, too."

Again she gave the American her Duchess look. It might be as well to introduce the man and ease him out the door, Rebecca decided. "This is Mr. Flynn, Gran. My grandmother, Mrs. Penberthy. Mr. Flynn was just leaving," she said briskly. "It *is* closing time," she added, speaking to the American directly. "I must see to my grandmother. I'm sorry I couldn't help you."

He nodded. He was frowning in his intense way at Bliss now and was apparently in no hurry to leave. Turning away, Rebecca checked the temperature of the paraffin in the tank, then helped Bliss push up the sleeves of her cardigan.

The older woman was as tall as her granddaughter and almost as slim, her posture regal. Her hair was iron gray, jaw-length, center-parted and held up at the sides with barrettes. Simon couldn't help but think that Dragon Lady was a more apt nickname. Her lined face had displayed a very unwelcoming expression when she first saw him, and her brown eyes, bright as a bird's, had flashed unfriendly fire.

Though undeniably handsome, she didn't look a whole lot like the glowing young woman in the photograph tucked in the inside pocket of his duffel bag. Which was hardly surprising. After all, fifty-two years had passed since that picture had been taken.

Bliss Penberthy certainly appeared to be in his grandfather's age bracket, however, and the old man in the Smugglers' Inn had seemed very sure there wasn't another woman named Bliss living in Penmorton.

But Simon was already convinced she was the woman he'd come to England to find. When she'd entered the store, he could have sworn his grandfather's voice had said yes, in his mind. A very fanciful thought for someone who saw himself as down-to-earth, he realized. Obviously either jet lag or the pure Cornish air was getting to him.

"We'll have your hands feeling better in a jiffy," Rebecca said soothingly as she helped her grandmother dip one hand in and out of the now liquid paraffin. Simon marveled at the love and compassion that shone on her face. He was beginning to realize that Rebecca Penberthy was much more attractive than he'd first thought.

The dragon lady was smiling just as fondly at her granddaughter, which softened her gaunt face considerably. The fondness didn't extend to him, however; she was even now shooting him another withering glance. "Was there something you wanted, Mr. Flynn? Other than to hover about my granddaughter?"

Mama dragon protecting her offspring, Simon thought.

"Mr. Flynn's a visitor to Penmorton, Gran," Rebecca said, obviously flustered by her grandmother's suggestive remark. "He just happened to come into the shop." Ducking her head, she added in a fierce whisper, "You mustn't go round insulting customers like that, Gran."

"If he's a customer, what's he buying?" Mrs. Penberthy demanded. Then her face and voice softened again as she looked more closely at her granddaughter, whose cheeks had flared with color. "I'm sorry, love, I didn't mean to embarrass you."

Rebecca shook her head at her and began dipping her other hand.

"What exactly does the paraffin do?" Simon asked, wanting to change the subject.

"The heat takes the stiffness out of Gran's arthritis," Rebecca explained. "After the treatment, she's able to exercise her hands, which in turn keeps the joints from locking up."

Simon realized that Mrs. Penberthy, now holding both wax-gloved hands aloft, was staring at him with even more hostility. "You're an American," she said with the same ponderous tone a judge uses to ask a prisoner how he's pleading.

"Guilty," Simon answered impulsively.

"Gran doesn't like Americans," Rebecca said, a hint of a smile in her voice, though none showed on her face.

"Americans invade England every summer," Mrs. Penberthy grumbled. "Always in a hurry—have to see fifty towns in twenty-one days or die trying. Always complaining about the plumbing. One woman from California told the landlady at the Ancient Mariner that our plumbing was still in the Dark Ages. Loud, too, Americans are, wanting everything their way, saying nasty things about the food we eat, making remarks about royalty—and all the while their magazines have more stories about the royal family than ours have. They throw their money around as if it was confetti, too. Got too much money, that's the trouble—you can tell that just watching telly."

"Tourists are supposed to throw money around," Simon said with what he hoped was an amiable smile. "It's part of their job description."

Rebecca laughed out loud. Simon immediately tried to think of something to say that would make her do it again.

"We've met some very nice Americans, Gran," she protested. "Remember the woman who bought our whole stock of copper pans? She wanted to see the garden, and you and she sat on the bench and had such a nice chat about roses."

"Mm," Mrs. Penberthy said.

Encouraged, Simon told her he'd planned on staying in Penmorton for a while but had been unable to find a vacancy. "When you came in I was trying to persuade your granddaughter to rent me your cottage," he said.

How did she manage to look so haughty? It was partly her almost military posture, partly a naturally patrician cast to her features. "That old hut?" she said. "It would fall down if you looked at it cross-eyed."

"I wouldn't even blink," Simon promised.

Rebecca rewarded his facetiousness with another chuckle, but all he got from her grandmother was a narrow-eyed glance that indicated she suspected he was making fun of her.

"Look, Miss Penberthy and Mrs. Penberthy," he said hastily. "I wouldn't be any trouble. What exactly is wrong with the cottage, anyway?"

"It leaks," Mrs. Penberthy said with a great deal of satisfaction. "Torrents of rain come in round the French doors and the chimney."

"Hardly torrents," Rebecca murmured.

"You won't deny the whole thing leans," her grandmother said.

Rebecca smiled ruefully. "It does, I'm afraid," she said to Simon. "I think it might have slipped off its foundation. I'm not sure it's even safe to go in there."

"It probably just requires a few adjustments," Simon said. Whatever the relationship had been between his grandfather and Mrs. Penberthy, he wanted that cottage. He wasn't sure why it was so important to him. Maybe it was because he was beginning to feel the effects of his long day and he didn't want to drive those narrow lanes in search of lodgings. Or more likely because he didn't want Mrs. Penberthy to best him—he could be just as stubborn as she.

"I could probably fix the leak—and the lean," he suggested. "Maybe we can work out an arrangement, part rent, part repairs. I'm not a bad carpenter."

Mrs. Penberthy switched her distrustful gaze from Simon's face to his hands. He held them palm uppermost for her inspection. "Plenty of calluses," he said.

Mrs. Penberthy's upper lip curled. "You could be an ax-murderer for all we know. Ax-murderers might have calluses."

"I suppose they might if they axed enough victims," Simon agreed. "I can only assure you I'm a nice person without a murderous thought in my head. I'll admit I don't work as a carpenter for a living. I'm a developer. I find the land and raise the money and hire other people to do the building. I go to a lot of meetings and do a lot of paper chasing, too. But I'm pretty good at house repairs. I learned how to fix things from my... from a relative when I was a kid. It's not the sort of skill you forget. I can certainly manage to fix up a cottage."

He wasn't sure why he'd avoided mentioning his grandfather. But it was probably a good idea not to until he could find out a couple of things. Such as, was his grandfather in any way responsible for Mrs. Penberthy's aversion to Americans? He really didn't have any idea what might have happened between the two of them all those years ago. Paul might have stolen something from her, or beaten her up. Imagining either scenario was almost beyond Simon, but in theory, anything was possible.

In which case, it wouldn't be too wise to mention why he was here or who he was related to. Fortunately he didn't look anything like his fair-haired, fair-skinned grandfather, except for his blue eyes. So there was no way either Rebecca or her grandmother could suspect he might have ulterior motives here.

Rebecca was studying his face. He did his best to look like the nice person he'd claimed to be—which of course, he was. When she nodded, he felt as if he'd passed some kind of test.

"It wouldn't be such a bad idea to air out that old cottage," she said slowly. "It is clean, I keep after it, but it's still a bit musty. It would do it good to have the heater on for a while. Getting some repairs done would be a bonus. I've thought of having a go at them myself, but I never seem to have the time or the energy."

The dragon lady's sharp glance darted from Rebecca to Simon. He could almost see her brain ticking over as she stared at him. She was getting ready to come up with another argument, no doubt.

He met her gaze as calmly and unthreateningly as possible. For a full minute, she stared at him, her brown eyes without expression, then to his surprise, she suddenly capitulated. "I suppose the money would be useful," she said.

"I can take care of our bills," Rebecca said indignantly as she began gently stripping the paraffin gloves from her grandmother's hands. "I'll take you to inspect the cottage as soon as I've finished here," she told Simon. "If you still want it after you've seen it close up, we'll decide on terms."

"Great," Simon said, and was amazed at the relief and pleasure he felt.

TOUCHING EACH of the fingers on her right hand one by one against her thumb, Bliss patiently pressed and released, pressed and released. Then she started on the left hand.

She was standing by her bedroom window, looking down at the walled courtyard. Usually she loved gazing at the pinks and reds and yellows of her tulips, her nodding daffodils, her tubs full of bluebells, feeling a sense of achievement; but this evening she was too distracted to notice more than a blur of bright color.

They were still in the cottage, Rebecca and the American. Simon Flynn. She was willing to bet he was going to take the cottage, even if it smelled of mildew from here to high heaven. She had seen the determination in his eyes.

Why was he so anxious to rent the cottage? There was more here than just needing a place to stay, she was certain. He had an ulterior motive. Which probably had something to do with Rebecca.

In her mind Bliss replayed everything the American had said. His wasn't a broad American accent by any means, but it had bothered Bliss's ears. Had Rebecca found it attractive?

Bliss hadn't liked the way he'd looked at Rebecca a couple of times, either. When her granddaughter laughed, for example. Bliss wasn't so old she couldn't recognize that certain way a man looked at a woman.

Those eyes. He had beautiful blue eyes. Was that why she'd given in over the cottage? Surely not.

He was just passing through on holiday. He wouldn't be in Penmorton long enough to do any harm.

Ha! That was a laugh. It didn't take a man any time at all to turn a woman's world inside out and backward.

She'd keep her eye on him. If he did anything to make Rebecca unhappy, she'd run him out of town personally. She didn't want anyone making Rebecca unhappy. Especially an American.

She clenched her fists, then opened her hands wide and clenched them again, telling herself she was still exercising. Something was trying to come through from the back of her mind. A door that had been closed had opened just a crack, not enough to let anyone look in, but just enough to release the sound of what had once been her favorite song.

Standing there, still looking out of the window, still not really seeing the bright flowers or the dilapidated cottage with its ominously closed door, she swayed a little from side to side, keeping time to the music playing in her memory, singing softly the words to "As Time Goes By."

How thin her voice seemed. It had never been a strong singing voice, but it hadn't sounded reedy when she was young.

How sad it was that voices changed. How sad that people got old. All of youth's bright promise gone.

The song had made her eyes water. That was silly. Remembering was silly. It never did any good to remember.

All the same, it suddenly seemed necessary to leave her bedroom and go up the narrow flight of stairs that led to the attic.

The shoe box was in the attic, she was sure. She distinctly remembered putting it in the attic.

CHAPTER THREE

"WHAT OUR COMPLEXIONS need, you see, is regular exfoliation—the stripping away of dead skin cells," Rebecca said to the teenager.

Simon was standing in front of the glass-fronted refrigerator unit where he was pretending to study the labels on milk cartons and containers of yogurt and yeast and wheatgerm. He glanced sideways at the chubby girl in the white blouse and school tie and navy blue skirt. Almost tipping backward with the weight of her backpack, she was gazing with rapt attention at Rebecca's face.

"Scrupulous cleanliness is the first step," Rebecca told her. "Exfoliation is the next. It cleans the skin and helps it to breathe. You apply this lotion with a very gentle scrubbing action. I use it myself, so I know it's good. It'll clear up those little spots straightaway."

Simon had watched Rebecca with uncharacteristic patience and increasing admiration as she dealt with customers on several occasions over the past few days. Whatever their age or gender, she treated them with total respect, warmth and sympathy.

Apparently she also knew the answer to almost every question her customers asked. He'd noted, though, that she was quick to recommend a visit to the doctor if the question warranted it.

Earth maiden, he dubbed her in his mind. Nurturer.

As soon as the now smiling schoolgirl had paid for her purchase and left, Simon grabbed a carton of plain yogurt and took it to the counter.

"Good morning, Mr. Flynn," Rebecca said gravely.

No sooner were the words out of her mouth than the inner shop door opened and Bliss Penberthy sailed in, head held high.

Either there was some kind of signaling device that alerted Rebecca's grandmother whenever Simon dropped into the store, or the dragon lady had extra-sensitive antennae. It seemed he was never going to have a chance to talk to Rebecca in private.

"Still here, Mr. Flynn?" Mrs. Penberthy asked, affecting pained surprise, as she did whenever she saw him.

"Still here, Mrs. Penberthy," he agreed resignedly.

"I should think a young and vigorous man like you would be bored with Penmorton by now."

"I haven't really had a chance to see much of the town," he pointed out. "I wanted to fulfill my part of the bargain and get the cottage in good shape first."

Judging by the look Mrs. Penberthy gave him, she was not impressed by his selflessness.

Rebecca smiled at him, however, and to be blessed by her luminous smile was well worth putting up with her grandmother's prickly protectiveness. "It's nice to be able to look at the cottage without tipping my head to one side like a bird," she said. "How did you straighten it up so quickly?"

"The girders beneath the floor joists are supported by concrete piers," he told her. "One of the piers had sunk a little, so I put in a shim."

"I heard hammering outside early this morning," Mrs. Penberthy grumbled.

Simon nodded. "I replaced the flashing around the chimney. Yesterday I found a box of roof tiles in the crawl space under the house, so that took care of the bare spots. And Mr. Matthews at the hardware store—sorry, the ironmonger—cut me a piece of glass for the window that was missing. I'm going to caulk around the French doors this morning."

Rebecca awarded him another smile. "I'm grateful to you, Mr. Flynn. The place looks much better. I think perhaps we should dispense with the rent—considering all the work you've done."

Simon shook his head. "I'm about through with the repairs, but I'm planning to stay on awhile longer."

The dragon lady seemed to want to comment on that, but just then the bell on the front door tinkled and a customer entered, an elderly woman with a rosy-cheeked infant in a stroller. She came immediately to the counter to visit with Rebecca, the baby raising his arms to be picked up. Rebecca obliged, her radiant smile leaving no doubt how she felt about children. She immediately started talking to the child in a sensible, straightforward, grown-up way that pleased Simon. He couldn't abide grown-ups talking squeaky baby talk to children or animals.

"I can help you with your purchase, Mr. Flynn," Mrs. Penberthy said sharply. Trying not to show his frustration, he had no choice but to reach into the back pocket of his jeans for his billfold and pay Mrs. Penberthy for the yogurt. Her arthritic fingers made her awkward with the coins and cash register, he noticed, but she managed both without making a big deal of it. He admired her for that, but wished she'd quit interfering with his plans to get Rebecca alone.

But then, as he was on his way out, he heard her say to her granddaughter, "Are you going to the shops this afternoon, love?" and he forgave her everything. He was going to get his chance.

Perking up his ears, he heard Rebecca answer, "Right after lunch. Make me out a list, will you, Gran? The fat pen you like is next to the register there."

As he closed the door behind him, Simon checked the hours of operation on the brass plaque. Closed all day Sunday. Early closing on Friday. Today was Friday.

As soon as he finished his lunch, Simon put on fresh jeans and a blue T-shirt and took up a position behind a gnarled old tree from where he could keep an eye on all exits without being seen by the dragon lady.

It was a half hour before Rebecca came out through the wrought-iron gate holding a string bag. She'd swapped her usual neat skirt for French-cut jeans, which showed her trim figure off to great advantage. Her black hair, tied back with a white ribbon rosette today, shone like ebony in the sunlight.

Not bad, Simon thought. Not bad at all. "May I offer you a ride?" he asked, stepping out as she drew level with him.

She was obviously startled, but recovered quickly. "Thank you, no," she said, and headed downhill. He swung into step alongside her. "I could have driven myself, Mr. Flynn," she said. "I have a very reliable car. But I like to be out in the sunshine when I can, and I need the exercise."

She glanced at him sideways, her lovely mouth taking on a mischievous twist. "Gran and I need some food items. We can't live on yogurt alone, as you seem to."

"Would you consider calling me Simon?" he suggested without commenting on her pointed remark.

She seemed to mull over his suggestion as they walked. He liked watching her face as she did so. Her expression started out solemn, but as she reached a decision her eyes brightened behind her oval lenses as though they'd filled with light from some inner source.

"Simon," she allowed, and he felt as if he'd aced another test.

He was surprised—and pleased—when they did not head in the direction of the supermarket, the only place he'd shopped so far. "You don't shop at the supermarket?" he asked.

She made a face. "Not today. Only when I need a lot of things in a hurry. Soulless places, supermarkets, don't you think? I like small shops where I know the owners and where their stuff comes from and what it's made of."

They lapsed into silence. Simon couldn't seem to think of a thing to say. What had happened to his social skills?

Still, walking along in the sunshine with a woman whose long legs could almost match him stride for stride was extremely pleasant.

"Have you always lived with your grandmother?" he managed at last.

She shook her head. "Dad and Mum and I all moved in with Gran when my grandfather, Foster Penberthy, died. I was nine. My parents helped run the shop for five years."

Travis and Nell Penberthy. The old man at the pub had mentioned them.

"Mum and Dad were killed in a car accident when I was fourteen," Rebecca continued. "They owned a rather ancient car, and the brakes failed." Her face was sad for a moment, but then it cleared. "I'm afraid my father wasn't much of a mechanic. He was a bit of a dreamer, always forgetting to get things checked. Mum wasn't much better. Gran and I were ever the practical ones. But Mum and Dad were wonderful people for all that, loving, friendly, very popular in Penmorton."

She was surprised at herself for telling him more than he'd asked. She'd done that before, when he'd asked if she'd always lived in Penmorton. Because he was easy to talk to, she supposed. He listened without interrupting, something a lot of people couldn't manage.

He also watched her a lot when he thought she wasn't aware of it. He kept coming into the shop to buy yogurt, which he subsequently threw, uneaten, into the dustbin. He must have disposed of four or five containers. Apparently he wanted to talk to her, but the opportunity hadn't presented itself.

Until now.

She felt a little thrill go through her, but whether it was a thrill of fear or pleasure she couldn't have said. All she was sure of was that Simon Flynn had something on his mind. As characters frequently said in American television dramas, he had his own agenda.

Wondering what it could possibly be, she missed the curb as they started over the pedestrian crossing at the foot of Robin Hill. At once his hand shot out to steady her, but as soon as she'd regained her footing he released her.

Her heart bumped against her rib cage. His large, warm, competent-looking hand cupping her bare elbow had activated interest in her inner regions. She'd already felt a tingle or two when he was around. This time there'd been enough of a response to raise the fine hairs on her arms. As if he'd scuffed his feet on a carpet just before he touched her. She smiled to herself. Such a romantic image.

But perhaps the interest was all one-sided. His hovering about her may have had nothing to do with attraction. Trouble was, she didn't have any recent experience to judge by. She was dreadfully out of practice in man/woman relationships. Perhaps it was simply the unaccustomed experience of walking along next to a man that was affecting her, making her feel... feverish. Especially considering that the man in question was extraordinarily attractive.

She was determined, however, to avoid relationships, even if her body seemed to be developing a mind of its own. Any sparks of electricity were best stamped out before they became bothersome flames. Actually she was surprised she had any sparks left. She'd thought she'd closed down all systems when her longtime boyfriend Todd Trevelyan had stormed off in a huff because she couldn't get away for the weekend he'd planned without consulting her.

Lawrence Brent, the boyfriend before Todd, had resented her lack of freedom just as much and had given up on her several months before Todd came along. She'd liked Todd, but she'd really loved Lawrence. It still hurt to think about him. She supposed she couldn't blame either man for getting tired of coping with her situation. But that didn't mean she wanted to go through all that heartache again. Conjuring up an image of her grandmother's walled courtyard, she mentally locked herself away inside it.

"You and your grandmother seem very close," Simon said. "I gather she's fairly dependent upon you?"

Rebecca gave a short laugh. "She wouldn't like hearing you say that. There isn't a dependent bone in her body. In many ways she's self-sufficient. But she has to rely on me quite a lot, yes. Her arthritis is crippling, especially in her fingers and wrists. She's not able to manage clothing that buttons or snaps, and it's difficult for her to do things that require lifting or gripping. She can wash dishes, though—the hot water helps—and she can cook and dust and make beds well enough to suit both of us. She does her bit, believe me, and she keeps active. She takes a walk almost every morning."

Rebecca paused for a moment. "The most worrying thing is her heart condition. She had a severe attack of rheumatic fever when she was twelve, but the cardiac damage didn't really show up until well after my parents were killed. That was a dreadful time for both of us, but we managed to muddle through. But then out of the blue, just about the time I finished school, she had a heart attack, and I almost lost her, too."

Am I talking too much again? she wondered. Probably. But when did she ever get a chance to talk to someone sympathetic? She mustn't whine, though. "Most of the time Gran's just fine," she said firmly. "As long as she gets plenty of rest and takes her medication and isn't exposed to stress. She says I fuss too much, but I don't really. I just keep an eye on her. Somebody has to."

He didn't say anything for a moment or two, then he asked, "You don't resent being . . . tied down?"

She shook her head. "Looking after Gran isn't just a duty, it's a loving commitment. She took care of me when my parents died. Now it's my turn to take care of her."

She hesitated. She'd always valued honesty, and she wasn't living up to her own standards. "There *are* occasions when I feel a bit put upon," she admitted. "I'm no saint. But those feelings never last. I love my grandmother, and I want to do everything I can for her. It's been me and Gran against the world for many years."

She hesitated again. "I'm sorry Gran isn't nicer to you. It's not you personally. She's that way with a lot of people, even locals. I think it's some sort of defense mechanism. She's not had an easy life, and her health problems make her feel useless. She'd much rather be completely independent, you see, and that's not possible. So she compensates by being—"

Rebecca broke off.

"Cranky?" Simon supplied.

She laughed. "She also has this thing about Americans."

"I've noticed." Simon grinned. "I admire that part, to tell you the truth. I like people with an attitude. And tourists *can* be obnoxious. Anyway, think what a scary world it would be if everyone went around with a happy face all the time."

He frowned. "I'm sorry to hear about her heart problem, though. That makes it..." His voice trailed off.

She felt his gaze on her face again and turned her head questioningly. How incredibly blue his eyes were in the sunlight. And how intense his gaze was. He was going to say something very intimate, she was sure. A surge of feeling went through her, and it was difficult for her to look away. Maybe she'd better imagine a locked room, rather than a courtyard. A locked room without any windows. Or maybe a castle with a moat.

"Was your grandmother in this area during World War II?" he asked.

Oh, dear. She really did need to keep a rein on her imagination. Stifling her disappointment, she said, "I expect she was."

"You don't know?" Normally she liked the way his dark eyebrows slanted upward when he was puzzled, but she was feeling slightly miffed that he appeared more interested in Gran than in her. She also wondered what on earth he was leading up to.

"Gran doesn't ever talk about the war," she said. "She always insists she doesn't remember anything about it. It was very traumatic for a lot of English people. There weren't any air raids in Penmorton, and of course most of the blitz centered on London, but bombs were dropped on Plymouth, I've been told. Being right on the English Channel, it must have been nerve-racking all along this coast. For a while everyone was expecting the Germans to land on our shores."

He didn't comment.

She resettled her glasses on the bridge of her nose—they had a tendency to slip. Simon Flynn wasn't looking too happy. Perhaps he was bored. Perhaps he'd just been making idle conversation and hadn't really wanted to be told about wartime England.

"That was an odd sort of question to ask," she found herself blurting. "What made you wonder if Gran was here during the war?"

He seemed taken aback by her question. Once again his intense gaze met hers. "I don't... I really didn't... I was just curious."

Which wasn't much of an answer. Tit for tat, she thought. It was her turn to question him. If he was married it would be easier for her to zap her burgeoning chemical reaction out of existence. "Do you have a family, Simon?" she asked. "A wife, children?"

"Well, of course I—" He broke off. "Whoa!" he exclaimed. He'd stopped walking and was staring ahead in astonishment. Following his gaze, she could see nothing out of the ordinary about the High Street. Had her question about a wife and children startled him so?

It's the picture on the postcard, Simon thought. He must have driven past the *other* end of the High Street when he arrived in Penmorton. It hadn't even occurred to him to look for it. And here it was. There was that graceful curve of the street, the small shops, the Cock and Fox pub, the restaurant with the bay window.

It was an odd feeling, looking at the actual street. Sort of déjà vu. Except for the vintage of the few cars parked on one side, the High Street didn't appear to have changed much.

His grandfather must have often gazed at that postcard after he returned to the U.S., Simon thought. And he'd probably stood here in this very spot looking at the street. More than fifty years ago. At a time when he was, according to Simon's grandmother, a whole different person. Young and happy-go-lucky...

Paul Carmichael must have watched sea gulls that were just as lively and vigorous and clamorous as those soaring and dipping and screeching above the stone buildings now. He must have seen the sun glinting on the water in the harbor at the far end of the street to his right, felt the warmth of the Cornish sun on his head.

The High Street would have been crowded with men and women in uniform then. Simon blinked; he could almost see them. He blinked again and saw, instead, townspeople and tourists dressed casually in bright colors. He felt a sudden closeness to his grandfather, which he'd rarely felt when the man was alive.

He became aware that Rebecca was staring at him. Which was hardly surprising. "The architecture, all that gray stone," he murmured as they walked on, hoping she'd accept admiration as a reason for his sudden trance.

She smiled. "My father used to say that if a man hereabouts in the olden days had the strength to lift a stone he must have been assured of a lifetime job. All the old houses and public buildings and churches are made of stone and granite, some of them dating back to the sixteenth century. Then there's that enormous harbor wall and the quays and the bridges. Think of the thousands and thousands of stones that had to be moved from one place to another without a lorry in sight."

He nodded, still feeling slightly stunned by the unexpected familiarity of the street. Rebecca glanced at him again. "You were going to tell me about your family?"

Glad to be able to cover up his reaction to the High Street, he launched into a description of his father's and grandmother's obsession with golf, his mother's recent skiing accident. He went on to tell her about his grandmother's new condo in Arizona, but still couldn't quite bring himself to mention his grandfather.

"You've not said anything about the wife and kiddies," Rebecca said with a sidelong amused glance when he finally ran down.

"That's because they don't exist," he told her. "Much to my mother's disappointment, I haven't even come close to getting seriously involved."

"You're prejudiced against women or just marriage?"

Was that a tactful way of asking if he was gay? Simon wondered. It was amazing how many women thought that if you weren't married you had to be gay. *You see a man over thirty who hasn't married yet, he has red flags all over him,* Laurie Bergstrom had said soon after she'd met him. She, who was thirty-two herself and still single. Ha!

"Mostly I've been too busy to think about getting married," he said, which was true, though some of his busyness had been play. "Circumstances..." He didn't really know what to say, so he simply let his voice trail away into mysterious silence.

Rebecca nodded as if she understood.

While she took care of her shopping, Simon bought a few items to justify staying with her. All the store-keepers knew her, of course. And obviously liked her. They asked after her grandmother, with respect it seemed, rather than affection.

When the shopkeepers looked curiously at Simon, Rebecca introduced him as a visitor to Penmorton who'd taken lodging in her cottage because all the bed-and-breakfast places were full. Which was the truth as she knew it.

He was beginning to feel guilty about deceiving her, but he still hadn't a clue how to broach the subject of the relationship between his grandfather and Bliss. It had been a blow to hear that Mrs. Penberthy had forgotten the war years. How could anybody forget a war? Did her memory loss apply only to traumatic incidents? Had his grandfather been a traumatic incident?

Worst of all, how on earth could he question the old woman if she wasn't supposed to be exposed to stress-ful situations? He sure didn't want to trigger a heart attack.

"Simon?" Rebecca said.

He gazed at her blankly for a moment, then looked around. They'd just emerged from Corwin's Grocery. He had no memory of being inside the shop. Better just start talking and see if an idea presented itself, he decided.

First he insisted on carrying the string bag full of groceries. Then, as they started back the way they'd come, he said, "I've always wanted to visit an old English town. I'm very interested in the urban-village concept—the idea of developments complete in themselves, with stores and restaurants and schools and police and fire departments and entertainment. That arrangement seems far preferable to building residential suburbs that require people to drive long distances to the nearest town or city."

In his nervousness, he was probably talking too much. But Rebecca seemed interested, or at least was polite enough to pretend interest, so he carried on, though he kept looking for a way to confess his real reason for coming to England.

"A lot of people object when you want to build apartments here and there," he explained as they started back up Robin Hill. "But some people can only afford an apartment. I always try to make sure the apartments blend in with the neighborhood and that nothing I do harms the environment. Right now I'm waiting for the result of a study to determine the best way to build in order to preserve the ecological balance of a river."

"That's wonderful, Simon!" Rebecca said with great enthusiasm, smiling warmly at him. "There've been too many developers who've gone ahead with their plans thinking only of the financial gains, rather than the environment."

Behind her glasses, her eyes were shining. In the clear afternoon light, they were the color of amber, the kind once obtained by the ancients from the shores of the Baltic Sea. Simon gave himself a shake. Cornwall's sea air was still stimulating previously unsuspected poetically inclined brain cells.

"Tell me some more about your work," Rebecca urged.

He felt guiltier than ever. He'd been trying to get her alone for so long, and now that he had her he was too cowardly to get on with the business he'd come here to settle. "Well, my current project is a fairly good example, I guess," he said slowly. "I was approached by the development association of a rural Washington town. It used to be a thriving timber area, but now the logging regulations have changed in order to protect what's left of the old-growth forests and the wildlife that depend on them. The group want me to come up with some ideas for a shopping/restaurant/hotel complex that would attract tourists. The site is ideal, by a river, as I said, but there's not much in the way of entertainment. No movie theaters, interesting stores or decent restaurants. You can't even rent a boat."

"What you need is another Penmorton," Rebecca suggested. "We have all those things. Not that I ever have time to make use of them." She laughed. "Our beaches are famous, but I don't know when I last had sand in my shoes. Gran's always on at me to get out more, but it never seems possible."

Simon nodded his understanding. "My mother complains because I don't take enough time off, either." He shifted the string bag to his other hand. Better not mention that wasn't the only complaint his mother had about his behavior. "When I agreed, er, when I decided to make this trip, she and my business partners acted as if the end of the world was imminent." He grinned, remembering what a hard time Biff and Christopher had given him: *You trust us. You really trust us!*

"It would be quite a challenge to build Penmorton in Washington State," he said, "But unfortunately transplanted cultures always seem to end up looking like theme parks."

She laughed again.

How had he ever thought her not beautiful? She was really quite lovely, in spite of her earth-maiden clothing and manner. For a moment he was distracted, but then he realized the health store was in sight and he still hadn't told her why he was in England. "I wonder," he said in desperation, "if you could possibly go out to dinner with me tonight. There's...something I'd like to discuss with you and..."

She was already shaking her head. "It's Gran's physical-therapy night. I have to drive her into Plymouth for it. Tomorrow perhaps...No, that wouldn't work, either, nor would Sunday, and Monday's the eighth of May and I promised Gran—" She broke off, looking thoughtful.

Just as Simon felt his frustration mount, she flashed him one of her mischievous smiles and said, "I've an idea, but I'm not sure you'll think much of it. I'm wondering if you'd like to join me on Monday. I promised Gran I'll take part in this celebration we have going on. As I told you, she's forever nagging me to get away from the house and the shop. So I said I'd go and I will, but it would be much more fun if I had a partner."

"I'd love to be your partner," he said at once.

She laughed. "You'd better watch accepting before you know what's involved, Simon. It's a big day on Monday. An annual event called the furry dance. Ours isn't as grand or formal as the one in Helston, but it's a lot of exercise."

"Monday?" he queried. "The health store isn't open on Monday?"

"Nothing will be open while the furry dance is on." She put out a hand for her string bag as they approached the shop door. There was a car parked at the curb, Simon noticed, a white car with a blue stripe along the body, a blue light on the roof. It belonged to the Devon and Cornwall constabulary.

"The furry dance?" he asked, not really paying attention. What were the police doing here? Shopping? Well, maybe. Police officers needed to stay healthy too.

"I've no time to explain the furry dance now," Rebecca said. "You'll have to wait and find out on Monday. Just wear jeans and trainers—gym shoes—like today. Come over at eleven-thirty and we'll—"

She broke off as the shop door opened and the bell tinkled.

Mrs. Penberthy's radar at work again, Simon thought, then realized Rebecca's grandmother was not alone. Standing beside her in the doorway, an inch or two shorter, was a police officer. He was young and plump and earnest, with country pink cheeks.

"You're Simon Flynn?" the constable asked.

CHAPTER FOUR

EVEN AS HE confirmed that he was Simon Flynn, Simon wondered why perfectly honest people like him should feel guilty when confronted by a police officer.

"There's a message for you," the officer said, handing him a folded piece of paper. "Came in an hour ago." Touching a polite finger to his hat he nodded to Rebecca and Mrs. Penberthy and headed for his car.

The message read, "E.T. phone home."

The caller wasn't named. She didn't need to be. Ever since Simon had graduated from college and moved into his own apartment, his mother had been leaving that message on his answering machine whenever she felt neglected. Occasionally she had news to impart, but he had a suspicion that wasn't the case this time.

Libby had called an hour ago, according to the time written on the paper. It was now nine o'clock in the morning in Seattle. He showed the note to Rebecca and explained the message.

"Could there be something wrong?" she asked as she led the way through the shop to the door in back. "Now there's a daft question. How would you know?" She opened the door and gestured to her right. "The telephone's there."

"I'll charge the call, of course," he said, wishing there was more privacy. The hallway led to a set of stairs to the living quarters above, but Mrs. Penberthy had sat herself down on a bench in the hall, her spine marvelously straight as always. She looked as if she had no intention of moving for some time to come.

"We have to hurry, Gran," Rebecca said, looking down at her grandmother worriedly as Simon worked out the instructions in the phone book. "We've dinner to cook, and we have to go to Plymouth for your treatment, remember."

"Dinner's already on," Mrs. Penberthy said. "The potatoes had those nice thin skins, so I could scrub them and didn't have to wait for you to peel them. I'll just sit a minute and catch my breath if you don't mind. Opening the door to that policeman was a shock. It was enough to give me another heart attack."

She gave Simon a sidelong look. A heart attack would have been his fault obviously.

Just as obviously his mother was in excellent spirits when he got through to her, which he did surprisingly quickly. "I was beginning to wonder what happened to you," Libby said, sounding as if she was in the same room. "I couldn't stand the suspense, sitting around here, waiting. All this inactivity. I am so *bored*, Simon. Did you find your grandfather's other woman?"

"You mean you sent the police out to get me just to find out—" He broke off in exasperation. He couldn't say much else when "the other woman" was sitting only a few feet away.

"Well, I had no idea where you were staying, darling," Libby said reasonably. "The police officer I talked to was very nice about it. Said he could quite see why I'd worry about my son not getting in touch after going so far away and it was a shame the way people nowadays treated their parents and he did happen to know there was a young American man staying with

Mrs. Penberthy and it was no bother at all to have someone go up and see if it was you.''

She finally took a breath. ''He had a great accent. Kind of buzzy and earthy. I do love English accents. So, Simon, did you find her?''

''I think so,'' he said.

''You think so. Can't you do better than that? How did you find her? Was it difficult? What's her last name?''

''You said it.''

''I did? I didn't say any... Wait a minute... You mean Penberthy? That's Bliss's name, Penberthy? How did you manage to get to stay with her? That's very clever of you, darling. I didn't know you had it in you. What's she like?''

''If you'd ask one question at a time, I might manage to answer,'' Simon said.

Evidently reassured there was no personal emergency, Rebecca headed up the stairs. Her grandmother continued to sit, posture impeccable, eyes fixed on the opposite wall, one accusing hand still pressed to her heart. Simon could almost see her ears straining to hear.

''You sound stilted,'' Libby said. ''Is someone listening?''

''You catch on quick, Mom.''

''No need to be sarcastic, Simon. I wasn't thinking. Have you asked her about your grandfather?''

''Not yet.''

''Why not?''

Simon sighed audibly, hoping the sound would give his mother a clue to his problem.

''Why not?'' she repeated.

''It's not that simple, Mom.'' God, it was impossible to sound natural when someone was listening in.

As though she'd heard his thought, Mrs. Penberthy finally stood up and went past him toward the stairs, giving him a withering once-over on the way. She climbed the stairs slowly.

"Well?" Libby demanded.

"I'll write you, Mom."

"You can't talk? Oh, I get it. Bliss herself is listening. God, this is exciting. Can't you find another phone? How about a pay phone somewhere?"

"I'll write you, Mom," he repeated. "Tomorrow. It's all very complicated."

It was Libby's turn to sigh. With acceptance apparently. "You have found her, though?"

"I'm fairly sure, yes."

Before she could ask any more unanswerable questions, he gave her the Penberthy address and phone number, and she let him go.

Picking up his own bag of groceries, Simon headed for the cottage. It was too bad Rebecca didn't have any spare time before Monday. He'd just have to hope the furry dance, whatever it was, would provide an opportunity for conversation.

WHATEVER ELSE he'd expected, it wasn't this, Simon thought on Monday morning. He and Rebecca had just joined the line of expectant dancers who were enjoying the sunshine outside the church at the top of the steep hill. As they'd made their way up the hill earlier, Rebecca had explained the occasion to him.

The furry, or floral, dance was held to celebrate the coming of spring. It was why many of the doorways in town were decorated with green boughs and flowers. The most famous furry dance took place in Helston, Cornwall. There, men dressed in top hats and tails, and women wore crinolines and full-length print dresses and garden-party hats gay with flowers.

Recognizing a good tourist gimmick when they saw one, Penmorton residents had adopted the dance, too. Theirs was less formal, but no less joyous, Rebecca said. People of all ages took part. And it was danced out-of-doors.

The festivities started promptly at noon, with the town's brass band leading the way, the tubas' Oom-pah-pah establishing the rhythm.

The pattern of the dance was simple enough, featuring a few easy steps, a twirl of your partner. Almost like country-and-western dancing. Whoever wasn't dancing had turned out to watch. People were gathered in front of houses and shops and in second-floor windows, where they clapped and shouted encouragement.

A gray-haired woman in a flowered apron handed Simon a small bunch of violets, which he presented to Rebecca. Smiling, she pulled the stems gently through a belt loop on her jeans, then glanced up at him with a look that was grave and yet aware. The combination caused all kinds of interesting things to happen in a certain part of his anatomy.

Surprised, Simon looked at his partner with radically increased interest. Was there a possibility...? For the first time, he missed a step and stumbled over a cobblestone. *Concentrate on the dance steps, Flynn*, he scolded himself. At the moment there wasn't any room for lustful thoughts.

When they'd been waiting for the dance to begin, he'd imagined it would proceed in a straightforward manner downhill. Instead, the long line of dancers heel-and-toed and pranced forward along every street and alley and tree-shaded lane, in and out of a few gardens, even straight through a pub, somebody's very large house and what looked like a courthouse.

"How long does this go on?" Simon asked after the last digression. They weren't far from the health store.

Rebecca gave him the mischievous smile he'd learned to watch for, her amber eyes full of light. "As long as it takes," she said.

Pulling on her hand, he spun her twice as fast as usual as punishment for teasing, but she just laughed at him. Somewhere along the route she'd lost the rosette that had held her long black hair neatly in place, and now the thick strands swirled around her face as she danced, making her look more like a woodsprite than an earth maiden.

He found himself imagining that long, black hair spread on a white pillow, those amber eyes shining gold as she looked up at him leaning over her...

Beyond Rebecca, he suddenly caught sight of Mrs. Penberthy sitting bolt upright in a straight chair outside the store, staring at him. He immediately swept his mind clean of all fanciful images and tried not to look guilty.

Oddly enough, for once Mrs. Penberthy's expression didn't show disdain, but rather confusion, as though something about him puzzled her.

And then he and Rebecca danced past and the moment was lost before he could speculate further.

Like him, Rebecca wasn't the least bit out of breath, he noticed. It was midafternoon now, and there was pleasure in the knowledge that they were still going strong, while ahead and behind people were dropping out and walking alongside.

There was pleasure, too, in watching Rebecca's expressive face, the healthy color tinting her high cheek-bones, pleasure in the gradually acquired compatibility of their two young bodies moving fluidly in unison, turning at just the right moment.

It was odd, Simon thought, that such unromantic music could produce such a romantic result. The street was crowded with dancers and onlookers, and he and Rebecca were dancing ahead of a couple of German tourists—a portly man and even stouter woman—both of whom had alarmingly red faces. In front of them were a pair of tangle-footed Scandinavian teenagers in very short shorts who every once in a while threatened to bring down the whole line like dominoes.

And yet, despite the crowd and the craziness, something was happening to him and Rebecca as the dance continued. Something magical. They'd stopped laughing. Their eyes kept meeting. The clasp of their hands seemed more intimate. It might have been a moonlit evening and the two of them alone, enclosed in a magnetic force field, in which they touched each other, let go, touched again. Their bodies swayed, turned, came together, parted, their glances meeting again, holding again, eyes glistening....

It was a long time before the dance ended, yet not long enough, even though Simon and Rebecca were both beginning to falter. As he reluctantly let go of Rebecca's hand, Simon saw that they'd stopped at the bottom of Robin Hill, right outside the Smugglers' Inn, which seemed a very appropriate place to be, considering the thirst he'd built up.

Unthinkingly, only glad to have a chance to spend more time with Rebecca now that his thoughts had taken such a surprising turn, Simon followed the rest of the dancers inside to the cool, dim comfort and a welcome place to sit.

"That was lovely," Rebecca said as she collapsed into a chair. "You did very well for an outsider, Simon. We'll have to make you an honorary citizen."

"I'll settle for a beer," he said.

She shook her head. "You have to drink cider—it's traditional."

Simon frowned. "I'm not all that fond of apple juice."

Laughter rippled out of her, as musical as wind chimes in a breeze. Simon didn't know what had amused her, but he felt undeniable stirrings again and made no attempt to suppress them. He was enjoying the day, the woman, the place, more than he'd enjoyed anything in a long time.

Still chuckling, Rebecca lifted her hair from the back of her neck to let some cool air touch the skin there. He wanted to touch it, too. She had a lovely, slender neck, he'd just now noticed. She also had a strong jawline and a smooth tanned throat that he wanted to kiss.

"You call Cornish cider apple juice and there'll be a general uprising against America," she said, obviously unaware of the images chasing around in his salacious mind.

No, not completely unaware. Her eyelashes fluttered slightly as he kept his gaze on her, not in a flirtatious way, but as if a sudden tremor had taken hold of her.

A glass mug appeared in front of Simon, served by a young man who hadn't been in the pub that first day. Clinking the mug with Rebecca's, Simon took a long, thirsty swallow and set the glass down with a satisfied sigh. It was then he realized he should have sipped it, instead.

"Whoa!" he exclaimed, immediately understanding the reason for Rebecca's earlier laughter. "Let me guess, this is the hard stuff."

"We call it Scrumpy," she informed him, her eyes wide with mischief.

"I take it it's fermented."

"To a fare-thee-well. It's rough cider, with a fairly high alcohol content."

He laughed and so did she, and their glances met and held again. This time an awkwardness that was not at all unpleasant came between them. "I ought to get back," she said at last. "I have bookkeeping to catch up on, and it's getting close to dinnertime."

Simon nodded, but neither of them made a move. After a moment, he reached out a hand and covered hers where it lay on the table. Then they just sat there, looking at each other. Simon felt he could sit there with her forever, having no need to talk. Wasn't there something he'd meant to tell her? He'd forgotten.

Memory returned abruptly when Clytie, who'd been busily serving the hordes until now, suddenly showed up at their table wearing a richly patterned Japanese kimono, her hair done up in a knot with a couple of lacquered chopsticks thrust through it.

She said a very friendly hello to Simon, provoking a surprised glance from Rebecca.

Suddenly realizing the danger in this situation, Simon tried to gather himself together, realizing he must get Rebecca to leave right now, before Clytie could say another word.

He was too late.

"So aren't you the sly one, then, Mr. Flynn, my darlin', killin' two birds with one stone," Clytie said.

He managed what felt like a very weak grin and tried to think of a graceful exit line, but his brain had turned to mush.

Clytie had already turned to Rebecca. "It was a good thing Mr. Flynn 'ere asked about a woman named Bliss when old Corny Cornwood was in the pub. I'd never have known your grandmother's Christian name was Bliss. Mrs. Penberthy, I always call 'er when I'm in the 'ealth shop. That's pretty that is, Bliss Penberthy. But Mr. Flynn might never 'ave found you if old Corny 'adn't known straightaway 'oo Bliss was."

She beamed at Simon, who was wishing desperately he could disappear through the floorboards. "And you found a place to stay, I 'ear," she went on. "Lucky it was, too, that Rebecca wanted a lodger just when you wanted a room."

Bestowing another smile on both of them, she asked if they wanted more cider, then went cheerily on her way when they stiffly refused.

Rebecca didn't say a word until they were outside and starting up Robin Hill. Simon's legs were beginning to ache. So was his head. "Would you mind explaining yourself, Mr. Flynn?" she asked. Her voice and expression were so frosty it was obvious for the first time that she'd inherited more than a couple of genes from her grandmother.

"It's a complicated story, Rebecca. It might be better if..." His blue eyes were asking for understanding, but she wasn't going to give him an inch of it.

"It might have been better if you'd said straight out when you came into our shop that you were looking for a woman named Bliss," she said hotly. "Asking all over town for her and then never telling us..."

When Rebecca thought of how much pleasure she'd had in the furry dance with him, how she'd even begun to think she could maybe open the gate to the court-yard she'd locked herself into and let him come at least partway in...

"I didn't ask all over town," he protested. "I only asked Clytie because she was friendly and I thought she probably knew everyone. Then Mr. Cornwood volunteered the information that Bliss was your grandmother's name."

He paused for a breath, then added, "I asked you to come to dinner with me on Friday night, remember? I was going to tell you the whole story then. I tried to get you alone in the shop on several occasions, but your grandmother kept coming in."

There was some truth in that, Rebecca realized, but all the same... "There's nothing you can tell me that you can't say in front of Gran," she said flatly.

"But you told me about her heart attack and how she shouldn't be exposed to stress," he pointed out.

Rebecca had to acknowledge the truth of that. "What possible stress could you be causing her, then?" she demanded.

Simon stopped walking. "Look Rebecca, we're almost to the shop. I can't possibly explain such a complicated story out here in the street."

He looked at her in that intense way of his and put his hands on her shoulders. "I assure you I mean no harm to your grandmother."

"I'll be the judge of that," she said, shaking him off. "I'll come to see you in the cottage the minute Gran and I get through with dinner."

She walked on quickly and was grimly pleased that Simon had to exert himself to keep up with her on the steep hill. She was so incensed her anger had driven the tiredness out of her legs. Evidently he was still feeling his. Good.

To think she'd actually allowed herself to begin to feel a little interest in him when all the time he'd had an ulterior motive in asking to rent the cottage.

"I'll be there in a couple of hours," she said over her shoulder as she opened the shop door. "And if your story isn't a good one, you'll be out of our cottage before you can say Jack Robinson."

She felt filled right to the top with anger, not just because he'd deceived her, but because she'd come so very close to deceiving herself.

CHAPTER FIVE

TWO AND A HALF HOURS later Rebecca banged the brass knocker set next to the French doors of the cottage. Simon opened up so promptly she wondered if he'd been watching for her through the window.

He looked deeply apologetic, almost hangdog, as he gestured her in. He was in fresh jeans and a short-sleeved shirt that showed off his biceps very nicely. He smelled of soap, and his black hair was damp and brushed into neatness, which made him look boyish and appealing. She wanted to pat his troubled face and say, "There, there."

She hardened her heart.

"I'm sorry about the shower in here," she said when he didn't seem to know how to begin. "Gran and I know Americans like their showers, and ours isn't very efficient,"

"It works fine now," he said. "I soaked the head in vinegar for several hours. It was clogged."

He waved her to the settee. He was keeping the cottage very tidy and clean, she noted. There was only the one room, except for the bath, but it seemed spacious because of all the windows. It was plainly but comfortably furnished with overstuffed chairs covered with cabbage-rose chintz, the aged, down-filled white couch she was sitting on and a few mismatched but usable antique tables. The bed that jutted out from the far wall was probably not long enough for him, but it was a double, with a good mattress and box spring, so he could lie diagonally on it, she supposed.

Why on earth was she making an inventory of the furniture?

She pushed her glasses into place and looked up at him.

He ran a hand through his hair, then stared at his palm as though surprised to find it had come away damp. "May I get you some coffee?" he asked, wiping the hand on his jeans. "It's freshly made. Or would you prefer tea?"

"Coffee would be fine," she said, her voice stiff.

He brought her a mug, offered milk and sugar and a spoon, which he dropped on the carpet and had to replace. He was so awkward she kept wanting to soften her attitude, but wouldn't allow herself. She took a sip of the coffee, which was far better than any she'd ever made, set the mug down on a mat on one of the antique tables and looked at him again.

He picked up an envelope from the sideboard, took out a postcard and handed it to her, then sat himself down in an armchair and reached for his own coffee, holding the mug in both hands as though he needed the warmth.

He'd given her a picture postcard of Penmorton, an old one, by the look of it. "My grandfather died recently," he said. "My maternal grandfather, Paul Carmichael." He paused as though expecting her to recognize the name.

She didn't. Was Paul Carmichael some kind of celebrity? she wondered. Was that why Simon had thought she might know him?

"Just before he died," Simon continued, "my grandfather showed a photograph and that postcard to my mother. He came here during World War II. Specifically 1943 to 1944. He was a sergeant in the Army Air Corps, as the United States Air Force was called then. An engineer/gunner."

"He came to Penmorton? I don't think there was an American base here. At least I've never heard of one."

"We don't know how long he was here or why he came. We only know he did visit and that while he was here he met a woman." Setting down his coffee, he took something else from the envelope and passed it to her.

She studied the photograph for several minutes. There was a teasing familiarity about the young woman in it. "That's a land-army uniform," she said slowly. "I've seen pictures in magazines and newspapers. There were a lot of stories and photos published for the fiftieth anniversary of the end of the war."

Quite suddenly she sat bolt upright, not an easy task on the soft settee. She stared at Simon. "You asked me if Gran was in Penmorton during the war. You asked Clytie Belyar at the pub if she knew a woman named Bliss."

Simon nodded. "The woman in the photograph is named Bliss. My grandfather didn't tell my mother the woman's last name. But that photo was in the envelope with the postcard of Penmorton and he said if he hadn't left Bliss behind in Penmorton, he might have been a happy man. He also said he loved her. Bliss."

"My grandmother." Rebecca couldn't quite seem to take in what he was saying. She was hearing all the words, but not putting them together. She looked at the photograph again. "I've never seen photographs of my grandmother when she was this age," she murmured.

"People didn't take so many photos then, of course, and I imagine film might have been in short supply during the war. As well, Gran tends to be very secretive about her past. I asked her once if she didn't have a photograph of her wedding, but she just shrugged and said if she ever had, it had probably got lost."

"Then it is your grandmother?" Simon asked. "I was pretty sure, but I couldn't be certain, even though she's named Bliss. That was one reason I didn't want to say anything too soon."

"You should have told me straight away why you were here," Rebecca said, looking him in the eye. "You had no business coming here, pretending to be a casual visitor, when all the time you had a secret purpose."

She frowned and held up a hand as Simon started to protest. "Wait a minute, I've just now realized what you were telling me. Your grandfather was in love with my grandmother during the war? Did she love him back?"

"I don't know. My family doesn't know. We don't know much more than I've told you."

"But it was so long ago and such a long way to come. Why does it matter to you?"

"It matters to my mother. It's a long story, I'm afraid."

"I've got all night." Rebecca felt heat rush to her face, but decided to ignore it. She'd spoken innocently.

Simon stood up and began pacing, rubbing the back of his neck with one hand. "My grandfather was a very admirable man, Rebecca. He inherited a lot of money from his father who came from a California family that did very well in the gold rush, but instead of living on his wealth, he became a builder, a very fine builder. Mostly he built low-income housing, subsidizing it himself. We've both always preferred to provide affordable but attractive housing for people who work for a living or people in unfortunate circumstances—single mothers, senior citizens living on social security—rather than showplaces for the rich. My grandfather also founded a hospital for poor people, as well as an orphanage."

"That's all very impressive, Simon, but what does it have to do with my grandmother?"

"I'm setting the stage," he said, and she let him go on without interruption while he told her of the cheerful man his grandfather had supposedly been when he went away to war in 1943, the sorrowful man he'd become when his year-long tour of duty was over, the cold and distant man he'd turned into as the years passed.

"My grandmother thought it must have been Paul's war experiences that soured him, and my mother always believed that, too—until he was dying and blurted out that he might have been a happy man if he hadn't left Bliss behind."

Rebecca was looking at him in a puzzled way. "Your grandfather was married to your grandmother *before* he came to this country? Before he met Gran?"

Simon nodded. "Paul and Jane married just after the bombing of Pearl Harbor. December 1941. He became a father less than a year later. My mother was six months old when he left for England."

He went on to explain that his mother had intended coming here in search of the story, but then she'd been injured while skiing and had persuaded him to come in her place. "My mother's a very persuasive woman," he said. "And I was very much in need of a change of... I was overdue for a vacation."

What had he been about to say? Rebecca wondered. He'd definitely changed his mind about something in midstream.

"So you came to spy on my grandmother," she said in an attempt to resurrect her anger, which seemed to be dissipating.

"I'd hardly call it spying," he protested weakly.

"Were you ever going to ask Gran about your grandfather?"

"I intended to eventually." He lifted a hand in mute apology. "It's hardly the kind of thing you can blurt out as soon as you meet someone, Rebecca. 'Excuse me, Mrs. Penberthy, my name is Simon Flynn, and I want to know. Did you have an affair with my mother's father fifty years ago?'"

"You could have told me," she said again.

"Like I said, I kept trying to get you alone. It seemed impossible."

Okay, he had a fair argument. That didn't mean she had to forgive him for being so devious. "Gran would have been twenty-three years old in 1943," she said slowly. "I didn't even know she was in the land army. I certainly never heard that she'd had an affair with a married man."

"Maybe she didn't know he was married. When did *she* get married?"

"Well, I think it was at the end of the war, which would have been 1945, but I'm not really sure. Gran's always been very vague about dates."

She sighed. "My paternal grandfather was Foster Penberthy. I didn't know him very well. About all I recall is that he smelled funny. He died when I was nine— I think I told you that before. Mum and Dad and I came to live with Gran right after."

She spread her hands, palms upward. "Gran loves me, but there are parts of her life she's kept secret. Which is her right, of course."

Rebecca glanced out the window that looked onto the courtyard, but she was thinking of her grandmother, rather than seeing the tubs of flowers and herbs. More to herself than to Simon she said, "If she really doesn't remember, it might upset her to be asked, which could be dangerous to her heart. And if she's *pretending* she doesn't remember, she must have good reason, and her wishes should be respected."

When he didn't respond, she glanced his way and found him gazing at her with an expression on his face she couldn't interpret.

"What?" she asked.

"I've never seen a face show compassion as clearly as yours," he said. "It's a remarkable thing to see. It's obviously not pity, but a deep sympathy, a sort of caring and wanting to comfort and not wanting to hurt all mixed together. I saw you look at a schoolgirl like that a few days ago, and you often have the same expression when you're with your grandmother. I admire you for the way you connect with people. I've never quite learned how to do that."

"Oh." She felt embarrassed, but pleased, also, because he sounded truly sincere and it felt good to be admired.

His gaze held hers, his eyes very blue in the late-evening light striking through the window. Most of the time there was a smile playing around his mouth, but it was absent now. As she gazed back at him, her heart seemed to swell. For a long while she couldn't look away.

"I have to go wash the dinner dishes," she said, standing up. *Coward,* a small voice in her mind accused. *Too true,* she responded.

"I thought you said you had all night." The teasing tone was back in Simon's voice.

"A figure of speech," she said.

"I see." The smile was back, too. "So what do you think?" he asked. "I guess we can't take the direct route to this mystery, but tell me this, aren't you the least bit curious yourself?"

She allowed herself a smile, the first of the evening. "When I was a little girl, my dad used to say I had a bump of curiosity a mile wide. It's still there, and it's itching like mad."

Simon laughed and looked more relaxed than he had since she'd entered the cottage. Probably she was letting him off too lightly, but it felt much better being friends again.

"So as they say in the tabloids, inquiring minds want to know," he said. "What shall we do?"

"Well, you're not to talk to Gran just yet," she said firmly. "This has been a bit of a surprise to me, and I need some time to take it all in before I agree to anything."

He nodded and got to his feet, also.

For a moment the two of them stood facing each other. "You told me you'd noticed I was a compassionate person," she said slowly. "What I wonder is, is that why you told me you had difficulty connecting with people? So I'd feel sorry for you and agree to help you?"

He winced. "I'm not sure I can answer that," he confessed. "Sometimes it's difficult to analyze your own motives. I *think* I just wanted to be open with you."

Their gazes held. Rebecca prided herself on being a good judge of character. All that was honest and honorable seemed to be there in his clear blue eyes. After a moment she nodded, but was still unable to look away. Tension crackled between them. Rebecca had no idea how to dispel it, or even if she wanted to dispel it. It seemed to her that this eye contact was significant. She was reminded of the old films she liked to watch on television where the only way you knew two people were attracted to each other was when the camera kept going from his eyes to hers and back again.

"I'd best be going, then," she said at last, her voice unnaturally throaty.

She thought for a minute he was going to offer his hand for her to shake, then she saw he was looking at her mouth and thought he might be considering kissing her good-night. But in the end all he did was open the French doors and let her out.

The funny thing was, she didn't feel all that disappointed. Like the plot of an old film, she thought, it was best just to be patient and let it play itself through.

CHAPTER SIX

UPSTAIRS, BLISS SAT in her favorite chair at the bay window of her room, watching as her granddaughter came out of the cottage. Rebecca's dark hair gleamed briefly under a stray ray of late-evening sunlight, then she crossed the courtyard and entered the house through the back door.

Bliss listened to her footsteps climbing the stairs, followed her with her mind as she entered the kitchen, then heard the sounds of dishes clinking as Rebecca started the washing up.

She could relax now.

Rebecca had spent a considerable amount of time with the American. What did they find to talk about? Bliss hoped they *had* been talking; though she'd been pleased that Rebecca had taken part in the furry dance, she hadn't much liked the idea of the American doing it with her. What on earth had possessed Rebecca to invite him?

Sighing deeply, Bliss looked down at the old shoe box in her lap, wondering why she'd dug it out of the attic, why she was letting buried memories surface.

It had something to do with Simon Flynn, she felt sure. Something to do with his American accent, his blue eyes, reminding her of someone else whose eyes had been just as blue, bringing that old song back to her mind. "As Time Goes By." No, she wasn't going to sing it, not even in her mind.

There were a few restaurant menus in the box. Not much to choose from during the war: Spam that was supposed to taste as good as ham, which never would in a million years; beef in such short supply all a chef could do was throw a small piece in a pot of vegetables and hope the resulting soup would have some flavor. Halves of tickets from cinemas. They didn't make films like those anymore. *Mrs. Miniver.* Katherine Hepburn in *Woman of the Year.* Ingrid Bergman and Humphrey Bogart in *Casablanca.*

Casablanca. The best film ever made.

There were no letters. Not one.

There was a photograph of herself in her land-army uniform. How funny that hairstyle looked now, but it was practical at the time. Look at those ugly boots. She could remember clomping round in them.

Here was her diary.

It was too painful for her arthritic fingers to try to take hold of the tiny key, let alone fit it into the lock, but that didn't matter. It wasn't necessary to open the book. She could close her eyes and picture her neat rounded handwriting, dark against the ivory pages, picture that first evening as though it were happening again....

London, England—September 1943

THE AMERICAN was still watching her, but Bliss wasn't quite ready to let him know she was aware of him. It was more fun to stand in apparent innocence at the side of the dance floor, swaying slightly to the music, prolonging the delicious suspense, wondering when he'd approach her and what he would say.

The club was crowded, the air blue with cigarette smoke. Men and women sat around small tables, talking, gesticulating. An RAF officer nearby was apparently demonstrating a spitfire dive complete with antiaircraft—ack-ack—gunfire. Several people besides Bliss were watching three couples jitterbug to "In the Mood," played by a first-rate five-piece band.

Most of the birthday-party guests were in military uniform, but a few women, including Bliss, had managed to scrounge up enough ration coupons to buy a pretty frock for the occasion. Hers was utility rayon, of course, but with a matte finish, not the cheap, shiny kind. It was a soft, golden mustard shade that flattered her rolled-up black hair and brought out the gold starbursts in her brown eyes.

She'd even acquired a pair of silk stockings, the seams of which she had lined up at the exact center back of her long, shapely legs. She felt positively elegant. Thank God for the black market, she thought. It was all very well to take notice of all the posters telling you to make do and mend, but once in a while you just had to have something new.

Although she was twenty-three, this was her first trip to London, which made the party qualify as an event, even though she didn't know the guest of honor from Adam.

An elbow jabbed her ribs. Her red-haired cousin, Josie, who was five years older and had wangled their invitations through a friend of her soldier husband, murmured, "Don't turn your head, but there's a Yank watching you."

Bliss allowed herself a small smile. "I know."

"Smashing-looking chap," Josie commented, then wandered away.

Bliss slid her gaze to the left. He wasn't much older than she was. Army Air Corps, the American equivalent of the Royal Air Force.

Most men looked good in uniform, of course, but there was something dashing about this man. He was tall, nicely put together, slim, very fair.

Bliss counted the stripes on his right sleeve, three, plus another one curving underneath. Staff sergeant? His left arm was in a black sling.

He'd caught her staring. He was coming toward her. She took a calming gulp of her tepid gin-and-lime and pretended a deep interest in the couples gyrating on the dance floor.

"Where did you find the sun?" he asked. He had a lovely voice that caused some essential part of her insides to turn to gelatin. He looked like Leslie Howard in *Gone with the Wind*. His blond hair had a wave to it, and his eyes were incredibly blue. And knowing. The sling gave him a jaunty devil-may-care appearance.

Bliss gazed at him blankly, giving him credit for an original line, though she had no idea what he meant by it.

"The sun?" he repeated, his gaze moving down from her face to the low V-neckline of her dress. "You have a great tan."

Her brain seemed completely fuddled.

"I've been frozen ever since I arrived in England," he went on. "I've been here through July and August, which I've always thought of as summer. July was the worst. I had to wear my overcoat! Until I saw you standing here all bronzed and gleaming, I didn't believe the sun ever shone in this country."

Bronzed and gleaming. Was that how she appeared to him? Bliss felt terribly flattered, even as she began to blush. "I'm outside a lot," she told him awkwardly. "I'm in the women's land army, stationed at a farm owned by a man named Tom Garland. It's just a few miles from my home in Cornwall. Our climate is a little milder than other parts of England—we even have palm trees. We've had quite a good summer."

He had smooth, light eyebrows that slanted upward above a nice straight nose. "Isn't Cornwall near Devon?" he asked.

"Next door."

The American seemed pleased, but didn't explain why. Instead, he asked her to dance. She wasn't at all surprised to discover he was an excellent dancer, despite the sling, and easy to follow. He somehow managed to telegraph every move to her before swinging her out and back and around, so that she danced better than usual herself. "Lucky it's only one side that's banged up," he said during a pause in the music, as if an injury could have any luck attached to it.

She caught Josie watching the two of them and grinned at her. Josie winked, then headed toward the bar with her army officer friend. Obviously she didn't think Bliss needed her company any longer. She was right.

"Paul Carmichael," the American introduced himself once he'd found them a small table against the wall. He'd brought fresh drinks for both of them, carrying a glass in each hand. He wasn't wearing a wedding ring, Bliss noticed as he awkwardly removed the drink from the hand in the sling.

"Bliss Turner." She raised her glass in a small toast and waited for the inevitable comment about the unusualness of her Christian name.

It didn't come. This was an unpredictable man. "Bliss, indeed," he said, gazing deeply into her eyes, smiling.

She felt a shiver go through her that had nothing to do with the temperature of the room and everything to do with Paul Carmichael's smile. It occurred to her that it really wouldn't be all that bad if the war went on forever. Which was a blasphemous thing for an Englishwoman to think, especially now that the tide had turned and the Allies were sure to win.

They talked for ages, leaning across the little table toward each other, forming a tight circle that shut everyone else out. As if by unspoken consent, they didn't talk about air raids or the lack of petrol or any of the dreary wartime subjects people never seemed to get tired of going on about. They didn't drink much, but they smoked a lot of Paul's Lucky Strikes, of which Americans always seemed to have an inexhaustible supply. Lately Bliss had been smoking some horrible fags that tasted as if they were made of hay. Manure, Josie said.

She found out he was from Southern California, not too far from Hollywood he agreed when she questioned him excitedly. He was a builder and carpenter, in partnership with his father and his father's best friend. He'd left his share of the business in their capable hands when he enlisted in the Army Air Corps the day after Japan attacked Pearl Harbor. He hated the regimentation of military life, but loved flying. He was an engineer/gunner on a B-24.

Bliss thought about that for a few moments, then asked, "What's it like, shooting at people?"

"I don't shoot at *people,* Bliss," he said in a chiding tone of voice. "I only shoot at planes."

They danced again. He did the foxtrot beautifully, softly singing all the words to "As Time Goes By" in a pleasant tenor.

Lord, but he was easy to talk to. When they returned to their table, Bliss told him about desperately wanting to play on the field-hockey team in high school, but not being able to because she'd had rheumatic fever, with a resulting heart condition. She'd joined the land army for the same reason; the heart problem had kept her out of the other services.

She told him she loved the land army, had always liked grubbing in the dirt. And old Tom Garland, the farmer she and several other women worked for, was especially good to her. "He's sweet on me, silly old man, and him forty if he's a day. But there, he's nice enough, and kind, bless him, so I don't fuss when he makes sheep's eyes at me."

Her dad hadn't wanted her to join the land army— not because he didn't want her to help the war effort, but because he'd felt Bliss would have been more useful helping at home. In reality, Bliss confided, Dad just didn't like her being away from his influence. And now he was in the army, himself, because there was a need for clergymen.

Dad was Penmorton's rector. Mum owned a little grocery shop. People said her mum had been lucky to make such a wonderful match; he was a man who'd been to college and who spoke like the people on the wireless. Bliss wasn't so sure her mum had been lucky. Her dad was strict, always lecturing Bliss *and* her mum about what he called decorum. She loved her dad, she assured Paul, but there was no getting away from the fact that he was terribly old-fashioned, seemingly dedicated to making abso-bloody-lutely certain Bliss never enjoyed herself.

Away from home, she went to the cinema two or three times a week, more if the flicks were American. America seemed ever so glamorous to her, all oil wells and orange groves. "What wouldn't I give for an orange!" she said.

She recalled one film where the star had a huge oval bedroom window that was draped with ruffled white muslin curtains. She'd made up her mind she'd have a window like that some day.

"I'll make it for you," Paul promised, looking at her as though he was falling for her, which later he'd said he was. "My parents are strict disciplinarians, too," he told her. "My father's very straitlaced and Mom's not exactly easygoing. If they knew what I was thinking right now, I'd be grounded for life."

Bliss wasn't sure what "grounded" meant in that context, but seeing the expression in Paul Carmichael's eyes, she got the general idea.

"What happened to your arm?" she asked to cover her sudden breathlessness. She'd wondered about the sling all along, but thought perhaps she shouldn't bring it up.

He laughed. "I was hit by a machine gun."

"You were *shot?*" Her voice squeaked.

His blue eyes glinted. "Not what I said." He shrugged. "It was kind of a freak accident, nothing heroic. We were flying over the coast of France, bombing sub pens, when we were jumped by an Me-109. While I was shooting at the Messerschmidt, the clamps that held my machine gun in its mount popped open. So far nobody's figured out why. The gun slammed into my left shoulder."

Bliss winced.

"It's not all that bad," he said. "More of a nuisance than anything else. Better my shoulder than my teeth." He smiled and she silently agreed it was a good thing that such beautiful teeth had been spared.

"The best part is that I need to have some specialized treatment for my shoulder," he went on. "Can't be done in London, I found out yesterday."

"They're sending you back to America?" Bliss felt a severe pang of disappointment, which was ridiculous, considering she was going straight back to Cornwall herself the following day and would never see him again.

His eyes held hers. "They're sending me to Devon a week Monday. The doctors reckon the course of treatment should take about a month."

It was a moment before she took in what he was saying. Then her face must have shown her dawning understanding, for he chuckled softly.

"Where in Devon?" she asked through a throat gone dry.

"Plymouth."

A gurgle of laughter bubbled irrepressibly up inside her as though that one word had struck a well of happiness. "What an amazing coincidence," she said. "Penmorton's less than twenty miles from Plymouth. Just the other side of the River Tamar."

That was a suggestive smile he had. Reaching across the table, he took hold of her hand, turned it over and began tracing the lines on her palm with one strong finger. "It says here you believe in fraternizing with the Allies."

"Depends what you mean by fraternizing," she said with a deliberately flirtatious flutter of her eyelashes.

His wonderful blue eyes held hers again. And again she felt a delightful shiver of anticipation travel up her spine.

"There's another coincidence," she said softly. "I'm going to be on leave, starting a week Monday."

"Would you by any chance be spending your leave in Penmorton?" he asked.

"Of course." Until that moment she'd fully intended spending it anywhere but. It wasn't necessary for him to know that, however.

"Perhaps you'll have a chance to visit while you're in the area?" she suggested. "I'll be home for a fortnight."

"A fortnight," he echoed, still staring directly into her eyes.

Bliss felt as if she'd climbed into a car on the big dipper and was about to rattle off over the rails. Things were happening very quickly between Bliss Turner and Sergeant Paul Carmichael.

It was wartime, she reminded herself. It didn't do to postpone happiness or action until tomorrow. It didn't do to postpone anything until tomorrow. A bomb could drop, an enemy plane strafe the streets, a land mine explode and send a hundred people sky-high. Tomorrow might never come.

CHAPTER SEVEN

Dear Mom:

Herewith ET progress report. As you so astutely guessed, I am staying with Bliss Penberthy, aka Dragon Lady, and her granddaughter Rebecca. Well, not exactly *with* them, but in a cottage on their property. Mrs. Penberthy owns a health store in Penmorton. Rebecca has helped her with it ever since her parents, Travis and Nell Penberthy, died in a car accident some time ago. She appears to be a very helpful girl.

It seemed preferable to give the impression of Rebecca as very young. If his mother didn't think too much about length of time between generations, it might work.

Unfortunately, as you also guessed, Mrs. Penberthy was listening in when I talked to you. Also unfortunately, she has a heart condition and is not supposed to be exposed to stress. Which makes it impossible to question her directly. She's also very touchy about Americans. I don't know if that's because of Grandfather Paul, but it seems possible. I'm hoping the granddaughter might come up with some leads. Best if you don't call here—

there's no privacy where the sole telephone is situated.

AFTER EXPRESSING concern about her physical condition and describing Penmorton in great detail, Simon signed off with love.

Giving Rebecca time, he decided to do some sightseeing. On Tuesday, after mailing his letter, he explored Falmouth, but didn't care for it much—he kept getting lost and traffic was heavy.

On Tuesday night he watched television. He sat through an old rerun from the original "Star Trek" series, a couple of comedy shows he kept missing the point of and the nine-o'clock news on BBC1.

On Wednesday he drove to Polperro, where he parked as commanded by signs at the top of a steep hill. Evidently the streets of the ancient fishing village were even narrower than those in Penmorton, and it wasn't possible to drive in them at all. Simon rode down with several very large and jolly ladies in a vehicle that was more like a pickup with a canopy than a bus.

Polperro featured many small stores and restaurants and galleries, but had retained the aura of its past. If he were to turn quickly, Simon thought as he walked, he would surely see smugglers—free traders, the local guidebooks called them—climbing up the narrow, twisting streets from the harbor, where their boats, built for speed, bobbed innocently at anchor. Loaded down with their "imported" spirits and tea and silks and tobacco and salt, they would nod a greeting to him as they wended their weary way home to the small, stone houses on the steep, terraced hillsides.

Odd how real the images seemed, he thought. It was almost as if the stone streets and alleys and houses had retained the imprint of the past, or else, instead of passing into history, the smugglers were merely hidden behind a curtain that occasionally became transparent enough to see through.

Nearly everyone, he learned from his guidebook, had helped with the smuggling in the eighteenth and nineteenth centuries, mayors, magistrates and ministers included. No one had looked upon it as a crime, except perhaps those who'd made the laws against it.

He had a "ploughman's lunch" at an ancient pub: some superb Stilton with lettuce, sliced onions, tomato, watercress and cucumber, topped with flavorful chutney and accompanied by two sturdy hunks of bread and butter and a pot of tea strong enough to stand a spoon up in.

Afterward, he walked around the harbor, wishing he owned a camera, thinking he ought to buy one and behave like a regular tourist. He'd never taken the time to learn anything about photography, but some of the photographers he and his partners had hired as needed had used automatic cameras—they'd seemed fairly easy to operate.

Certainly he could appreciate the pictures that were there for the taking. The tide had gone out, and brightly colored fishing boats lay tilted on their keels in the sandy harbor, hitched at the bow by long cables to the seawall. Up on the cliffs, he was greeted by spectacular views of rocky headlands. By the time he returned to Penmorton, he felt that the salt-scrubbed wind had cleared his brain. *Something* had provided him with inspiration.

Around five o'clock, Rebecca showed up at the cottage door wearing her working uniform—white shirt and slim black skirt—her hair tied smoothly back.

"What do you know about Mr. Cornwood?" he asked as she set a loaded tea tray down on a low table.

Straightening, she looked at him blankly.

"Clytie mentioned him, remember?" he said, gesturing for her to sit on the sofa. "She called him Corny. He was at the Smugglers' Inn the day I arrived. It was Mr. Cornwood who told me your grandmother's name was Bliss. He seemed to know some stuff about your family, your name and the names of your parents, too. I remember thinking he was kind of an oral historian. I liked the idea. History has always interested me. It's always there behind us, shoring us up, pushing us forward, reminding us of our mistakes and of our moments of greatness."

He shook his head. "Sorry. I didn't mean to philosophize. Anyway, Mr. Cornwood is this little old man. Eighty maybe, hard to tell—he wears his cap pulled down so low it's difficult to see his face. Reminds me of Andy Capp in the comics."

Rebecca laughed and leaned forward to pour the tea. "I didn't know you had Andy Capp in America."

She was silent for a few moments, apparently trying to recall Mr. Cornwood, giving Simon another chance to watch the interesting play of expression on her mobile features. "I remember," she said at last, her eyes brightening behind her glasses. "A Mr. Cornwood used to own the newsagent's shop in the High Street. He retired several years ago."

"He might be a good source of information, don't you think?"

She took a sip of tea before answering, then looked at him over the rim of the cup. "You're taking it for granted I'm going to help you research Gran's story."

"You're here."

She laughed. "So I am." A frown puckered her fore-head. "Excuse me a minute." Setting her cup down on the tray, she left the cottage but returned moments later with a telephone directory.

Sitting together on the sofa, they pored over it, but could find no listing for Cornwood in Penmorton or any of the nearby towns.

"He must be ex-directory," Rebecca said, and Simon marveled, not for the first time, at the differences between American and English usage. "Not listed," Rebecca said after a glance at his face.

"We could contact him at the Smugglers' Inn," Simon suggested. "Tonight maybe."

Rebecca looked at him appraisingly for a minute, then nodded.

They left a couple of hours later, after Rebecca had seen her grandmother into bed. By mutual consent, they drove. Simon had climbed several hilly streets in Polperro, and Rebecca had been on her feet in the shop all day. On top of which they were still suffering from the shinsplints brought on by the furry dance a couple of days earlier.

The pub was crowded. Just a plain old Wednesday-night crowd, Clytie told them. They should see it on Friday and Saturday nights. She was wearing a Chinese cheongsam of jade green brocade this time, her bangs dyed to match.

"Corny isn't 'ere," she said, "but 'e's bound to show up sooner or later. Just take it easy and enjoy the entertainment."

The entertainment consisted of a three-piece band, a very pretty young woman with bright red hair playing a lively guitar, a long-haired drummer and a middle-aged black man at a keyboard, who kept giving Clytie

the eye. Several couples were dancing cheek to cheek on
the postage-stamp dance floor. An elderly man solemnly twirled a plump, equally solemn woman dressed
in a purple dress that was straining alarmingly at the
seams.

Sipping their beer, Simon and Rebecca watched the
dancers. It seemed to Simon he could remember being
a pretty good conversationalist not too long ago. When
had he lost the art? When had he become so tongue-tied
in the presence of a woman?

"Would you like to dance?" he said impulsively when
the band began a new set. "Maybe it'll loosen up our
calf muscles."

Amused by his less than romantic way of asking, Rebecca agreed. It really was peculiar, she thought, as they
began to move together to the music, that it was perfectly all right for a man and woman who didn't know
each other well to assume such an intimate position, in
public, with nobody thinking anything of it at all.

Except maybe Clytie, she amended, as she caught the
bartender's speculative glance.

"The band's good," Simon said, sounding strained.
"Yes."
Brilliant conversation.

Simon was a graceful man. Just as he had in the furry
dance, he found the rhythm in the music and moved
easily to it. It was a pleasure to move with him. She
hadn't danced for ages, and now she'd done it twice in
one week. She'd almost forgotten how much she enjoyed it.

This was more intimate than the furry dance, though.
She didn't recognize the slow number the band was
playing, but it had a romantic feel to it.

She was glad she'd kept her skirt and heels on after work; it would have been impossible to dance in the trainers she'd contemplated wearing. And Simon looked even better than usual. He'd caught the sun, and looked healthy and strong. He smelled of the outdoors, clean and windswept. He had been newly shaven when he opened the door of the cottage to her, but stubble was already showing up. Was anything as sexy as a dark-haired man with a five-o'clock shadow?

His hand was warm against the small of her back. Not unpleasantly so. Whenever he was going to change direction, she felt the pressure of his hand increase in a gentle signal. She was conscious of his broad shoulders, his flat stomach almost touching hers. She could feel his breath stirring her hair. It made hers catch in her throat.

"There he is," Simon said just as the guitarist announced an intermission. Rebecca looked toward the bar.

A minute later, Simon had gathered up their beer glasses and was on his way to the bar, Rebecca trailing behind, feeling mildly disoriented.

"Hi, Mr. Cornwood," Simon said as he settled on a stool next to the man. Rebecca crouched down to pet the man's dog. "Remember me? Simon Flynn," Simon said above her head. "We met here a little while back. I couldn't find you in the phone directory, so I thought I'd catch you here. This is Rebecca Penberthy. I believe you know her grandmother."

Mr. Cornwood nodded as Rebecca stood up. How on earth could he see with that cap brim pulled so low? Rebecca wondered as she sat down on his other side.

"Not in telephone book," he said, "because I live with my married daughter." He took a hefty swallow of beer. "Flynn," he repeated. "The name fits. You've the map of Ireland on your face."

So he *could* see, then, Rebecca thought.

"My father's parents emigrated to the United States from County Cork," Simon told him.

"Lot of Irish went to America, I understand. Potato famines and such."

"*Do* you know my grandmother, Bliss Penberthy?" Rebecca asked to get the conversation on track.

"Memory's not what it once was," the old man said. He took another long slow swallow of beer, draining his glass, then set it down with great deliberation on the counter. "Beer seems to help, mind you. Gets the old circulation going, you might say."

"Let me buy you one," Simon suggested, and got no argument.

Clytie rolled her dark eyes. "Talk about a subtle 'int," she muttered.

Mr. Cornwood ignored her. "You ever play darts, lad?" he asked.

Simon smiled at him. Simon had lovely teeth, Rebecca thought, and she really liked his smile. It was always rather wry, but in an attractive way. It was a good clue to his nature. She'd always believed people's looks hadn't much to do with their own efforts until at least their late twenties, but after that they began to reveal the person inside.

Once in a while, Simon's smile looked just a little wistful, which puzzled her because he didn't seem the type who'd have anything to be wistful about. Except he'd said something about not making connections with people. What had he meant by that? Oh, well, a little puzzle to a person wasn't such a bad thing. Open books could be dull.

"I'm known for my darts playing all up and down the West Coast," the puzzling person was bragging to Mr. Cornwood. "There are plenty of dartboards in American taverns and pubs nowadays."

He turned to look at the dartboard on the far wall. "I've only played electronic darts, though. I imagine the traditional board is different?"

"Wouldn't take long to catch on, you," Mr. Cornwood said. "I used to be a bit of a champion player myself."

"Now 'e's a champion moocher," Clytie said. "Get on with you, Corny. You can't be taking advantage of visitors. Not in my pub."

"Wasn't going to suggest playing for money," the old man said indignantly. "Just wanted to get a match going. Nothing wrong with getting a match going, is there?"

"Nothing at all," Simon said with another of his wry smiles.

"It might help with my circulation, too," Corny said. "Exercise sends oxygen to the brain—I heard that on the telly."

Simon laughed. "Well, then, by all means, let the games begin."

The dog rose as soon as his master slid to the floor and followed majestically at heel, not even deigning to turn his head as an English spaniel woofed at him from under a table.

They played a couple of games of 301. Corny Cornwood lifted his cap brim only a fraction in order to see the board, Rebecca was amused to note. He played well, she had to give him that. Every dart found its mark with a solid thunk.

Rebecca wasn't a bad darts player herself, but she'd decided to sit this match out. It seemed a good time for some male bonding.

It took Simon a while to get used to the heavier darts. As he had with the furry dance, he seemed to search for and find the necessary rhythm, then program it into his body. It was a pleasure to watch him. He was graceful, he had good eye-hand coordination, and his broad shoulders followed through perfectly. He gave the game his full attention. By the second game, when he wanted a double, he got one; when he aimed for a triple, the dart flew straight and true into the triple ring.

Their match attracted other players. By the time the band returned to the floor, a regular tournament was in progress. But finally Simon persuaded Corny to a table in the far corner with the promise of beer.

"Haven't seen Bliss Turner in many a year. I knew her mostly when she *was* Bliss Turner," Corny said after wetting his throat thoroughly and looking hopefully at Simon. "Pretty lass, she was."

He smirked as Simon signaled Clytie for a refill. "All Cornish lasses are pretty lasses. You'll've found that out."

"I sure have," Simon said, and he gave Rebecca a smile that took her breath away.

"Bliss wasn't active in sports in school," Corny said. "Didn't look it, but she was delicate 'twas said. Heart, I heard. Had a younger brother went to school with her. She was smart, he said, a hundred percent on all her papers near enough. And she was in the land army during the war, I do recall. Bit of a surprise that, with her heart and all. But all the lasses were in something, couldn't keep 'em at home no more than you could keep the lads. I was in the army myself. Royal Army Medi-

cal Corps. Stationed up in Scotland. Larbert, Sterling-
shire. Got to be a corporal, I did. Hated the army,
though. Bloody hell, it was."

The cap bill turned toward Rebecca. "Pardon my
German, miss."

"Where was Gran stationed or billeted or whatever
it was called?" Rebecca asked before he could get carried away again with his own history.

He swallowed some more beer. "North of here, not
too far. On a farm. Bloke named Tom Garland owned
it—still does, far as I know. Bliss came home regular.
After the war she helped her mum at the shop, just like
you help *her* now, miss, so I hear."

"Were you away all during the war?" Simon asked.
"Did you get a furlough—a leave—at all? Particularly
in 1943 and 1944?"

"I was home D day, that I do remember," the old
man said. "That would be June 1944." He shook his
head. "Bravun days they. Gone now."

Quite suddenly he sat up very straight and turned his
cap toward Rebecca again. She pushed her glasses into
place and studied his face. She could barely see his eyes
gleaming in the shadow of the bill; they were small and
dark, like those of some forest animal. "Stand me right
now," he said abruptly. "There were some talk of a
scandal, weren't there?" His voice was suddenly harsh.
"Bliss Turner. Rector's daughter. What was that about,
then?"

Apparently expecting Corny to empty his glass pretty
quickly, Clytie had come over and was industriously
wiping the table with a checkered cloth. "I don't know
anything about a scandal," Rebecca said sharply.

Corny sat back, apparently thinking. After a minute
or so, Clytie gave up and wandered back to the bar.

"I'm not sure I remember what it was," Corny said, sipping again. "I do remember people talking. You know the way people talk in this town. Too many old women. Always was. I think I did know what it was about once, the gossip. But I've been to bed a time or two since then."

"Another beer?" Simon asked, evidently thinking the pump might need priming, but Corny shook his head. Apparently he had a limit after all.

"PERHAPS WE SHOULD just forget the whole thing," Rebecca suggested as they drove up Robin Hill.

Simon glanced at her in surprise. "We've hardly begun."

"I don't feel right digging round in Gran's past. If there was a scandal, what right do we have to stir up gossip again? There's no knowing if your grandfather was even involved, Simon."

"He was involved in a big way in something. My mother heard such anguish in his voice when he talked about Bliss. He wasn't the kind of man to show emotion."

"Well, I was a bit put off the whole idea by Mr. Cornwood's innuendoes. It's really none of our business."

"Yes it is." Simon surprised himself by his immediate response. He tried to explain it as much to himself as to Rebecca. "Every once in a while, since I've been in England, I've felt my grandfather's presence, prodding me on. He wasn't a happy man. He was missing certain emotions. I think maybe I'm missing them, too. It may sound dumb, but I feel as if finding out the truth about what happened between him and Bliss might help me as much as him. I've come to look upon it as a quest."

He glanced her way, half expecting her to laugh, or at least to look at him as if he was nuts, but instead, she gazed at him solemnly for several moments, then agreed to go on at least a little longer.

"Does your grandmother not have friends her own age?" Simon asked. "There must be other people who've known her all her life. This is a small town."

Rebecca frowned. "I don't know of any friends she's kept through the years. She was always so busy. After my parents died, there were just the two of us, and she concentrated on taking care of me and the shop and being home when I was home. I don't think she had time for friends in those days. She never was one for visiting back and forth. I suppose she's lost touch with the people she used to know well. It happens if you don't stay in touch."

Simon pulled the Peugeot into the lane behind the cottage and cut the engine. He hadn't been any more successful than Bliss in keeping his friendships in good repair, he thought. His work had always come first, and the people he saw socially were always on the move, new people coming in to take their places. People born in the sixties were a restless lot.

"We could try the old Guildhall," Rebecca suggested.

He looked at her questioningly. Evidently he'd missed something.

"The local historical society has quite a collection of historical artifacts," she explained. "It includes old newspapers. If we look at the relevant years we might find something."

It was dark in the car. There were no streetlights in the lane. No door light on this side of the cottage. Even though he could only see Rebecca in outline, he was very conscious of her sitting beside him. She still seemed troubled.

He could smell lavender. He'd noticed it in her presence before. When he was a child, one of his Irish aunts had grown lavender in profusion in her wonderful Seattle garden. In that same garden, nasturtiums had concealed caterpillars under their leaves, and mushrooms had popped up overnight in damp, shady places. How exciting the world had seemed to him then.

He blinked. Where had that thought come from? "You smell of lavender," he said softly.

Her voice sounded tense when she answered, and just a little husky. "Gran dries it every year. She used to make little satin sachets for our dresser drawers when she could still manage to sew. Now we just keep it in envelopes."

"We aren't going to do anything to hurt your grandmother," Simon promised.

She was silent for a moment, then said, "Thank you for understanding, Simon."

He wanted to kiss her, but he wasn't sure how she'd react. He wasn't always that great at interpreting women's responses. He had acted precipitously once or twice, which had made him wary. A few years ago a young woman he'd taken to had kicked his shins so hard his eyes had watered. Yes, relationships were tricky these days. You had to watch your step.

"Well," Rebecca said, opening her door, rendering his hesitation superfluous. "It was an interesting evening."

"Corny's quite a character," he said as he emerged from his side of the car. He sounded stilted again, he realized. Why couldn't he just relax with this woman? She was probably the most relaxing woman he'd ever been around, but he felt keyed up, tense, whenever he was with her.

"We should probably go to the Guildhall soon," she suggested. "I don't suppose you can hang round Penmorton too long. When are you due to leave?"

"I've an open ticket," he said. The truth was, he didn't want to think about leaving. Now that he'd finally taken a vacation, he didn't want it to end. "Is the Guildhall still open when you get through working?" he asked.

"I was thinking we might go on Friday afternoon after I close the shop. It's my early-closing day, remember?"

"You're sure that's okay with you? I mean, I could just go ahead by myself if you—"

"I don't think that's a good idea," she said at once.

"You don't think I'd be discreet?"

"I didn't say that," she said, which wasn't the same as a denial. "I just mean to be with you in this."

Because she *wanted* to be with him? Didn't trust him? Wanted to satisfy her own curiosity? All of the above?

He was beginning to remember that one of the difficulties of seeing too much of one woman involved working out what her apparently simple statements meant. When emotion was involved, simple statements sometimes had several layers of meaning.

Emotion? Since when had emotion replaced plain old everyday lust in his thoughts? The word had always made him nervous. He thought of it as being right up there with other forbidden words such as commitment, relationship, love.

CHAPTER EIGHT

BY FRIDAY AFTERNOON a steady rain had turned the old stone streets of Penmorton into waterways. In spite of the weather, traffic was brisk. Pedestrians hurried along, stooped under umbrellas or hooded raincoats.

Simon had to drive several blocks beyond the Guildhall to find a place to park, and then there was only one slot, barely big enough for the Peugeot. Luckily Rebecca had brought along a sturdy black umbrella and was willing to share it.

According to a plaque on the wall of the entranceway, the old Guildhall had overlooked the harbor since it was constructed in the year 1500. The caretaker for the historical society's collection was Mr. Medlicott, who would have been perfectly typecast as a butler in a murder mystery. A very old, very stern man, wearing an old-fashioned suit and stiff-collared shirt, he took their entry fee and, when Rebecca told him what they wanted to see, showed them to a cubicle on the lower floor.

Copies of the Penmorton *Weekly Guardian* were stacked on floor-to-ceiling shelves on three sides of a small desk with two straight chairs set side by side. The whole area wasn't much bigger than a closet.

"I daresay one day we shall have all of this on computer," Mr. Medlicott said. "That day is not yet here, however. Indeed, it may never come to Penmorton." He sounded pleased with the prediction. "I shall return when I am ready to show you the rest of the collection." Giving them each a frosty glance over his glasses, he added sternly, "Handle with care."

"Mr. Medlicott used to be the Penmorton elementary-school headmaster," Rebecca whispered after the old man had closed the door. "It seems to have left him with a permanent distrust of anyone younger than himself. Imagine him thinking we were the kind of people who would damage precious old newspapers."

"Well, you never can tell," Simon said mildly. "I might be longing to fold, staple or mutilate."

Shaking her head at his teasing, Rebecca took off her glasses and began drying them with a tissue pulled from her jeans pocket.

"Aha," Simon said. "I wondered when we'd get to this. Isn't it that significant moment in old movies where the heroine takes off her glasses and lets down her hair so the hero can finally notice how beautiful she is?" He was relieved that his tongue had finally come untied.

Rebecca squinted at him. As usual, a smile was playing around his mouth. It had a hint of wickedness to it this time. "I'm afraid the hero would be sadly disappointed if he was expecting beauty," she said as she replaced her glasses.

"No, he wouldn't," Simon said firmly. "He has already determined that the heroine is absolutely gorgeous. He thinks it remarkable that said heroine can look so gorgeous with her hair pulled straight back."

She chuckled. "I call this my peeled-grape look," she said.

His gaze wouldn't let hers go. "I don't blame Mr. Medlicott for his lack of trust," he went on. "I'm not sure I trust myself in a closeted situation like this. Seems to me if we *were* in a movie, this would be the perfect opportunity for the guy to make his move. Maybe Medlicott sensed that. Maybe that's what he was referring to when he said, 'Handle with care.'"

Simon's dark eyebrows slanted up in the way that intrigued her. "Something started between us during the furry dance, Rebecca," he said. "It was there again on Wednesday night. It's here now. You can't deny it."

She took a shaky breath. "I can postpone it," she said. "We came here with a purpose in mind."

Her voice could have been stronger, but he took her at her word, anyway. "You're a hard taskmaster, Rebecca Penberthy," he said. "Did you learn that from Mr. Medlicott?"

She shook her head. "He retired while I was still in nappies. But my dad and mum had him. They used to bring him up whenever I complained about school. Said he was so strict he wouldn't start morning assembly until he could hear a pin drop. He would literally drop one to make sure. And he had an absolute obsession about contractions, insisted they should be banned from the English language. Lazy speech made for lazy minds, he said. He never used a strap on a student, though, and there were plenty of teachers who did in those days."

As she talked her way out of her nervousness, she'd been sorting through the stacks and had accumulated two slippery piles of plastic-sealed newspapers on the desk. "I don't see how we can look up the whole war. Fifty-two multiplied by six years makes more newspapers than my eyes will hold out for. Why don't we concentrate on 1943 and 1944, the period your grandfather was in England?"

Nodding, Simon pulled out a chair for her, then seated himself. There was hardly room to breathe. "This is claustrophobic," Rebecca said, feeling nervous again.

She could smell the ginseng soap she'd provided him with. She smelled of it herself, had always loved the clean, pleasant tang of it. She could even detect the faintest odor of the coffee he'd drunk with his breakfast. Looking sideways she saw that his five-o'clock shadow had begun, though he'd probably shaved that morning. She wondered if his face would feel rough to her hand, thought it probably would and caught herself stroking the tips of her fingers with her thumb as if she'd actually touched him.

His glance caught hers before she had a chance to look away, and his mouth curved into a crooked smile as he shook his head. "Not claustrophobic. Cozy," he said.

Intimate, she amended silently.

Their gazes held, and once again there didn't seem to be enough air in the small space.

"I suppose we'd better start or we'll be here all day," Rebecca managed to say.

"Not such a bad fate," Simon said softly. "We could pretend we're in an elevator stuck between floors and everyone's gone home so we can't be rescued for a couple of days. And nights."

Rebecca shot a glance at him. His expression was completely serious. For once, no smile hovered around his mouth.

She swallowed, then forced herself to look away from him and open the folder in front of her. "Well, this room is certainly small enough to be an elevator," she said with a false-sounding laugh.

"Rebecca," he said.

"Mm." She pretended a deep interest in the page in front of her, though in truth either her glasses or her eyes seemed to be slightly blurred.

He put a hand over hers where it lay on the desk. "Thank you for going along with me on this project," he said. "I'm not sure I can explain why, but it *is* important to me. I'm really grateful to you."

She dared a swift glance. His face was very close to hers. Still not smiling. Close enough that she could feel his breath on her skin. She nodded uncertainly, then looked back at the newspaper. For another second or two she felt his gaze on her, then he removed his hand, pulled a newspaper toward him and began studying it. For a long while the only sound was their breathing. Rebecca concentrated on not letting her fingers tremble.

She was very much afraid the lock on the courtyard gate was in danger of falling off.

After half an hour in the cramped space, Rebecca found a brief mention of Bliss Turner, the rector's daughter, who had joined the land army at the start of the war. She was coming home for a fortnight's leave. The date was September 21, 1943. There was no other mention of her during the rest of the year.

Simon kept getting caught up in articles. He read aloud instructions for staggering the planting of carrots in the dig-for-victory campaign, another about potatoes flourishing at Hampton Court, once home to Henry VIII. There were many exhortations to save waste paper, budget ration points, several pieces that offered wartime lighting suggestions. Finally he read an account of D day, when the largest air and sea invasion force in history set off across the English Channel, determined to take Europe back from Adolf Hitler.

There was a compelling immediacy to the story. It *was* June 6, 1944 and the invasion was happening now, today, in front of their eyes, the bombers taking off before dawn, planeloads of paratroopers dropping into Normandy, waves of troops racing from landing craft to the beaches under heavy enemy fire.

They were silent for several minutes. Then Simon tidied his pile of papers. "Grandfather Paul wasn't involved in the invasion. When the Seattle newspapers were running stories on D day's fiftieth anniversary, I asked him about his war service. I knew he'd been in the Army Air Corps, but he'd never said much about it. He told me he was an engineer/gunner and that he only got injured once, when his machine gun broke loose from its mounting and banged into his shoulder. He also told me a hair-raising story about a student pilot who goofed up and sent their plane into a spin. They couldn't reach the lever that would open the bomb bay doors so they could bail out, because they were caught in the centrifugal force. Grandfather thought he was going to die, but the instructor pilot managed to bring the plane out of the spin and they landed safely."

He could see his grandfather's face as he'd told that story. His expression had been more lively than Simon had ever seen it. He'd tried to keep Paul talking about the war, but Paul had seemed to tire of the subject.

"The only other thing he told me was that his tour of duty was already over when the invasion began. He was waiting somewhere on the northwest coast of England for a ship to take him back to the States. The *Louis Pasteur*, a French liner that got out of France before the

Germans could take it over. He left England about four days after D day."

"Well, we've gone way beyond that in the newspapers, so it would seem that whatever happened between Paul and Gran didn't warrant a story," Rebecca said.

"That's good, isn't it?" Simon said.

She frowned. "I suppose you're right." She hesitated. "I didn't want to come across anything scandalous, such as Mr. Cornwood suggested, but I rather hoped we'd find out *something*. Gran's always been so closed up about that part of her life. It might be better for her if it *was* brought out. She might be happier for it." Rebecca sighed. "I would like to see her happier."

Simon reached over to take her pile of papers, his left arm brushing her shoulder. His face was close to hers. And she looked very woebegone.

He touched her cheek with gentle fingers. "Rebecca," he said very softly. Her pulse started racing.

"I am ready to show you the collection if you are finished there," Mr. Medlicott said behind them.

They both jumped and laughed nervously, then exchanged an amused, slightly embarrassed, wholly guilty glance.

The collection was fairly extensive, and Mr. Medlicott was prepared to explain it all. Simon learned about a form of match called a congreve that was introduced in 1832. He learned that an ell was an English linear measure of forty-five inches, or 111 centimeters, and had originally referred to the forearm, from elbow to tip of middle finger, which when multiplied by two was a measure for cloth.

The large but neatly displayed collection included the usual mixture of wartime relics, the most interesting of which was a whole suit of armor that implied a very short individual, plus a breech-loading cannon, late fifteenth century. Artifacts belonging to Penmorton's maritime past included a model of an Elizabethan ship that had sailed from Penmorton to join Sir Francis Drake's fleet in defending England against the Spanish Armada in 1588.

Mr. Medlicott's voice was dry as dust, but Simon was fascinated, anyway. History had always been a favorite subject of his.

"We're probably taking up too much of your time," he said after an hour had passed. The older man's voice was beginning to sound weary.

Mr. Medlicott shook his head. "It gives me pleasure to talk about the past, sir. Young people are not always interested, especially in the finer points. We get classes of schoolchildren in here occasionally, but all they want to look at are the old weapons and the suit of armor."

Then Mr. Medlicott went on to tell them a wonderful ghost story about a headless horse drawing an ancient, unoccupied carriage along one of Penmorton's alleys and another about a woman in a black veil who haunted the Guildhall staircase, weeping and wringing her hands. He had often seen her himself, he said without so much as a blink of an eyelid.

"Do you know my grandmother, Bliss Penberthy?" Rebecca asked when they were approaching the last few items in the collection.

Without a moment's hesitation Mr. Medlicott nodded. "I have not seen her for a number of years, but yes, I am acquainted with the lady, though I do not know her well. I consulted her once or twice about her son, Travis, who was a pupil of mine."

He looked at Rebecca, nodding. "Travis became your father, I believe. I actually taught Bliss herself for one year at the high school in Trosper, long before its title was changed to grammar school. A few years before World War II broke out, that would be. Perhaps 1936. After the war, I began teaching elementary school. Younger children are much more pliable, their young minds more open to learning."

He nodded thoughtfully. "Miss Turner she was then. A fifth former. Intelligent girl. Spoke well. That was always a problem with some of the children—the Cornish dialect..."

He cast his gaze heavenward for a few seconds. "Of course, Miss Turner *was* a minister's daughter. She was very courteous and studious, though perhaps a little—" He broke off, then finished the sentence, anyway. "High-strung? Well, perhaps not. Most girls of that age are given to fits of giggling. Then there was that unfortunate incident with the ammonia in the chemistry laboratory."

He sniffed audibly.

Rebecca, who had heard the story, tried not to smile. On parents' day, her grandmother had dropped a bottle of concentrated ammonia in front of the closed door to the lab. None of the mothers, fathers or students had wanted to go near the pungent vapors to open the door. They'd all had to climb out through the windows.

"Miss Turner was quite good at science actually," Mr. Medlicott continued. "Unusually so for a girl. Rather fragile in health, was she not? Rheumatic fever? As I recall, she was not allowed to take physical training or engage in sports. It was a source of great disappointment to her, though for the most part she was a bright and happy person."

He looked over his glasses at Rebecca. "I taught your mother, Nell, also. She and Travis were fine students and very well behaved, though Travis was admittedly a little, shall we say, relaxed, about homework."

"Do you remember all your students that well?" Rebecca marveled.

"Of course," he said matter-of-factly.

Simon took the photograph of Bliss from the envelope in the inside pocket of his leather jacket and showed it to the old man. Mr. Medlicott nodded. "Yes. I did hear that Bliss Turner had volunteered to serve in the land army. I remember feeling pleased that her health had improved." He shook his head. "Several of my pupils were later killed or maimed in action. So many fine young people died. Dreadful, dreadful."

He looked over his glasses at Rebecca. "We have some photographs taken at local schools. I'm fairly confident there are some pictures of your grandmother. Would you care to see them?"

He led the way to a rack where several large albums were filed and began studying the dates on their spines. A few minutes later they were looking at a photograph of a class of about thirty students, the front row kneeling, the next sitting, the rear row standing. Why did boys always fold their arms when someone pointed a camera at them? Rebecca wondered. A severe-looking teacher, not Mr. Medlicott, stood slightly off to one side as though to distance himself.

Mr. Medlicott indicated Bliss. She looked so much like Travis in this picture, Rebecca thought, and felt a rush of sorrow for her dead father go through her. The shape of Bliss's young eyes were like Travis's, and she had the same strong jawline. She wore a ribbon tied in a big bow high on her head, as did most of the girls in the picture. All were in uniform, the girls in pleated gym slips over white blouses, a sash knotted like a tie at the waist, the boys in navy blazers and gray flannels.

Mr. Medlicott pulled out each year's album and found Bliss's class. Then he came up with another picture from about the same era that showed Bliss with one other girl. It had been taken during the summer. Both girls were wearing the plain summer frocks that had been allowed for warmer weather, and both were squinting into the sun. Their arms were linked. The other girl was a little slimmer than Bliss, with hair that was just as dark but a mass of frizzy curls.

"Winifred Fairburn," Mr. Medlicott said. "She married a veterinarian. Dr. Stubbins." Taking the book back, he closed it gently and set it in its place on the shelf.

"Do you happen to know if Mrs. Stubbins lives in Penmorton?" Rebecca asked.

A frown creased his high-domed forehead. "Winifred Stubbins," he said. "I believe her husband died several years ago." He shook his head. "I seem to remember she came originally from Penmorton, but her husband was a Trosper resident. Possibly he had his practice there."

He glanced politely at Simon. "He never practiced in Penmorton—I would have known if he had. I cannot help you any further, I regret to say. I do not socialize a great deal nowadays, so I have lost touch with recent happenings. I *am* sorry."

"You've given us a lead at least," Simon said. "That's more than we came in with."

"A lead?" the old man queried.

"We're trying to trace my grandfather's movements," Simon told him. "He was in England with the

American air force, the Army Air Corps it was called then.''

"Here in Penmorton?"

"He wasn't based here, but he visited here."

"During the war?" Mr. Medlicott smiled. "There were a number of Americans round about then. Some of the local men resented them. It was said there were three things wrong with American servicemen—they were overpaid, oversexed and over here.''

He chuckled rather rustily at the old joke. Rebecca was amazed to hear him laugh at all. He didn't look as if he had much laughter in him, and according to what her parents had told her, he never had.

"I rather appreciated the Americans' being here myself,'' he went on. "We could not have won the war without them.'' He gave Simon a thin smile. "I have not been of much assistance, have I? I did not actually meet any Americans, you understand. I take it your grandfather did not accompany you?"

"He died recently." Simon looked at the old teacher hopefully. "His name was Paul Carmichael. Did you ever hear of him in connection with Bliss Turner?''

Mr. Medlicott shook his head. "I *am* sorry." He hesitated. "Was there a connection between your grandfather and Mrs. Penberthy?''

"Possibly," Simon said, which made Mr. Medlicott look puzzled.

"So what now?" Simon asked as he and Rebecca emerged into the street. It had stopped raining, he noted with pleasure. The sun had come out, and steam was rising gently from the pavement.

"I have to get back. I'll be taking Gran to therapy in Plymouth again as soon as we have dinner. We go every Friday night.''

She dropped her rolled umbrella onto the floor of the car and eased herself into her seat as he walked around to the driver's side. "I've never heard Gran speak of a Mrs. Stubbins or a Winifred," she said when he climbed in. She was frowning, twisting to face Simon as she tried to get the seat belt fastened.

"Perhaps we could work on tracking her down this weekend," he suggested.

"I've too much to do. Gran and I are going to dust the shop, and I've had a lot of new stock come in that has to be sorted and unpacked."

"Perhaps I could help?"

"It would take so long to show you my methods I could have the job done," she said, then darted a challenging glance at him. "I want to be there if you find Winifred." Yanking at the belt, she muttered, "Damn this thing—it keeps getting shorter."

He reached across her, eased more of the belt loose from its moorings, then snapped it into place. Taking her hands in his, he smiled at her. "We're a team, right? I promise not to talk to anyone significant without you."

She was looking at him worriedly, her hands tense in his. He wanted so badly to kiss her. Very gently he placed her right palm against his cheek for a second, then touched his lips to her wrist. "You have my word on it," he said.

Her whole face had softened. Her thumb began gently stroking the side of his face—he could hear the rasp of his whiskers. "I think this is the significant moment in the movie where the guy finally gets to kiss the girl," he said and suited action to words before she could object.

Not that she seemed to want to object. After the first tentative meeting of their lips, her mouth moved against his, slowly, with what seemed almost deliberate provocation. Her mouth felt wonderful against his, petal soft yet firm.

He put his arms around her, awkwardly because of her seat belt. Suddenly, unexpectedly, the air exploded between them, and the kiss became passionate as her lips parted to his probing tongue.

Heat charged through his entire body, making his grip tighten and his mouth harden on Rebecca's. He held her as tightly against him as he could manage, one hand fumbling to unfasten her seat belt so that it would no longer impede them.

Her hands clasped the back of his neck and tangled in his hair. Giving up on the seat belt, he let his hands move over her. They were both breathing as rapidly as they had when they'd danced down the hills of Penmorton.

Someone tapped on the window behind him.

Releasing Rebecca abruptly, he swung around. A middle-aged woman with a long, horsey face was peering through the open window on the passenger side of a vintage sedan pulled up next to the Peugeot. Her eyebrows arched politely.

Rolling down his window, Simon raised his own eyebrows questioningly.

"I say, parking spaces seem to be in terribly short supply," the woman said. "Would it be dreadfully inconvenient for you to surrender yours? If you are quite finished, of course."

Nothing in her expression or tone suggested she had witnessed their burst of passion, though it seemed obvious from her choice of words that she had.

"No problem," Simon said faintly.

She favored him with a very horsey smile. "Splendid. You are too kind."

Rebecca started laughing as he eased the car out into the street. After a moment Simon joined in. He could love this country, he decided.

CHAPTER NINE

"TELL ME THE NAME of Winifred Stubbins's business again," Rebecca said. "All I took in was that she grooms dogs."

Simon smiled at her. "The Stubbins Salon for Small Dogs."

They were in the Peugeot, driving the A38 through Bodmin, after which they would head northwest. It was midmorning on a gray and windy Monday. It had taken Simon until Sunday to trace Winifred Stubbins. He'd talked to several telephone operators before he'd thought to check business names. And there she was in a place called Tintagel, way over on the other side of Cornwall. As promised, he'd let Rebecca know immediately, then phoned Mrs. Stubbins to tell her they'd like to see her and why.

Meanwhile, Rebecca had contacted Mrs. Doreen Oliver, who lived on one of the streets that crossed Robin Hill. She used to manage a shop herself before her children were born, and every once in a while, to make a little pocket money, she enjoyed helping out at Penberthy's. And Mrs. Penberthy liked her, an important consideration. Rebecca had called her up right away and she'd been quite willing to fill in for Rebecca while her children were in school.

Rebecca had told Bliss she was accompanying Simon on a sight-seeing trip. They were going to Tintagel to see the castle. Protecting her young, dragon-lady Bliss had immediately begun to ask questions, which hadn't surprised Simon in the least. Rebecca had said quite evenly, "Gran, I just told you, we're going sight-seeing," and Bliss had subsided. Rebecca was devoted, but she was no doormat.

"Tintagel sounds familiar to me," Simon said now, trying to cut through the slight constraint that was present in the car. It was probably his own frustration that was causing the tension, he thought. Fate seemed determined to prevent him from getting close to Rebecca. He hadn't seen her all weekend, except for a few minutes the previous evening when he made his report. He'd spent his time profitably, taking care of the last repairs the cottage needed, watching some more TV. The comedy shows were beginning to make more sense to him. He'd stayed close to home, hoping Rebecca would show up with a tea tray again. She hadn't.

He was beginning to develop an obsession about getting close to her. Their one kiss had whetted his appetite for more, but there had been no opportunity for more. Not since Friday, anyway.

"Tintagel sounds familiar to everyone," Rebecca said, leaning back against the headrest. "Tintagel is the stuff that dreams are made of, the site of King Arthur's castle where he lived with Queen Guinevere and the famous knights of the Round Table—Lancelot and Gawain and Galahad, the White Knight. Not to mention Merlin the magician."

"Ah, yes," Simon said. "Arthur was the hidden son of Uther Pendragon, the king of Britain. Didn't Merlin hide him? And later he proved who he was by pulling the sword Excalibur out of a stone after no one else was able to budge it. Then he married Guinevere and set up housekeeping in Camelot. Isn't that all fiction? I always understood it was."

"It may be labeled fiction in America, but not in Cornwall," Rebecca said with mock indignation. "It's as true here as the fact that there are piskies and knockers and mermaids. As true as the legend of Jack the giant-killer, who slew the wicked giant, Cormoran, at St. Michael's Mount."

Simon wanted to keep this conversation going now that the former constraint had dissipated. "I've heard of mermaids, but piskies and knockers?"

The gray morning light glinted on her glasses as she flashed him a mischievous grin. "Don't you be poking fun at our culture, Simon Flynn. After all, yours has a leprechaun with a pot of gold in it."

"True. Is that what a piskie is? A Cornish leprechaun?"

"With a pointed hat rather than a flat one. A piskie is a little elfin creature who likes to be helpful to people, but may on occasion be quite naughty. Knockers are mine fairies—tin miners used to hear them singing and knocking and would follow the sounds to find good ore. Knockers can be quite vindictive, though, if you don't treat them with respect. There's a story of a man named Tom Revorrow who heard them rattling round a mine he was working and shouted at them to go away. After which a shower of stones fell on him and gave him a dreadful fright."

Simon laughed. "I'll try not to offend any little person I meet, just in case. I'd like to see King Arthur's castle if there's anything left of it and if we have time. I remember reading Chaucer's *Canterbury Tales* in school—under protest, I might add—and fancying myself as something of a knight."

He gave her a sidelong glance and she laughed. "Shades of Mark Twain and his Connecticut Yankee at King Arthur's court. There are castle ruins, yes, and we have to make the time to see them. I never lie to Gran— not directly, anyway—and I told her we were going sight-seeing. So we have to see some sights and report back."

He glanced at her again. She looked very relaxed now, and also very sexy in pale blue jeans and a black sweater, which she called a jumper. It was made of some kind of extrafine yarn and looked very soft. He thought it might be cashmere. He wanted to touch it to find out. He would find an opportunity to do so later, he thought. If the opportunity didn't come up, he'd make one.

Rebecca's shining black hair hung loose and straight from a side part. It brushed her shoulders when she moved her head, releasing the delicate scent of the lavender.

"I really thought somebody invented the story of King Arthur and the days of chivalry," Simon murmured.

"Only dull, boring people who lack imagination believe that," Rebecca said with a flash of her amber eyes. "And there has been a lot of fiction written. There was a man known as Hawker of Morwenstow who stayed at Tintagel for a month in 1823 with his much-older bride and then composed 'Quest of Sangraal,' about the Arthurian legend. Supposedly it was his verse that persuaded Tennyson to visit Tintagel and write 'Morte d'Arthur,' which was based on Sir Thomas Malory's 'Le Morte D'Arthur,' which was itself based on a saga written by the historian Geoffrey of Monmouth in the twelfth century."

She was counting off on her fingers. "Oh, yes," she added. "We mustn't forget the artist Turner who painted a wonderfully powerful and dramatic picture of the castle in 1818, nor Tennyson again, writing 'Idylls of the King.' Dickens visited Tintagel also, as well as Thackeray and Swinburne. And you must know 'Ave Maria.' A musician told me the words were written to a song that was originally about King Arthur."

Her voice had taken on a lilt that was almost like music itself. "The thing is," she continued, "there were stories about Arthur long before any famous storytellers became involved. And even if the stories about Arthur had more to do with the sixth century than the thirteenth, which is when this particular castle dates from, Cornish people don't worry about such anomalies. When we set our minds to believe, we believe. A little gap of seven centuries between a man and the house he lived in doesn't worry us in the least."

Simon laughed. "Okay, I'm not going to argue."

"The main thing is that people want to believe in such legends, and there's no reason they shouldn't. Tales of valor and chivalry and undying love, along with knights on white horses and good triumphing over evil, have the power to stir hearts. Which is not such a bad thing to do to a heart."

"No, indeed," Simon agreed.

She glanced at him again as though to check how he was taking all this. "It's also believed by many that Excalibur actually existed and that the noble knight Sir Bedivere really did throw it into Dozmary Pool after the king was killed by the traitor Mordred."

"Are we going anywhere near Dozmary Pool?"

"We won't get far enough onto the moor on this road. We wouldn't want to bother, anyway. It's just a pond really, nothing dramatic about it. I prefer to see it in my mind's eye, a wondrous bottomless lake, shining gold in the sunset, a hand rising above the surface to take the sword and shake it thrice before disappearing beneath the water with it."

As she said this, Simon could picture the hand and the sword and the golden lake. He quoted a verse from *Canterbury Tales* to her, to prove he really did have a nodding acquaintance with knights: "Once on a time a knight of high degree, though born in Pavia, dwelt in Lombardy."

"And there he lived a rich and prosperous life," Rebecca chimed in.

They both laughed. It came to Simon that Cornwall was bringing out of him every bit of poetry he'd ever read. It also came to him that he was happy. He couldn't remember when he'd ever actually stopped to wonder if he was happy, but now he was happy without even thinking about it. He was happy because he was wearing a comfortable rugby shirt and was with a lovely young woman with the enchanting name of Rebecca Penberthy, driving between patchwork fields that were even greener than those at home, talking about knights and ladies and thinking that with any luck she would later be in the mood for a little twentieth-century romance.

They found the Stubbins Salon for Small Dogs quite easily. It was located in the front of a large sprawling bungalow. In the distance magnificent headlands loomed dramatically against the lowering western sky.

There was an Open sign on the front door.

Winifred Fairburn Stubbins had become a very large, majestic woman with fine gray eyes and very few wrinkles in her plump countrywoman's face. She still had a mass of frizzy curls, but now they were white streaked with gray. She was wearing an all-purpose brown smock.

"Call me Fairy," she said briskly after Simon and Rebecca introduced themselves. "Everybody does. Always did."

She gestured them into a spotlessly clean, rather bare room. A couple of chairs were set up on either side of a round wooden table. Excusing herself for a minute, she brought out a tray set with a blue-willow teapot and cups and saucers, together with a matching milk pitcher and sugar bowl. There were also several good-size pieces of something studded with currants that looked as if they contained a couple of hundred calories to the square inch. Heavy cake, she called it.

"I'll keep on working if you don't mind," she said. "I was halfway through with Mackintosh when you arrived." Crossing to a tall table at the side of the room, she opened a traveling pet container and removed a jet black toy poodle with boot-button eyes. Attaching him by his red collar to a miniature hitching post, she set the cage on the floor and picked up a dog comb and a pair of scissors. "I have more customers due in this afternoon," she added with an apologetic smile.

She glanced curiously at Rebecca as she combed out one of the poodle's ears. "So you're Bliss Turner's granddaughter. You've a look of her. Her coloring. Height. Though she wasn't quite as skinny as you, or even me." She laughed. "You might not believe it, but there was a time I was nothing but a twig."

"We saw a photograph of you with Bliss at the Penmorton Guildhall," Simon said. "You were both sixteen or so."

"Then you saw me at my least," Mrs. Stubbins said cheerfully. "You may not have noticed, but there's a lot more of me now." She patted her ample chest. Simon wasn't sure he could bring himself to call her Fairy.

"Six children," she said proudly. "Four boys, two girls. Nursed every one. And with each one I got bigger and bigger. Stubby adored my chest," she added with a flirtatious glance at Simon. "Stubby was my husband. A veterinarian. A lovely man. Got me started with the grooming to go along with his clinic. In Trosper that was. I moved here to be near my eldest daughter after Stubby died fifteen years ago. Lungs. Intelligent man. Should have known better than to smoke, but since when did smokers have the sense they were born with? Sixty-four years old when he died. No sense at all."

She gave Rebecca a sorrowful glance. "I heard Bliss's husband died at sixty. I wasn't surprised. The way he drank, Foster Penberthy would never have made old bones."

"Granddad died nineteen years ago, yes," Rebecca said, a slight edge to her voice.

"Now there, love, I didn't mean to insult you," Mrs. Stubbins said. "Everyone knew Foster was a drinker. He always was, long before he married Bliss. It wasn't possible to keep it a secret. He should have been an innkeeper, then he could have lived in a pub all the time, instead of most of the time."

She broke off and began trimming the pom-pom at the end of the little dog's tail. "That marriage should never have taken place," she went on. "I told Bliss not to do it, but she wouldn't listen to me. We had a big row over it. Right after, Bliss pulled herself into herself. I never felt welcome after that. Such a shame, considering we were best friends through elementary school and grammar school and for several years after."

She looked wistful. "I've thought several times, since Stubby died, of visiting Bliss, hoping we could pick up where we left off. But it's hard for me to go anywhere, seeing I don't have a car and wouldn't know how to drive it if I did. One of my children or grandchildren would probably be happy to drive me, but I hate to impose on them. They all have busy lives. And to tell you the truth, since I got so fat I don't fit too well in most cars."

Her hands paused at her task. "Besides, it would have broken my heart all over again if Bliss hadn't wanted to see me." She looked directly at Rebecca. "Does she know you're here?"

Rebecca shook her head. "She knows we're in Tintagel, but I told her only that we were going sightseeing."

"You thought she might be angry if you came to see me?"

"I thought she might be angry about the reason." As she often did when she was nervous, Rebecca resettled her glasses on her nose. "Mr. Medlicott told us you were a friend of Gran's when she was young. Did you know her during the war?"

"Most certainly I did," Mrs. Stubbins said, one hand cupping the little dog's rump. "My goodness," she added on a long sigh, "those were good days. It might seem odd to say that about wartime, but there was a lot that was wonderful about that war, in spite of the bombs and standing in long queues for every blessed thing we wanted to eat. People pulling together, sacrificing for the good of the country, being kind to one another, everybody helping the war effort, even if it was only collecting aluminium pots and pans to be melted down for Spitfires. Winston Churchill making all those marvelous speeches. 'We shall never surrender.' Sometimes when I see the apathy of so many of our young people now, I think it wouldn't be all that bad to have another war.''

She glanced at Simon, her voice sharpening. ''You said when you rang me yesterday that Rebecca wanted to talk to me about her grandmother.'' She paused. ''But I'm a person who believes that what's past should stay past. Stirring it up never does a body any good.''

That was a warning if ever he'd heard one, Simon thought. He took another bite of the heavy cake, which was so delicious he knew it couldn't possibly be good for him. ''I'm afraid we do want to ask you about the past, Mrs. Stubbins,'' he said, swallowing.

The big woman didn't respond, just continued working on the tiny pom-pom, her plump hands moving with surprising delicacy. She was frowning fiercely.

Simon and Rebecca exchanged worried glances. Rebecca poured tea for both of them. Well, nothing ventured, nothing gained, Simon decided. ''Did you ever meet my grandfather? His name was Paul Carmichael. He was in England during the war. In the Army Air Corps. He and Bliss... spent some time together.''

Mrs. Stubbins's face tightened as if in recognition of his grandfather's name, but it took her a while to respond. After fluffing up the end of the poodle's tail, she began carefully trimming the hair around his tiny paws. The dog whimpered a little, and she paused to rub behind his right ear, murmuring softly to him until he subsided.

"I wondered when I heard your accent on the telephone," Mrs. Stubbins muttered at last, all warmth gone from her voice.

He was surprised at the rush of emotion her words sent racing through him. "You *did* meet my grandfather, then. You knew him."

"I knew him." She glanced at Simon appraisingly. "You don't look anything like him. Bliss used to say he was the spitting image of Leslie Howard. From *Gone with the Wind*." A shadow flickered across her face. "He was killed, you know, during the war."

Shocked, Simon set down his cake and shook his head. "No, Mrs. Stubbins, that's not so. Paul didn't—"

"Leslie Howard, I mean," she interrupted. "The airliner he was flying in got shot down over the Atlantic by an enemy plane."

She flashed Simon another appraising glance, then grinned unexpectedly, her plump cheeks dimpling. "You ask my opinion, you look more like Clark Gable than Leslie Howard. Which is all right with me. I always rather fancied Gable."

"My father's family is Irish," Simon told her. "I inherited more of their genes than Paul's, I guess."

Reaching into a drawer behind her, the woman took out a pair of spectacles with very fancy frames. Holding them up like a lorgnette, she squinted at Simon through the lenses, then nodded. "You do have eyebrows like Paul's. His were fair, almost invisible, but they slanted up to the bridge of his nose just like yours. And your eyes are similar. Paul had beautiful eyes. Incredibly blue. Like the other Paul. Newman."

"Was Gran in love with Paul Carmichael, Mrs. Stubbins?" Rebecca asked. Evidently she had trouble using the nickname, too.

Mrs. Stubbins was concentrating on the second of the poodle's tiny front paws, clipping meticulously. Simon thought at first she wasn't going to answer. "He was the love of her life," she said at last. "She thought the sun and the moon rose and set with him. Fair worshiped him, she did. She never got over him going away. Never." Her voice was flat.

Rebecca looked stunned. "But she got married, Mrs. Stubbins. She married my granddad, Foster Penberthy. She must have—"

"She never could have loved him the way she loved Paul. Never." Sadly she shook her head, her gaze unseeing, as though she was looking back through the years. Her face was really quite beautiful, Simon thought. Obviously her life had not been marked by the illness and sorrow that had aged Bliss Penberthy.

The poodle whimpered again, and Mrs. Stubbins abruptly came back to an awareness of her surroundings. She looked from Simon to Rebecca and back again. "I still dislike digging into the past this way," she said. "Bliss was my best friend once. If she wanted you to know about Paul, she would have told you about Paul, and you wouldn't be here."

"She's always said she doesn't remember anything about the war," Rebecca said.

"Perhaps she doesn't, then," the woman said sharply. She nodded several times, more to herself than to them. "I'm not certain I remember much about that time myself now that I think about it."

Unfastening the clip that held the poodle's collar to the post, she picked the little dog up and cuddled it against her bosom. "There now, that wasn't such a dreadful experience was it, Mackintosh love?" she crooned. The poodle's tail wagged like a metronome.

"Why don't you ask your grandfather about Bliss if you're so curious?" Mrs. Stubbins said to Simon.

"My grandfather died earlier this year," Simon said.

The woman sighed. "Paul Carmichael dead. It's funny, isn't it. If you don't see someone for fifty years you don't think about him aging or dying. You still see him in your mind the way he was. Golden Boy, Mrs. Turner called him."

She glanced at Rebecca. "Bliss's mum, I mean. I don't know that her dad ever met Paul. John Edward, the rector. He was off in foreign parts at that time, preaching to the soldiers, whether they wanted him to or not. Which was probably not. I heard him preach a time or two myself. He was that boring you wouldn't believe even God would pay attention. He's dead, too, of course, though he lived long enough to make years of Bliss's life miserable. He and Foster used to argue constantly, I heard. Drove Bliss wild, I heard. She knew there was no changing either of them, that was the worst of it. Only comfort she ever took was in her son, Travis, and look what happened to him."

Something flickered in her eyes, but then she shook her head in a mournful fashion. "Almost everyone I ever knew is dead. A time comes when you take a look round and realize you are older than anyone else you know. I'm even older than my mum and dad were when they died."

She sighed. "I always thought when I got old I would feel old on the inside, but you know, I don't at all. Inside I'm still sixteen, still wanting to go dancing or to the pictures with my best friend, Bliss."

She laughed suddenly, seeming to throw off the somber mood. "It's quite a shock when I look in the mirror in the morning and see my old aunt Tossie looking back at me. Who'd ever have thought I'd end up looking like fat Aunt Toss."

Still cuddling the little poodle, she smiled tentatively at Rebecca, her gray eyes gentle. "How *is* Bliss nowadays?" she asked.

Rebecca sighed. "She has very bad arthritis, Mrs. Stubbins. And she had a heart attack eleven years ago. She has angina spasms every once in a while. Unfortunately she's not a suitable candidate for surgery. But she manages to get along all right."

The woman moved her head slowly from side to side. "I remember how ill she was when she had rheumatic fever, and then afterward she had to be so careful. She always said her parents made too much fuss about her heart, but if it's still a problem they must have been right to fuss all those years ago."

She rolled her eyes. "I remember reading the rector's obituary in the *Cornish Guardian*. Made him sound as if he qualified for sainthood. Perhaps he did. He was terribly strict. I suppose as a clergyman he thought he had to be. Poor Bliss had a ghastly time with him."

"A man in Penmorton—a Mr. Cornwood—told us there was some kind of scandal," Rebecca said.

"With your great-granddad? John Edward Turner? Are you joking? Holier than everyone, that man. Especially thou." She laughed heartily at her own small joke.

Simon was almost certain the woman had deliberately misunderstood Rebecca's remark.

"I was talking about Gran," Rebecca said firmly, and Mrs. Stubbins flushed a little and averted her eyes, confirming Simon's suspicions.

"I'm sorry, Rebecca," she said after a strained moment of silence. "I don't feel right talking behind Bliss's back to her granddaughter. I wouldn't want her gossiping to mine, and I never had anything—"

She broke off. She hadn't had anything for anyone to gossip about, Simon finished for her. Which meant Bliss had.

"Did Bliss know Paul was already married and had a child?" he asked.

For several moments the old woman stared at him, openmouthed. Then she sighed deeply, her eyes suspiciously moist. "Well, now, that would explain a lot, wouldn't it."

"You didn't know?" Rebecca asked.

"I never even guessed. And I don't think Bliss knew, either. She'd have told me. She told me everything in those days. Poor Bliss." She sniffed a couple of times. "That rotter. So that's why he let her down so badly."

Mrs. Stubbins pressed her lips firmly together. "No point stirring up all that past unhappiness, is there?" she reminded them. "I can't think why you'd even want to."

At that moment Simon wasn't sure he could think of a good reason, either, but still he felt compelled to try to persuade the woman to tell them anything more she knew. It soon became apparent, however, that she'd made up her mind to clam up and wasn't about to reverse the decision. Even when he explained that his mother had sent him to England specially to find out what he could about Paul and Bliss, she refused to say another word.

Simon considered telling her his grandfather's last words, thinking that might soften her attitude, but then he realized he wouldn't feel right about passing on such a private revelation. He was coming to care more and more about his grandfather's carefully preserved secret.

Rebecca also tried to pry some facts loose from Mrs. Stubbins, but her heart didn't seem to be in it. It was entirely possible, Simon decided, that they never would solve the puzzle completely. He was beginning to have an inkling of what the answer to the puzzle might be, but all the guesses in the world wouldn't do any good if they couldn't be confirmed.

CHAPTER TEN

FAIRY HAD ALWAYS THOUGHT of herself as a happy person. That was one of the reasons she still liked to be called Fairy, even though she could certainly understand why young people failed to see where the nickname fitted her. But sometimes her happy outlook was hard to preserve, in spite of her positive attitude. She'd felt a wave of sorrow for her old friend Bliss sweep over her as the salon door closed behind her two visitors. Things never had gone right for Bliss. Not in the long run.

A glance at the wall clock told her that her next customer wasn't due for half an hour. Putting the little poodle gently into his carrying cage, she cupped him with her hands until she felt him relax, then folded his blanket tenderly around him.

She needed a cuppa herself, she decided. Carrying the tray into the back room, she thought of the words of an old song about a nice cuppa tea and sang it softly under her breath as she refilled the kettle and put it on the burner.

Once the kettle boiled and the tea was steeped, she set up the tray on a side table. Sinking into her favorite armchair, which had been custom-made for her as a gift from Stubby, she sent up a fervent thank-you to the dear, dear man, not just for the chair, but for being so loving to her all those years.

She wished, oh, how she wished, that Bliss could have been as lucky. Chewing thoughtfully on a piece of the heavy cake, she gazed into the empty fireplace. As if the grate were a crystal ball, she could see Bliss Turner dancing round and round the Fairburns' old sitting room on Clara Avenue in Penmorton, her pretty face alight with excitement and anticipation, her brown eyes shining as if they'd been touched by starlight.

"His name is Paul Carmichael," she had said with the air of someone making a world-shaking announcement. "I'm in love, Fairy. I'm really, really, truly in love, and it's just as wonderful as we ever thought it would be."

Fairy sighed and poured a cup of tea. *Love.* Growing up, she and Bliss had talked hour after hour about love. They had expected so much from love. Perhaps too much. Even dear old Stubby hadn't quite managed to come up to her expectations, though he'd given it a valiant go. Prince Charming himself would have been hard-pressed to fulfill expectations fed by the films of the thirties and forties.

Love. Setting down her cup, Fairy hummed along as she heard Bliss's soprano singing sweetly across more than fifty years. "As Time Goes By."

"It's our song, Fairy," Bliss said. "Paul's and mine. You should hear Paul sing it. You *will* hear Paul sing it. He's coming to Penmorton next week. He's coming to be with me."

He was handsome, Paul Carmichael. Tall, slender, nicely put together. A little weak round the mouth and chin, but you didn't notice that at first because of his eyes. Eyes to die for, Fairy's youngest granddaughter would say. She watched far too much telly, that girl.

Paul Carmichael. Fairy had always wondered when Paul had managed to find time for his medical treatments in Plymouth during that fortnight Bliss was on leave. Bliss had explained after Paul had returned to his base that he'd hitchhiked into Plymouth every morning, had his treatment and hitchhiked back, riding on anything that would move, once on a greengrocer's horse and cart.

He and Bliss had spent almost every minute of those two weeks together, day and night.

Fairy had raised her eyebrows in the way she'd learned from Joan Crawford. "Night?"

Bliss put her finger to her lips, went over to the door and opened it so she could see if anyone was on the other side, then came back to the sofa where Fairy was sitting to whisper, "Paul stayed in the cottage."

Now that the rector had joined the military service, Penmorton had brought in a new temporary rector. Bliss's mother had moved back into the rooms above her shop, which she liked a lot better than the cold old rectory. The new rector was a dear old man. Everybody liked him.

"I crept out every night as soon as Mum was asleep," Bliss went on, then giggled. "Wonderful things, blackout curtains. They give you a marvelous feeling of security. No one can see in."

Fairy stared at her, impressed, absolutely chartreuse with envy. It was as though a wide crack in the earth had opened up between the two of them, Bliss on one side, twenty-three years old, ripe to bursting with knowledge, Fairy on the other, also twenty-three, but an ignorant virgin. "You never did, Bliss. You never slept with him!"

"Thank goodness Mum's such a loud snorer." Laughter, happiness, love made Bliss look more beautiful than Fairy had ever seen her. "And thank goodness my dad got the call to serve the army. Even if he'd let Paul stay at the rectory, I'd never have got past *him*. He'd have sat on the stairs all night or else locked me in the cellar."

Bliss's voice softened. "Mum really likes Paul. She calls him Golden Boy. Well, he brought his ration coupons with him, didn't he?"

Her eyes lit up. "He even brought oranges. God knows where he found them. All because I made some offhand remark about wishing I had an orange. *And* he brought popcorn and popped it in the frying pan. Mum thought it was ever so tasty. She put it in a bowl and took it round to share with all the neighbors, just a little bit each. A treat."

Bliss had saved some of the popcorn for when Paul was gone and Fairy came to visit. Fairy hadn't thought much of it. "Tastes like cardboard," she'd said.

"You've tried cardboard, have you?" Bliss had teased.

Bliss had cooked Paul's eggs for him. One for each of the two weeks. "Mum wouldn't use his rations. Those were *his* coupons, *his* eggs, she said."

Bliss had boiled his egg for three minutes exactly, timing it with her souvenir egg timer she'd bought on a school trip to Bournemouth years before.

Paul had never used an eggcup. She'd had to show him how to cut the top off the egg cleanly, how to dip out the contents with a teaspoon. They'd made a game of it, one spoon for him, one for her.

It had been like going to the pictures, hearing Bliss talk about Paul Carmichael. In 1943 Fairy hadn't yet met Stubby. She'd been kissed once or twice but had been too afraid to go any further, except in her imagination. Not like today when unmarried people went further on the telly in full view of a person than they used to do in private.

Bliss had always been good at telling stories, creating pictures in people's minds. Even after all these years Fairy could recall every detail Bliss had told her. Every scene was as clear as if it had been made into a film. She could feel the sun shining warm on her head, smell the salty air, hear the tumbling roar of the surf, as Bliss Penberthy and Paul Carmichael walked out together in Penmorton on a beautiful sunny day....

There was a rattling sound at the front door of the Stubbins salon, and then the bell tinkled as the door was opened. Fairy pressed down on the arms of her chair and hoisted herself to her feet, sighing. Another customer. Mrs. Rochester and her Pekingese probably, arriving just in time to interrupt the best part.

Remembering Bliss's story, she'd let her cup of tea get cold. "Coming," she called as she poured herself another and took one more bite of cake.

CHAPTER ELEVEN

IT WAS A LONG CLIMB, with steep footpaths and hundreds of stone steps. They talked as they climbed. "Do you suppose Paul ever told Bliss he was married and had a child?" Rebecca asked at one point.

"Hard to say." Simon stopped at a rare flat spot and bent forward to stretch his complaining calf muscles. "It seems likely that was the thing that broke them up, but we can't be sure."

"Perhaps that was the scandal Mr. Cornwood talked about."

"Only if Paul or Bliss told everyone in town he was married. Apparently Bliss didn't even tell Mrs. Stubbins, who was supposedly her closest friend, so it hardly seems likely word would get out."

"Unless some colleague of Paul's let it drop."

"That's a possibility, I suppose, but we haven't heard anything about Paul having a colleague while he was in town."

He sighed and they began climbing again. "The thing is, if Paul was the love of Bliss's life, and then she found out he was married and broke up with him, would that make him miserable for the rest of his life? Would that change his whole personality? We need to do a little more digging, I think. Have you any ideas?"

She stopped at the next flat spot and turned to face him. She was several steps ahead of him so he had to look up at her. The sky was still gray, but the light was bright enough to show him her beautiful skin and the planes of her cheekbones. His fingers ached to touch that face, to trace the line of her cheekbones. He wanted to kiss her again.

Rebecca shook her head. "I don't know where we can go next. I'll have to give it some thought."

Turning, she started upward again. They finally reached the top of the rocky promontory, three hundred feet above the sea. The trees up there were bent sideways from the prevailing wind. Seabirds soaring and calling above his head, Simon stood stock-still on the rough grass and stared in awe at the stark ruins of the medieval castle. "Whoa!" he exclaimed.

"It's splendid, isn't it?" Rebecca said.

Although there wasn't much left of Tintagel Castle, popularly known as King Arthur's Castle, it was still very dramatic. Walls formed of wedged hunks of jagged, black, slaty stone loomed roofless against the gray sky. Centuries of wind and rain had scooped and sculpted them into odd shapes and sizes. Openings that once were doorways or holes for arrows framed views of the Atlantic. Ancient steps that had known the tramp of thirteenth-century Norman feet now led nowhere.

A movement at the edge of the cliff caught Rebecca's eye, and she turned to see a puffin swooping down over the edge. Probably it was nesting there; the rugged cliffs were breeding grounds for many species.

The puffin's flight had brought her attention to the sky and she touched Simon's arm and gestured toward the horizon, which had turned the color of ink. Closer in and immediately above them, huge clouds with charcoal gray bases were building. A lock of hair whipped across Rebecca's face, and she realized the wind was becoming stronger with every minute.

"You're right. We're in for some weather," Simon said.

The words were hardly out of his mouth when the heavens opened and water, fast and heavy, pelted their defenseless heads. They stood openmouthed in shock for a moment, staring at each other. Then Rebecca pointed at a narrow alcove in the castle wall that had probably served in the past as a sentry post. Grabbing Rebecca's hand, Simon ran with her through the downpour.

There was a wooden bench in the alcove, obviously a more modern addition, and a very welcome one. As they flung themselves onto it, the downpour became a deluge. They seemed to be sealed in behind a wall of water, cut off from the rest of the world.

"It's like being behind Niagara Falls," Simon shouted over the uproar. "My mother and grandmother took me to see them when I was in fifth grade. It was great. We went down to the Cave of the Winds at the foot of the American Falls. We were issued oilskins."

They had no oilskins now. Although they'd spent only seconds in the rain, they were soaked to the skin. Even now, as the water hit the sill of the little alcove, it bounced in toward them, splashing their legs. Simon put an arm around Rebecca's shoulders and drew her against his side. They both pulled their feet in as far as they could. "It can't last long at this rate," Simon said in her ear as he put his other arm around her.

Her heart was pounding, echoing the beating of the rain. She wasn't sure if her excitement was caused by the suddenness of the cloudburst or from Simon's closeness.

In the dim interior of the alcove, his eyes were vividly blue. He was obviously enjoying this. She was enjoying it, too, and couldn't help laughing aloud at the sheer power of the storm. Simon joined her. Their laughter, like the storm, was elemental and primitive, and it produced a primitive response in Rebecca. In Simon, also, if the tightening of his arms around her was anything to go by.

His mouth was moving as though he was murmuring something to her, but she couldn't hear his voice over the racket of the downpour. She could barely hear herself think. She didn't want to think, anyway. She just wanted to feel.

Simon was looking at her mouth now. Anticipation thundered through her, and she raised her head just enough to make it easy for him to cover her mouth with his. As he did so, she felt all the breath go out of her in a long sigh of surrender.

No, not surrender. Surrender implied giving in to a stronger force, and there was nothing weak in her giving. Her mouth moved against his as urgently as his moved on hers, and her hands flew to his shoulders, then to the back of his head, her fingers tangling in his thick, wet hair, tugging his head closer.

With their damp bodies pressed so tightly together, Rebecca should have felt chilled to the bone, but instead, her blood was racing through her body, filling her with heat. Her lips parted farther, as Simon's insistent tongue demanded entry, and the kiss became hot and wild, unlike any Rebecca had ever experienced. It sensitized her, so that as Simon's hands moved over her, to her throat, her shoulders, her breasts, her buttocks, her blood raced to that area.

She heard herself making odd little sounds in her throat and wondered how she could hear them over the noise of the storm. Her hands left his hair and moved urgently down his back.

"We have to do something about this," he murmured against her lips.

"Yes," she answered.

Suddenly there was silence. The rain had stopped as abruptly as it had begun.

The tension in Simon's arms slackened. Cupping her face with his hands, he kissed her gently once, twice, then let out a ragged breath and leaned back. "Your glasses have steamed up," he told her.

"That's not terribly surprising," Rebecca said shakily. Removing them, she pulled a tissue from her shoulder bag and wiped them dry.

The smile that was so much a part of him played around his mouth. "That was some kind of storm."

Rebecca laughed. He was not referring to the rain and they both knew it. "Thunder and lightning," she said, though the storm outside had involved neither.

The smile spread to his eyes. "The *1812* Overture," he said, going her one better.

She grinned. She was familiar with the orchestral work by Tchaikovsky. Its climactic ending featured drums and guns and fireworks and ringing bells.

Simon got to his feet and brought her with him. "We're risking hypothermia," he said, looking down at his soggy shirt and jeans.

"I think my jumper has shrunk," Rebecca said ruefully.

He looked her over, light dancing in his eyes. "You may be right. It's cashmere, isn't it?"

"It was. It feels more like the original goat at the moment."

She looked outside. "If this was an old film," she said, repeating the jocular reference they'd made on previous occasions, "there'd be biblical rays of sunlight reaching down to touch a calm sea."

He took her hand and they stepped outside the alcove. The sky looked almost as stormy as it had earlier; if anything, the clouds were darker. And the sea, now an angry gray, was tossing up enormous waves topped with white foam.

"I think it might be a good idea for us to get out of here," Simon said.

Before the rain had come they hadn't been alone on the hill. Rebecca had noticed at least half a dozen other people scrambling around the walls or strolling the footpaths, and as they'd come up the last part of the climb, dozens of gulls had been circling and screeching overhead. But as soon as the storm had started, people and birds had disappeared. Rebecca hoped they'd found shelters as interesting as the one she and Simon had happened upon.

"You're shivering," Simon said accusingly.

She glanced at him and laughed. "So are you."

They started making their way down the hill, unable to hurry as the rain had made the footpaths and the rock and slate steps slippery. The wooden building where they'd purchased tickets on the way up was closed tight. Either the ticket taker was huddled inside, or she'd abandoned her duties the minute the storm paused.

The end of the pause was not far off, Rebecca thought as they reached the bottom of the hill and she glanced again at the dark, turbulent sky. Any second now they were going to get inundated again.

They hesitated before starting up the road to where they'd parked the car, looking hungrily at the café across the street. A poster on the side of the building announced, "If you want a genuine Cornish pasty baked by a little old Cornish biddy, come in."

"Sounds tempting," Simon said, "but I think we have to get out of these clothes."

"We could go back to Mrs. Stubbins's place, I suppose," Rebecca suggested.

He looked at her sideways.

"Or we could see if that hotel across from the car park would take pity on us and let us in," she went on.

"All in favor say aye," he said, and immediately added, "Aye."

Rebecca's heart thumped once, then settled down to a steady beat. "Aye," she said.

The weathered-looking desk clerk at the Queen Guinevere Hotel took their bedraggled appearance in stride. "Mekkin a lotta weet," he commented.

"It's making a lot of wet," Rebecca said, translating for an obviously mystified Simon. "He's a Scot," she added, then gestured toward the windows. The rain had returned and was pelting the mullioned windows.

"Last time we had a storm like this yin, it lasted nigh on a fortnight," the man said solemnly, then dipped his head and looked at Simon from under tangled and grizzled eyebrows. "Would ye be wantin' single or double occupancy, sir?"

"Double," Simon said without a moment's hesitation, then added, "We won't be staying overnight. We mainly need to dry out."

The desk clerk did a manful job of accepting that statement with a solemn nod, though there was a glint in his eye as he handed over the rather ornate room key. "Ye'll nae doot be wantin' a pot o' tea sent up," he suggested, then glanced at Simon again. "Wi' perhaps a wee drap o' whuskey to chase the chill."

Simon agreed heartily, apparently not needing a translation this time. "Do you have a restaurant?" he asked.

The man gave a sorrowful shake of his head. "I'm sorry, sir, but I'll see I canna find ye a wee bite."

The room was gorgeously decorated in blue and gold with an enormous four-poster bed dripping with brocade and gold tassels. The best sight of all was the fire laid in the hearth, needing only a match. Simon struck one and brought it to life.

Their clothing steamed as they stood before the blazing hearth. Obviously there was nothing for it but to strip completely. They looked at each other for a long moment. "Maybe you'd like to change by the fire while I strip off in the bathroom?" Simon suggested, sounding slightly hoarse.

Rebecca nodded gratefully. They were going to make love. She had no doubt about that. Nor did Simon, she was sure. But it wasn't something that could be rushed into.

While he brought her a couple of large terry towels from the bathroom, she bent to remove her shoes and lined them up by the fireplace.

After drying herself thoroughly and rubbing her sopping hair, she wrapped the extra towel sari-style around her body, then cleaned her glasses with a tissue from her bag and put them back on. Just as she finished combing out her hair, Simon exited the bathroom, a neatly tucked towel shrouding his lower half. His black hair, tousled and still damp, was matched by the mat of hair on his well-muscled chest.

His grin was slightly sheepish, which Rebecca found endearing. Her own smile felt stiff and shy. Gathering up her discarded clothing, she headed for the bathroom and hung her sodden things on the towel rails next to those Simon had used. He had turned on the wall heater. There was something very intimate about their jeans and underwear hanging side by side in that small room.

The tea and whiskey, scotch of course, arrived courtesy of an expressionless bellboy just as Rebecca emerged from the bathroom. The desk clerk had managed to come up with a pair of hot, heavenly-smelling Cornish pasties to add to the order. Each pasty was accompanied by an exotic-looking salad decorated with edible nasturtium blooms.

"Look at this mesclun!" Rebecca exclaimed over the greens. "Lollo rosso and endive and radicchio. Oh, and there's chicory, arugula and red-oak leaf."

Simon smiled at her enthusiasm. He liked the way she got maximum enjoyment out of little things.

Drawing up a straight-backed chair to each side of the fire, they held their plates in their laps and ate as though they were starved, which in fact they were. The tea was English Breakfast, robust and full-flavored, the scotch whiskey was nectar of the gods, and the blazing fire warmed them to the bone.

"That was fantastic," Simon said with great satisfaction as he swallowed the last morsel of flaky pastry and set down his plate. Then he looked at Rebecca and gave her a wicked smile. "If this was an old movie—" he began.

Someone knocked on the door.

Simon's answering frown was so black Rebecca couldn't help laughing. Hitching up his towel, he stomped to the door and flung it open.

A very young maid stood there. Obviously taken aback by Simon's bare, muscular torso with its thick mat of black hair arrowing down into the towel, she lowered her eyelids and her cheeks turned rosy. "M-Mr. MacDonald sent me up, sir," she stammered.

"The desk clerk?" Rebecca queried from her seat by the fire.

The girl peered around Simon and blushed again as she saw that Rebecca was also wrapped in a towel. "He's really the manager," she explained. "Robert should have been at the desk by now, but he probably got delayed by the storm."

"We experienced a slight delay ourselves," Simon said.

When the maid continued to peer beyond him, he asked, "Did Mr. MacDonald have a purpose in mind when he sent you up?"

"A purpose? Oh! Yes, certainly." She was really flustered now, staring up into Simon's face. "He wanted me to fetch your clothes."

Simon raised those speaking eyebrows of his.

"What I mean is, oh, dear, I should have explained, we have an electric dryer on the premises and Mr. MacDonald thought—"

"Say no more!" Simon swept off to the bathroom and returned loaded down with their damp clothes. "Your sweater shouldn't go in the dryer, should it?" he asked Rebecca, hesitating as the maid reached for the things.

"I don't suppose it makes much difference now," Rebecca said. "It's never going to be the same and I've got to wear something to go home in, so it might as well be dry."

"I'll have it all back directly, sir," the maid said.

"No hurry," Simon called after her, then closed the door and returned to his seat, scowling.

"Don't worry," Rebecca assured him. "In Cornwall 'directly' can take several hours."

The scowl was instantly banished to be replaced by a wicked grin. "That's good to know. Now where was I?"

"If this was an old movie..." Rebecca prompted, smiling.

"Oh, yes. If this was an old movie, this would be the part where the guy finally, after much trial and tribulation, gets the girl." He quirked his brows. "If you catch my drift?"

Rebecca shook her head, teasing him. "They didn't do what you're thinking of in old movies. Not on camera, anyway. They never got further than kissing under a tree by a river."

"Yes, they did," he argued. "The camera might pan the sky and the trees, but you knew *exactly* what was going on. And I recall that in the next scene, sometimes, the woman was pregnant—" He broke off. The scowl returned. "Now there's a thought."

Rebecca sighed. "It is indeed."

"Shows what kind of nineties guy I am," he said flatly. "I don't have any protection with me. I wasn't expecting... It's not the sort of thing I travel with and I didn't really..." He trailed off again. "If this was the

States I could go down to the men's room and find a machine. Do you suppose Mr. MacDonald . . . ?''

"You wouldn't dare ask him!''

He laughed, though without much mirth. "You're right. I wouldn't.''

"I truly appreciate your concern over this, Simon,'' Rebecca said solemnly.

Oh, she did love the way that smile hovered around his mouth. Leaning forward, she put her hand very gently against the edge of it and felt the sensual rasp of whiskers.

His hand immediately came up to cover hers, then he moved his head just enough to bring his mouth into contact with her palm. His tongue deftly touched and withdrew and touched again, sending a jolt of sexual heat through her.

"There's no reason we couldn't climb into that historic-looking bed and make a little history of our own,'' he growled into her hand. "We don't have to go all the way to war, but we could indulge in a minor skirmish. . . .''

"In the old films when lovers went to bed, they had to keep one foot on the floor so as to be decent,'' she told him.

He laughed, got to his feet, removed her glasses and set them down on the lunch tray, then picked her up off her chair as though she weighed next to nothing. "Frankly, my dear, I may be concerned for safety, but when it comes to decency, I don't give a damn.''

Leaning her against the edge of the high bed, he flung the covers back, then eased her gently onto the immaculate white sheet.

She pulled off her towel and dropped it on the floor as he made his way around the bed. He stretched out beside her and she pulled the covers over both of them. The sheets were cold, and at first they clung together for warmth more than passion. But soon the chill had dissipated completely and they were kissing deeply, savoring each other's taste. Then holding themselves just a little apart, they touched each other with delicate fingers.

"If we have to stop, we'd better be careful not to get too inflamed," Simon said with mock seriousness at one point. Then he cupped her breasts in his hands and teased her nipples with his thumbs, a move that threatened to do just what he'd cautioned against.

If someone had told Rebecca at the beginning of this day that she'd spend part of it in bed with Simon Flynn, she would not have been terribly surprised. But if someone had also told her that they would make love to each other for more than an hour without, as Simon had put it, going all the way to war, she'd have thought that someone was crazy.

Yet that was exactly what they did, and she was even more moved by Simon's restraint than she might have been by his passion.

"There'll be a chance to go to war another time," he said to her sleepily around three o'clock or so.

The two of them dozed for half an hour until a knock on the door signaled the return of the maid with their now dry clothes.

Rebecca was still a bit sleepy as she pulled on her jumper, which had shrunk something fierce and made Simon whistle with appreciation. Her trousers were all right, though, and she remembered she'd slipped a nylon windcheater into the car. Simon went down and brought it back so she could present herself in front of Mr. MacDonald without embarrassment.

The manager's face showed no expression as Simon paid their bill. Judging by the jerkiness of his grizzled eyebrows, though, Rebecca thought he might be indulging in a little speculation.

Simon was just as solemn as he signed the credit-card slip and thanked Mr. MacDonald for his assistance in the matter of the food and drink and clothes.

"My pleasure," the manager said.

"*My* pleasure," Simon murmured with a wicked sidelong glance at Rebecca as he escorted her through the door.

She managed not to chuckle until they were outside, then they both burst into gales of laughter and ran across the street to the car.

He was a love of a man, Simon Flynn, Rebecca thought. An absolute love.

The word "love" echoed inside her mind for the longest time.

CHAPTER TWELVE

"YOU DIDN'T HAVE any rain in Penmorton?" Simon asked.

The dragon lady balanced her watering can on the edge of one of the wooden tubs in the courtyard and squinted at him. "Sunshine all afternoon," she asserted, her expression still darkened by the suspicion with which she'd greeted their return.

"It was a tremendous storm," Rebecca said. "One of the worst I've ever seen. The rain was bucketing down."

"Mm-hmm." The suspicious regard was transferred to her granddaughter.

"We really had no choice but to wait it out," Simon offered.

Bliss sniffed and went back to watering her flowers and herbs, using both hands to manage the watering can. It was obviously a painful task for her, but though Simon's hands itched to take over the job, he knew better than to undermine her sense of independence.

"What did you think of the thatched cottages?" she asked him abruptly.

Simon frowned and glanced at Rebecca. She was gazing at her grandmother with an exasperated expression on her face. "I don't remember any thatched cottages," he said. "All I saw were stone and slate ruins. There was a café at the bottom of the hill, but it had a regular tiled roof."

Bliss's bright brown eyes slid in his direction. "My goodness, I'm so forgetful," she said. "I must be thinking of Launceston Castle."

Rebecca's audible sigh was almost a growl. Bliss had been checking up on him, Simon gathered. Dragon-lady tactics. She was making sure they'd really gone to Tintagel Castle.

He shook his head. "I'll see you later," he said to Rebecca. He wanted to send her a loving message with his eyes, but it was impossible with Bliss watching them like a hawk. He hoped Rebecca would remember to change her shrunken sweater before her grandmother saw her in it.

"I'll bring you the book I mentioned some time after dinner," Rebecca promised. Her voice was neutral, and she was looking at her grandmother's flowers rather than at him. The message came through loud and clear all the same. She hadn't promised him any kind of book. So she was promising something else. He would see her alone later. Which meant he should probably find a drugstore—correction, a chemist's—and do a little shopping.

"AREN'T YOU GOING to take off your jacket?" Bliss asked as Rebecca poked her head into the fridge looking for something for dinner. She hadn't thought to get anything out of the freezer section before going to Tintagel. She hadn't been thinking about much else than Simon. After all that had happened between them, it was still difficult to concentrate on mundane matters.

"I made fish cakes with yesterday's leftovers," Bliss said just as Rebecca caught sight of a plate covered with greaseproof paper. "They aren't perfectly shaped but they're probably edible."

"I love your fish cakes," Rebecca said sincerely, backing out of the refrigerator with the plate in her hand. "I love you, too. Thank you for thinking ahead. I don't know where my head was."

"Mm-hmm."

Bliss could pack more meaning into that innocent couple of syllables than anyone Rebecca had ever known. But right now Bliss's sarcasm had no power to bother her, and she was most relieved she didn't have to trot out to buy something for dinner. The day's activities were beginning to tell on her.

Hastily she blanked out the memory of some of those activities before Bliss could read them on her face, as she sometimes seemed able to do. "Thanks, Gran," she said, giving the older woman a loving hug. "I'll make a salad and we'll be nicely set."

"Aren't you going to take off your jacket?" Bliss repeated. It was becoming clear to her that Rebecca was working very hard to appear normal, which of course meant that something was not at all normal.

"Of course, yes." Rebecca's fingers went to the zipper of her windcheater, then she looked down at herself and hesitated. Two small but bright patches of color appeared on her cheekbones and she gave Bliss a brief, guilty-looking smile. "Perhaps I'll just take a quick bath and a change before I put the fish cakes on," she said. "I'm still chilled, and all that scrambling about on hillsides made me feel a bit grubby."

Before Bliss could comment, she hurried from the room.

Why, Bliss wondered, sinking onto a chair, would Rebecca suddenly decide to take a bath before dinner? She'd looked perfectly clean. Why should her suggestion that Rebecca remove her jacket make her blush?

And why had Simon Flynn kept glancing at Rebecca with such a soft look in his blue eyes?

Despair wrapped itself around her heart as if a hand was squeezing it. She might be getting on and her body might be weak in parts, but she wasn't daft. Her brain still functioned astutely. It was quite obvious that the thing she'd most dreaded had come to pass. Something had happened between Rebecca and Simon Flynn. The atmosphere between them had been thick with sexual tension. They'd avoided looking at each other. And there'd been a note in Simon Flynn's voice that hadn't been there before. A proprietary note. An affectionate note.

Oh, yes, she recognized all the signs. She'd experienced them. And she remembered them. The first time you made love with a wonderful man, a man you cared about, was not something you ever forgot, no matter how much you pretended to.

The first time...

They'd strolled on the promenade along Penmorton's seafront, walked to the end of the pier and back again, then hiked up the path to the clifftop. The sun shone in a clear blue sky. Once they reached the ancient bridle path they could see for miles in any direction.

"You were right," Paul had said, smiling. "It *is* warmer in Cornwall."

"Well, it's not always like this," Bliss admitted. "Quite often the wind could blow your head off up here. And it can get awfully chilly. It rains a lot, too— you can see that, just looking around at all the green. What's it like in Los Angeles?"

She couldn't believe they were talking about the weather. She wished she could think of fascinating things to say the way people did in films. Normally she wasn't a bit shy, but when she glanced at Paul as they walked along, when she saw that certain look in his blue eyes as he glanced back at her, her tongue kept getting tied in knots.

He told her Los Angeles was hot in summer, warm in winter, that he hardly ever needed an overcoat, but it did rain sometimes. He told her he'd taken aircraft mechanics at the California Flyers School of Aeronautics and had lived in a hotel right on the beach in Santa Monica. The whole L.A. area was bustling, he said; aircraft-manufacturing plants—Lockheed, Douglas, Northrup—were going full speed ahead with their war effort.

"Our palm trees are taller than yours," he added with a grin. "Our streets are a lot wider, too. And our houses look different—there's a big Spanish influence—stucco houses, red-tile roofs. Right now there are a lot of uniforms around, just like here."

They walked in silence for a while, then Paul looked sideways at her and said, "That's a pretty dress. Yellow is definitely your color."

It felt good to be wearing a dress, instead of those scratchy jodhpurs. This one was a brighter yellow than the one she'd worn when she first met him and had square, padded shoulders. She loved the way the fabric swished against her bare legs as she walked. A lot of women were delighted to be able to wear trousers now that there was a war on, but once the war was over Bliss didn't care if she never wore trousers again.

Paul was out of uniform, too. He had on casual cotton trousers, a shirt that matched his blue eyes, a Harris-tweed sports coat he'd brought in Plymouth, which he insisted made him look like an English gentleman. It

was draped over his left shoulder because his left arm
was still in a sling. Bliss's dad's old khaki rucksack was
slung over his right shoulder. Occasionally it bumped
Bliss on the hip. There were a couple of bottles of ale in
it and an extra packet of Lucky Strikes, plus a heavy
jumper for each of them in case the weather turned
chilly.

The channel was calm, glinting turquoise under the
sun, white ruffles showing here and there along the
edges like lace trimming on a petticoat. Hard to imagine that on the other side of the channel . . .

No, she wasn't going to think about the war while
Paul was here. She wasn't going to think at all.

Very casually he took hold of her hand. She was
amazed at how much feeling could come through a
person's hand. His grip was warm and strong. She suddenly felt more lighthearted than she could remember
ever feeling. Even as a child she hadn't been all that
carefree, what with Mum fussing about her heart, Dad
lecturing about the damage going to the pictures was
doing to the state of her soul.

"Tell me what it's like to fly," she said. "Do you like
it? Don't you ever feel afraid being up there alone in the
sky?"

"I'm much more afraid when we're *not* alone," he
said with a grin, then shook his head. "I love the sensation of flying. Leaving the ground behind. Leaving
your worries behind."

"Worries?"

There were little lines around his eyes she hadn't noticed before. "Everybody has worries, Bliss."

"I suppose that's true. It's just that you seem so
carefree. What do you worry about?"

He laughed. "I worry about getting killed. I'd just as soon not. Don't you worry about that?"

She considered. "I did at the start of the war, I think. Well, even before that—when your dad's a clergyman, you hear a lot about death. He used to make me say that prayer 'If I should die before I wake, I pray the Lord by soul to take.' Frightened me silly, especially with Mum always carrying on about my heart. But now I've survived this long, I don't even think about dying. Dad's always going on about the hereafter, but I'm not interested in that. I'm interested in what's going to happen to me while I'm alive."

"What do you want to happen?"

She thought about it for a minute. "Well, I'd like to get married someday. I mean, most people do, don't they?"

He nodded, then looked away and moved his neck a little as though the sling's knot was chafing his skin.

"Is anything wrong?" she asked.

"It doesn't seem much of a reason to get married, does it? The fact that most people do."

He was very serious all of a sudden. Had she put her foot in it? Did he think she was hinting? As if she would. Everyone knew men tended to get very edgy if they suspected a girl was hearing wedding bells.

Which was what Bliss had been hearing ever since she'd met this man.

"I just meant that it's sort of expected," she said hastily. "My mum's always on at me about getting married, saving myself for my husband and all that. I suppose there's not much else a girl can do, really. I don't particularly want a career, and I don't have the education for it. Mum and Dad couldn't afford college for me, and I wouldn't have wanted to go if they did. I mean, what's the point? I always hated school, anyway. After the war, if I'm not married by then, I suppose I'll go back to working in Mum's shop. Not that I'm in any hurry to get married," she added to reassure him.

He was still frowning. "Mostly I just want to have fun," she said, watching his face. "I don't even care if I never get married. I'll find something to do with myself, never fear."

He laughed and the little lines smoothed. "I like your attitude, Bliss Turner." Lifting her hand in his, he kissed her fingers, then her cheek.

She felt heat rush to the spot and wanted to reach up and touch it, but didn't want him to think she was making too much of it.

"How about a smoke?" she asked, gesturing just ahead to where there was a bench at the side of the path. There was nothing like a cigarette to get you over awkward moments.

After they'd lit up, they sat together looking straight ahead at the shining channel, smoking, not speaking. The light off the sea was extraordinary. Bliss could feel her heart thumping against her ribs. He was going to kiss her, she was sure of it. Because it was a Tuesday, there was no one else on the cliff to the right or left.

The bench was in the middle of a kind of valley, where a footpath led down to the sands, which meant even if anyone had been in the area they wouldn't have been able to see the two of them sitting there. It was a sheltered place. The sun felt very warm.

"What's that building over there?" Paul asked, looking beyond her to where the ground rose again.

She turned to see. "Oh, that's an old huer's house."

He smiled. He had lovely teeth, she thought—very white and even. A film star's teeth. Real people didn't have teeth like that. "And a huer is?" he asked.

She frowned. "Well, I suppose the word has something to do with hue and cry, wouldn't you think? Years ago, whoever had the job of lookout, the huer, would keep watch up there till the great pilchard shoals came in, then he'd sound his horn and all the fishermen would go out in their boats to cast their nets."

Paul looked toward the hut, squinting against the dazzle of sunlight on white-painted wood. "Is it locked?"

Her heart thumped even harder as she realized what he was thinking. She had daydreamed all week about the two of them making love, but hadn't been sure what was possible, considering his injury. The hut had a wooden floor. It wouldn't be very comfortable, though they did have heavy jumpers in the rucksack. And Paul had his tweed jacket.

Heat washed through her whole body as her mind leapt ahead and produced a vivid image of herself and Paul naked, wrapped in each other's arms. The sun would shine in through the hut's one window, turning Paul's hair to gold. She remembered what he'd said when she first met him, how she looked all bronzed and gleaming.

"I wouldn't expect the huer's house to be locked," she said carefully. Her voice sounded hoarse as if she'd caught a cold. "It's a sort of historic building. People go in it."

"Not too many people around today."

She nodded agreement, not trusting herself to speak.

For a moment their eyes held. A question passed between them and was answered affirmatively without a word or gesture. Suddenly aware that this was a momentous decision, Bliss shivered slightly.

At once Paul slipped his jacket off and put it around her shoulders. She could feel the heat of his body still in it, smell the peaty odor that was always present in Harris tweed.

Dropping his cigarette to the ground, Paul crushed it under his shoe, hoisted the rucksack, which he'd dropped at his feet earlier, then stood up and put out a hand to her. She took it and let him pull her to her feet.

His blue eyes danced with mishcief—and something else. It was the something else that was taking Bliss's breath right out of her body and causing her heart to rattle around in her chest.

The promise of passion.

Holding her cigarette butt between thumb and first finger, Bliss drew one last lungful of acrid smoke, then dropped it to the ground and crushed it under her shoe just as he had.

As though this was a symbol of some kind, Paul smiled, then put his right arm around her shoulders, pulling her in to his side, a little awkward because of the sling on his other arm and the jacket wrapped around her.

"You are so beautiful, Bliss," he murmured as his head came down toward her and his lips met hers.

Warmth spread outward from her heart to every last part of her body. No one had ever called her beautiful before, and she had never thought of herself that way, but quite suddenly she *felt* as beautiful as anyone in the world.

SIMON PICKED UP his pen and began to write:

Dear Mom:
Herewith ET update. Corny Cornwood, pub habitué, darts champion, beer drinker extraordinaire, declares there was "some kind of scandal" connected with Bliss Penberthy, née Turner. Museum curator Mr. Medlicott, former teacher and one time headmaster of Penmorton's elementary school, confirms that girl in photograph is Bliss Penberthy and identifies uniform as British land army.

~~We~~ I discovered Mrs. Winifred Stubbins of Tintagel, dog groomer, old school friend of Bliss Penberthy's. She admitted under questioning that Bliss and Paul had an affair and that Paul was "the love of Bliss's life," then decided she ~~shouldn't~~ wouldn't say anymore, "because it wouldn't be ethical," Wise lady, Mom.

It seems clear that either Bliss discovered Paul was married and had a child—you—or Paul confessed he was married and had a child. Either way, Bliss was a minister's daughter, which had to be a big deal in small-town 1943. So she probably gave him his walking papers. She's apparently anti-American, so it would seem he probably done her wrong in some way.

I could probably come home now—mission accomplished—but I haven't yet figured out how to let Bliss know Paul loved her. As I told you earlier, it's not possible to bring any of this up directly because of Bliss's heart condition. We may have to forgo that part of the mission.

However, I'm quite enjoying England, so I'm not in any particular hurry to leave. As you've been nagging me to take a vacation, I'm sure you'll be happy to hear that.

A master stroke, he thought.

It's interesting to see the old towns and how they were laid out. They're certainly aesthetically pleasing, though not always convenient. Then again, the Cornish terrain is very hilly, so builders didn't have a lot of choice. All the same, quaint-looking stone cottages are usually cold and damp.

Was that enough subterfuge, or would Libby read between the lines with that eagle eye of hers and notice that he'd left something out? Which he had, of course. He hadn't once mentioned Rebecca.

P.S. Bliss's granddaughter has been very helpful and cooperative.

There!

P.P.S. Be assured ye sleuth is still hot on the trail. More later.

REBECCA WAS HOLDING a book in her right hand. "It's about King Arthur country," she said.

Simon took it from her without looking at it and set it down on a nearby table. Then he closed and locked the cottage door. He'd already drawn all the curtains and turned off all the lamps except the one next to the bed. He saw her notice that.

"Well," she said, sounding breathless.

With some ceremony, he removed her glasses and set them carefully on the nearest table. Then he took her hands in his and raised them to his mouth, kissing her fingers one at a time. She had lovely long fingers, he thought, tapered, artistic, the nails short and unpainted but neatly manicured.

"I don't want you to think..."

"What?" he asked.

"That I came here just to..."

"Didn't you?"

She laughed. "Gran's already tucked in," she informed him.

Placing her hands around his waist, he pulled her as close to him as he could, his hands cupping her wonderfully firm posterior. Her own arms tightened around him. Without her glasses, her eyes looked softer, but just as full of light. She was smiling. She'd replaced her jeans and ruined sweater with beige pants and an open-neck, long-sleeve, navy blue shirt. She looked impossibly slender and elegant. Her straight hair hung loose from its part, framing her face with ebony.

"I preferred the shrunken sweater," he murmured.

"Typical male," she said.

"I've never pretended to be otherwise. I'm willing to bet the knights of the Round Table, with all their gallantry, would have appreciated that sweater."

She laughed, her honey-sweet breath touching his skin like a caress. Her amber eyes glinted.

"I visited the chemist," he told her.

"Did you now."

He was barely breathing. He couldn't remember ever having been affected in quite this way by a woman. He was excited, yes—that was becoming more demonstrably obvious by the second—yet he was conscious of a kind of delicate restraint that was new to him. He wanted to take his time, savor every moment, delay satisfaction as long as possible, because he didn't want to be satisfied. He wanted to desire her as much afterward as he did now.

And this was something totally new to him.

The exact center of her full lower lip was caught in her teeth, tempting him with its ripeness. Delicately he touched his tongue to the spot and felt her tremble. She was holding herself back, also, he realized, not from shyness or reluctance, but because she knew as he did that once they unleashed the banked emotions that had flared between them earlier in the day there would be no stopping them.

She took a shaky breath, parting her lips so that his tongue could find entrance. Gently he touched just the tip of it to the soft flesh inside her upper lip, then to one corner of her mouth.

"Simon." His name came out of her mouth on a soft moan. His mouth brushed hers, still gently, though not tentatively, then moved down over her chin. Her head tilted back so that his lips could find and explore the tender hollow at the base of her throat.

Her body had gone loose. If he let go of her, he was sure she would fall. He marveled at her trust, even as he tightened his hold on her.

The navy blue shirt had a low neckline. He could see the shadow between her breasts. It was obvious she was not wearing a bra. Kissing her smooth, warm skin, he nudged the blouse fabric aside and let his tongue trail over the softly swelling breast he'd exposed, searching for and finding the nipple, already erect and waiting.

As his lips closed over it, she moaned again. Heat flashed through him like a lightning bolt, and he pulled her hard against him and kissed her again on the mouth. This time the kiss was hot and demanding.

She met his ardor with her own, her mouth drawing his breath from him, pulling it into herself as her hands tugged his shirt loose from his jeans, then moved over the bare flesh of his back.

Somehow his own hands were active on her naked skin. He had no idea if he had unfastened the buttons of her shirt or if she had done it herself. It didn't matter. Soon his own shirt was undone, and he felt the exquisite sensation of her firm breasts sliding gently against the mat of hair on his chest.

Once again she was making little incoherent sounds deep in her throat. She'd done that before, in the stone alcove at King Arthur's Castle. The sounds excited him and threatened to destroy the patience he'd sworn to hang on to.

She had long, slender bones and she was tall. Looking at her, the words willowy and lissome came to mind. She couldn't be called petite, yet there was something so delicate about her his hands felt overlarge touching her, and he was afraid of seeming clumsy.

With great care, he eased her off her feet and into his arms. This was the second time he'd carried her to bed, like some macho movie lover. He'd never done that with a woman before, but it seemed natural with her, as long as he used great care and was absolutely sure she was willing to go along with him.

The amber shining of her eyes left no doubt that she was.

Playfully she elected to take off the rest of his clothes, lightly slapping his hands away as he moved to help her. He lay back, letting her have her way, enjoying the unusual sensation of being treated as if he was helpless.

He had expected she'd give him leave to take over when she was done, but she shucked her pants and blouse and sandals so swiftly and neatly he didn't have a chance to get involved.

Grumbling, he pulled her down onto the striped sheets that smelled, as always, of rosemary, or so Rebecca had told him when he'd asked about the subtle odor. Kissing one closed eyelid, then the other, he decided to forgive her, though he couldn't remember what he'd been grumbling about. He leaned over her and stroked her body with strong, slow motions that made her shudder and open her eyes.

"Are you ready to go to war?" he asked.

Her soft gurgle of laughter stirred his private parts to even more compelling attentiveness. "All the way this time, then?" she murmured.

He gazed fondly down at her, his eyes brimming blue in the light from the bedside lamp. Those black eyebrows of his had assumed the slanted position that made him look so devilish. "The trumpets have already sounded, my lady," he said as his thumb worked over her lips, and his lower parts pressed insistently against her hip. "The ramparts are manned."

So, he was back in Tintagel, was he? Very well, she'd join him there. Reaching up, she put her hands at the back of his head and tugged it gently down until his mouth hovered over hers.

"I want it to be slow," he said.

"I've got all night," she answered, smiling as she remembered saying the same thing to him under less friendly circumstances.

His mouth touched hers, lightly at first, then more demandingly. It was a longer kiss this time, a serious kiss. She felt she never wanted to let his mouth leave hers. Was the smile still hovering around it? she wondered. She thought it might be. She could almost taste the smile in the kiss.

Once upon a time she'd thought kisses were, on the whole, awkward things. Noses and chins got in the way and you ran out of breath and it was generally wet and sometimes your teeth bumped his... Whatever romance had been there at the start of it was destroyed.

But this kiss wasn't some awkward physical fumbling; it was a communication, a joining, a giving and a taking. It was Rebecca telling Simon she'd come to feel a great affection for him and so felt she could trust him with her body, even her soul. It was Simon telling her he had strong feelings of his own but was trying to hold them back, to make their lovemaking last.

Pushing himself up on his arms, he gazed down at her face, the smile she'd imagined tasting minutes earlier tugging gently at the corners of his mouth. "I'm not sure I'm going to be able to keep this as slow as I wanted to," he said. "The spirit's willing as all get out, but the flesh is weak."

Looking down at her breasts, he moved a hand to touch one, his fingers becoming suddenly impatient. "You are so incredibly beautiful," he told her.

And then he touched her lips. She felt his fingers tremble and was moved to an extreme of tenderness she'd never experienced before. It was perhaps at that moment that she admitted to herself, only to herself, that she was falling in love with Simon Flynn.

Not about to let herself worry about the idiocy of falling for a man who was a temporary visitor to her life, she let herself relax into the glory of it, instead, and raised her face for another kiss.

Afterward she had no idea how long they made love that night. Occasionally they talked, not about anything important. Mostly they wove together bits of fantasy for each other, adding to their excitement with references to the knights and fair ladies who had surely witnessed their encounters at the castle and the hotel and might even be watching approvingly now.

They touched and stroked and kissed any part of each other that became available, at first with great passion, later lazily but no less enjoyably.

Once, twice, perhaps even three times, Simon brought her to the brink of explosion, then touched her with masterful precision in just the right place so that the pressure was released in great, throbbing bursts. Following which, he entered her and held her and moved with her until his own release came.

Before the night was half-done she had explored his body with her fingertips and her mouth so thoroughly she could have drawn a map of it. She could find no flaw in him.

Eventually they became sleepy. Rebecca's body was tangled inextricably with Simon's, and it occurred to her that they should really straighten themselves out or they'd be cutting off each other's circulation. But there was no energy left in her, nor any desire to move her flesh away from his. "My very perfect noble knight," she said softly.

"*Canterbury Tales,*" he answered.

"Mmm-hmm."

"So that I have my lady in my arms," he murmured.

"Canterbury Tales," she murmured back, feeling warm and secure and very, very sleepy.

Letting go of all thought, she felt herself sliding irrevocably into the deepest, darkest, sweetest sleep she'd ever had.

CHAPTER THIRTEEN

THE SOLUTION CAME to Simon the moment he awoke the next morning. He'd often found that if he had a problem with one of his building projects, he could think it over just before going to sleep and find in the morning that his subconscious mind had popped up with at least the beginning of an answer.

The solution in question had to do with the relationship between Paul and Bliss, of course. He'd begun suspecting the answer some time ago but hadn't really put it together. Now that he had, he felt it had the ring of truth. He could hear his grandfather saying yes in his mind again.

His theory also fitted the known facts, and it explained Paul's unhappiness and Bliss's anger far better than just the fact of his deceiving her about having a wife and child back home in the States. Simon felt quite pleased with himself.

Rebecca stirred in his arms, then came awake all in an instant. Sitting bolt upright and looking alarmed, she pushed her tangled hair off her forehead, her high cheekbones still flushed with sleep. "What time is it?"

Sunlight was barely filtering in around the edges of the curtains. Gulls squawked raucously overhead. "It's okay, it's only five o'clock," Simon said, having just a minute ago checked his watch.

The tension went out of her body and she smiled down at him, totally unself-conscious about her nudity. He liked that. "I slept remarkably well," she said, touching his lips with a finger.

He grinned at her and took the finger into his mouth, nipping it lightly between his teeth before letting it go. "Me, too. Maybe we could market the concept, suggest everyone throw away their sleeping pills and try sex, instead."

A shadow crossed her face. "Sex," she said flatly. "That's all it was to you? Just sex?"

He'd forgotten that women were inclined to be particular about semantics. Making love was a cut above sleeping together and a vast improvement over having sex. Kissing and cuddling was better than necking or making out. The roads to male/female harmony were strewn with such land mines.

"I'm not belittling what happened between us last night," he hastened to add with complete truth. "It far transcended anything I've ever experienced."

Smiling forgiveness, she put a hand on his chest and stroked it lightly with her fingertips, setting up a delightful friction that to Simon's amazement aroused interest in distant parts. He groaned. "Mercy," he said. "I'm too drained. I don't think there's a milligram of testosterone left in my body."

Pulling her down beside him, he kissed her lingeringly, then leaned his head back. "I've something to tell you—I think I may have come up with the reason Paul and Bliss split up."

Her gaze fixed gravely on his face, she pushed a pillow up against the headboard and settled herself against it, pulling the covers up. Simon followed suit. The cottage had turned chilly in the night, though he certainly hadn't noticed it while they were having—making love.

Taking her hand, he lifted it and kissed it lightly, then held on to it as he returned it to the comforter.

"Try this scenario," he suggested. "Bliss doesn't know Paul is married. They have an affair. Bliss gets pregnant. That's when Paul confesses he has a wife and child and can't marry her. Bliss is left to handle the pregnancy alone. Her father, the rector, can't have been thrilled. This was 1943, after all, and pregnancy without matrimony was a big deal in those days. Furthermore, Penmorton is a small town. So everyone would soon have known she was pregnant, thus the scandal Corny mentioned. According to Mrs. Stubbins, Bliss's marriage to Foster Penberthy was a mistake—maybe she did that to give the baby a name. Paul goes home to his unloving wife and his little daughter, and spends the rest of his life regretting he left Bliss behind."

Rebecca was staring at him as if he'd suddenly grown an extra head. Her face had turned the approximate color of buttermilk. All the golden light had gone out of her eyes.

"Hey, listen," he said, putting an arm around her bare and lovely shoulders. "It's all ancient history. I know you love your grandmother and you don't want to think about her having such a hard time, but at least—"

He broke off as Rebecca leapt out of bed and began dragging on her underwear.

"It's not that bad," he assured her. "Think of the possible alternatives. It could have turned out that Paul got in a fistfight with Bliss's father or beat up on her or something. He wasn't the most patient guy in the world."

Rebecca was still yanking on her clothing. Simon looked at her incredulously. "Didn't it occur to you that Paul might have gotten Bliss pregnant?" he asked.

She was fastening the button of her waistband, tucking in her silk shirt, pushing her feet into her sandals. She stopped only long enough to look at him blankly, seemed about to speak, evidently changed her mind and simply shook her head. Putting on her glasses, running her fingers through her hair to tidy it, she looked at him again, this time with horror, then dashed out the door as if someone had sounded a fire alarm. For a minute Simon even thought maybe someone had. He couldn't think why else she'd behave so oddly.

Leaning back against his pillow, he sighed and wondered why women were sometimes so irrational.

BY MIDMORNING, he still hadn't decided what to do. Judging by previous experience, if he went to the shop and confronted Rebecca, either Bliss would show up or the place would fill with customers. Probably he should wait until evening and hope Rebecca would be ready to share the reasons for her strange reaction.

In the meantime he thought he might give his mother a call, rather than mailing her the letter he'd written the previous day. He could try his theory out on her and see what *her* response was.

He wouldn't be able to call from the house, though; that one phone in the hall was too open. He'd have to find a more private phone. Clytie, he thought. She might be willing to help him out.

She was. Happy to see him, looking very striking in an Indian sari, she showed him into her tiny office and indicated the phone with a graceful, Eastern-inspired gesture that seemed to imply that all she possessed was his for the asking.

Libby listened without comment to the developments Simon had outlined in his letter and then to the conclusion he'd reached overnight. When he finished he was met by silence. He could almost hear his mother's formidable brain checking over everything he'd told her, adding nuances he'd missed, dotting every *i* and crossing every *t*.

"This is really exciting!" she exclaimed finally.

He took the receiver away from his ear, looked at it and put it back. This was not the reaction he'd expected. Surely she should have been shocked that her father might have left an illegitimate child behind in England.

"Exciting?"

"Good Lord, Simon, sometimes you can be so dense," she said, which seemed a very unfair remark. "Haven't you figured it out? If your theory is true, it means we're related to the Penberthys. Well, not to Bliss, but to the granddaughter—what was her name? Rebecca? How old is she, anyway?"

"Twenty something," he said vaguely.

"Really? I got the impression she was much younger. I hadn't realized she was a grown-up. I suppose you must have called her a girl. You really have to stop doing that, darling. It's just not politically correct and—"

"What do you mean, related?" Simon interrupted. He closed his eyes. *Oh, my God, yes.* He knew what his mother was going to say. A buzzing started in his ears.

"If Paul fathered Bliss's baby—what was its name?"

"Travis." The buzz had become a roar.

"That would make Travis my half brother if he were still alive," his mother went on. "And even though he's dead, that would make Rebecca my niece and your cousin."

Cousin. In some places that was considered a fairly close relationship. Maybe even a taboo relationship. Other places it was probably acceptable. It? What was he calling 'it'? Sex. Having sex. Sleeping together. Making love.

He and Rebecca. Cousins.

So that was why she'd fled the cottage.

"Are you there, Simon?" his mother asked. He had the feeling she'd asked it a time or two before.

"I'm here," he said weakly.

"Do you get it?"

"I've got it." Sitting behind Clytie's elaborately carved desk—elephants, why would anyone want elephants lumbering around the edge of their desk, each one's trunk hanging on to the tail of the one behind it—Simon tried desperately to pull himself together.

"Listen, Mom, I want you to keep this under your hat for now, okay?" he said. "Don't go calling the Penberthys and burbling about being kissing cousins. We can't take the risk of shaking Bliss up and affecting her health. She's kept this thing a secret from Rebecca all these years. Let's not blow it for her."

"I'm not that indiscreet, Simon," his mother said indignantly.

Hurriedly he threw out several soothing remarks, added half-a-dozen excuses for why he had to hang up the telephone, then did it before Libby could object, thankful she didn't know where he was calling from so couldn't call him back.

Feeling dazed, he thanked Clytie, refused the offer of a Guinness on the house—before lunch was a little too early even for a man reeling from a severe shock—and stumbled off to his car.

Where to? was the question. He didn't feel up to facing Rebecca until he had this whole incredible development sorted out in his mind.

Should he go talk to Winifred Stubbins again? Come back to the pub later and see if Corny Cornwood was around? Beard Mr. Medlicott in his museum?

None of the above, he decided. He would simply start the Peugeot and drive to wherever fate led him.

WITH A HALF-EMBARRASSED glance at Simon's face, Rebecca carried in the tea tray she'd prepared and set it on the low table in front of the settee.

He closed the door and came to sit beside her. She could feel his eyes on her as she poured but concentrated on pouring the tea. "You went for a drive, Gran told me," she said.

"To Bolventor."

"Daphne du Maurier country."

"Yes." He hesitated. "I investigated the remains of a tin-mine engine house on the way back. Interesting."

Rebecca nodded. The atmosphere was thick with tension and she wasn't sure how to break it or even if she should attempt to. Handing him his cup, she asked stiffly, "Did you see Jamaica Inn?"

"I had lunch there, along with several busloads of tourists. The sight-seeing buses were called charabancs, according to the sign in the parking lot."

"The last part's pronounced as if it has a g," she told him. "Charabangs."

"Really?"

This was a ridiculous conversation.

"Daphne du Maurier wrote at a Sheraton desk," Simon contributed.

Rebecca glanced at him again and found he was looking at her with a sort of questioning intensity, his blue eyes very focused and direct. Nervously she picked up her cup and sipped some tea. "Did you visit the museum there?" she asked.

He made a sound that was somewhat derisive. "I didn't stay long. I've never liked the idea of real animals being stuffed—'mounted,' I guess, is the proper term. It's bad enough with wild animals, but this place includes people's pets. One man donated his cat for the purpose after it died. There were dioramas set up like tea parties..."

His voice trailed away as if words had failed him. "What on earth would a fine writer like Daphne du Maurier think of having such a place at Jamaica Inn?"

Rebecca shook her head. In spite of the tension between them, she was pleased that his reaction to the display had been the same as hers.

"I found Dozmary Pool," he told her.

She darted still another glance at him.

"I didn't see the hand waving the sword, but I thought the place was fairly atmospheric. I could imagine Bedivere throwing Excalibur into the water." He paused. "I wished you were with me."

She took a deep breath and set her cup down on the tray. "I behaved badly this morning, Simon. I want to apologize."

"No need. Once I figured out what the problem was, I understood why you were so shocked. I was pretty shocked myself for a while."

"You're not now? The fact that we may possibly be cousins doesn't bother you? Considering..."

He reached for her hand and held it between his own. "The point is, Rebecca, it's not exactly a fact. It's a possibility. There's not much sense getting upset about it until we know for sure there *was* a baby involved."

"But it seems pretty obvious."

"Only because it explains everything. Which doesn't mean it's the *only* explanation."

She shook her head. Withdrawing her hand in as casual a manner as she could, she said, "I don't feel right about..." She had no idea how to express what was in her mind.

"Our having a relationship if we're related?"

She nodded, feeling inexpressibly sad. And lonely. It was as though she'd flung the gate of that symbolic courtyard wide and opened her arms and heart to love, only to hear the gate clang shut again.

"Even if there is a blood relationship between us, it's not exactly close," Simon pointed out. "We'd only have one grandparent in common, not two."

"All the same." She looked at him directly. The smile that usually played around his mouth was completely absent. The groove between his brow seemed more pronounced. He'd gotten a little more sun on his trip to Bolventor, which made his eyes seem vividly blue. His black hair was as shaggy as always. There were lines bracketing his mouth she hadn't noticed before.

"It's not just the possibility that we're cousins, Simon," she said slowly. "Though that's certainly a barrier where I'm concerned. In England it's true that there's nothing illegal about cousins, well, cohabiting, shall we say, but it's certainly not looked upon with any favor. There's also this—it seems apparent that your grandfather ruined Gran's life. Even if your theory isn't true, how can I possibly carry on a…romance with you, knowing that? What if Gran was to find out you're Paul Carmichael's grandson and that I'm involved with you even though I know you're his grandson? She'd be mortified. Heartbroken. Her heart has been broken enough already."

"Paul's own life wasn't exactly terrific," Simon said. "He was such a loner, Rebecca. He worked hard, had many brilliant ideas, was well-thought-of, but although he had hundreds of acquaintances, he didn't have a single close friend. He shut people out. Even his family. I'd say he also gave a pretty good imitation of a person with a broken heart."

"But it seems as if the problem was of his own making."

Simon put his hand under her chin and turned her face up to his, his expression filled with so much pain she felt her heart swell with answering pain. "You're holding me responsible for my grandfather's behavior?" he asked.

About to deny any such thing, she hesitated. That *was* what she was doing in a way, though her main motivation was to prevent any hurt to Bliss. She found she couldn't meet his gaze. Very gently he released her.

"You want me to leave Penmorton?" he asked.

Her stomach contracted as though all the air had gone out of her body. "No…yes…no…of course not. Well, you're the only one who can decide what you should do," she stammered.

"Well, as long as you've got your mind made up," he said, amusement edging his voice for the first time since she'd entered the cottage.

She sighed. "I don't know what to do, Simon," she admitted.

"Well, I do," he said briskly. "First we work at finding out if my stupid theory is actually true."

"I won't have Gran—"

"Then we find another way. She must have had other friends besides Mrs. Stubbins. We just have to track them down."

Rebecca looked at him, wanting so badly to touch his sad face, his stern mouth, but she couldn't do it. Besides feeling uneasy about the possible blood relationship, she couldn't quite separate him from Paul Carmichael and the terrible thing Paul might have done to her grandmother. Against such strong opposition, a newborn love didn't stand a chance.

All the same he was right to want to pursue this; they had to know for sure. Slowly she nodded agreement. "But in the meantime..." she began tentatively.

"In the meantime, we'll follow the good advice of Lord Byron." He grinned wryly. "Here I am again, about to spout poetry. I've been doing it ever since I landed in this country. Anyway, Lord Byron gave some fairly forthright counsel right after he'd broken up with a woman. He said, 'The best way will be to avoid each other without appearing to do so, or if we jostle, at any rate not to bite.'"

Simon hesitated. The smile had returned for a moment, but it disappeared again as quickly as it had arrived. "Don't look so worried, Rebecca. It'll be okay.

Until we know what's what, we'll be good friends, fellow detectives, nothing more.''

"You mean that?"

He gave a short laugh. Somewhere in that laugh, Rebecca suspected, was a sigh. "On my word as a perfect, noble knight," he said.

CHAPTER FOURTEEN

THE MORNING was clear and sunny. Penmorton's surrounding patchwork of fields shone green and gold like a Constable painting. On such a day it was almost enough just to be alive, even if your hands and wrists and knees ached and your chest felt tight.

Bliss didn't always enjoy her morning walk. It was something she did for the sake of her health, a duty, rather than a pleasure. But this morning there seemed a quality to the light that was reminiscent of long-ago mornings, long-ago walks.

She had taken the bus down to the harbor for a change, then walked slowly to the seafront promenade, comfortable in her sturdy walking shoes, tights, wool skirt and warm jacket. The tide was all the way in. The promenade looked different from the way it had during the war. Then it had been edged with rolls of barbed wire to keep the enemy out. Now it was abutted by huge blocks of concrete set at various angles, an effective and even strangely artistic way of keeping the coastline from being eroded.

The pillboxes—roofed concrete gun emplacements—had been removed decades ago, along with the barbed wire.

The pillboxes. She caught herself on the edge of smiling and frowned, instead. She'd come here to sort today out, not think about yesterday.

Something was bothering Rebecca. Her pretty face was drawn with tension and unhappiness. If there was one thing Bliss recognized, it was misery. In this case, she didn't have far to look for the cause. Simon Flynn. She'd known he meant trouble right from the start. What was she to do about him? That was the question. How was she to get him out of her house and out of her beloved granddaughter's life before he caused irreparable harm?

Aware that her legs were beginning to ache, never a good sign for her circulation, Bliss sat down to rest on the slatted wooden seat of a concrete bench and gazed out at the English Channel.

"The sea has great therapeutic powers," Paul had said once. "Watch it for a while, and troubles just drop away."

The water shone more blue than green this morning. There were a few feathered wisps of cloud overhead. She recalled Paul saying, "Little weather change for the next twenty-four hours."

He'd known a lot about weather and had taught Bliss what to look for, letting the names of cloud types roll off his tongue like poetry: cirrocumulus, nimbostratus.

Tilting her face to the sun, eyelids half-closed, Bliss imagined she could really hear his voice. Vibrant, confidently masculine, it seemed to haunt the edges of the clouds.

"Hey, listen, don't worry, honey. I'm going to live forever."

She'd worried, anyway. Now that his shoulder was healed he was flying daylight raids over Germany, dropping bombs, getting shot at, shooting back. How could she not worry? Lying in her narrow bunk in the barn/dormitory she shared with three other land-army girls, clutching her lumpy feather pillow and occasionally crying into it, she was convinced that he'd be killed, that he'd never again hold her in his arms, never again make love to her. She loved him and had told him so, hoping he'd tell her the same. He hadn't. He'd be killed any day now, and she'd never know if he loved her or not.

All of this, of course, was before the dreadful quarrel.

Bliss closed her eyes so tightly she could see purple splotches. No, she wasn't going to think about the quarrel. She had avoided thinking about it for more than fifty years.

She'd rather think about pillboxes. When they wanted to make love in the daytime and Bliss's mother was very much in evidence, tending her vegetables in the courtyard, working in the shop or sewing in her bedroom with one eye on the window that looked down at the cottage, they'd depended on pillboxes, with an occasional visit to the drafty Huer's house for sentiment's sake. What the pillboxes lacked in comfort they made up for in privacy. Nobody ever went in them at that stage of the war, especially the one at the far end of the promenade. And Paul and Bliss always carried or wore, depending on the weather, thick jumpers—"sweaters" Paul called them—and jackets with padding in them. Lying on their makeshift bed in the concrete structure, they spent hours talking, kissing, touching.

"You have a great body," he told her often.

His own was tight and hard, though not bulging with muscle. Bliss's tan, which was limited to her arms and hands, face and throat, was fading as the weather changed, but he seemed to have a permanent tan, with only one band of white between his waist and thighs. "Californians get tanned through to the bone when they're kids and it never washes off," he explained with a facetious grin. "Best part is the white part," he added. "Feel free to explore."

"Shouldn't we use something?" she asked him.

He wrinkled his nose. "It's not necessary," he told her. "I have a very low sperm count."

She blushed, even though by now she was used to the way he said things straight out. "Most Americans are straightforward," he'd told her. "We don't hide things the way English people do. We like to get everything out on the table so everyone can see."

"How do you know?" she brought herself to ask. "About the, er, sperm count, I mean."

"I had it tested." For a second his eyes narrowed and a cloud drifted over his face, then he shrugged. "My father's always been anxious for me to have sons, to keep the family business going through the generations. I keep telling him I'm not in any hurry. But it's possible I won't have any—" He broke off and abruptly looked away.

Bliss's heart contracted. Paul was obviously upset at the idea that he might not be able to provide the children his father wanted. Probably, she thought tenderly, he had the silly idea that his masculinity was in doubt. Men worried about that a lot, she'd heard. But why had he had his sperm count tested? she wondered. She found herself asking him.

He shrugged again, but still didn't look at her. "It was just one test among many. They put you through a bunch before they let you in the army."

Sperm counts part of army medicals? American authorities were thorough, that was for sure.

Paul was evidently tired of talking. Leaning over her, he began kissing her, his hands roaming familiarly over her naked body. By now he knew just how to touch her breasts to bring her to maximum excitement. He delighted in watching her face as he touched her secret places, smiling as she in turn touched him, something she'd been very shy about in the beginning. She wasn't sure it was something nice girls did, but Paul had assured her it had nothing to do with nice or naughty and everything to do with satisfaction.

As they made love, it started raining. Bliss could hear the rain drumming on the concrete roof of the pillbox. She welcomed it, for not only was the danger of someone coming lessened, it added atmosphere to the primitive accommodation. Not that they needed atmosphere to arouse them.

There had been excitement between them always. Perhaps because of the war and its threat of death always hovering over them, perhaps because of the secretive nature of their lovemaking. Occasionally a thrill of fear shot down Bliss's spine when she heard footsteps nearby and thought for sure this time someone was going to catch them "in flagrante delicto," as Paul was fond of referring to their passionate coupling.

"It's not exactly a crime," Bliss protested.

"Depends on your point of view," he teased her. "Your father the rector, for example. How would he look at it if he saw us?"

As a sin. A deadly sin. Punishable by turning errant daughters into pillars of salt. Bliss shuddered and changed the subject.

Later in the year when the wind off the channel whipped into the pillbox and the huer's house, they'd had to satisfy themselves with night-time loving, after

Mrs. Turner had gone to bed and Bliss could sneak across the courtyard. And that was only when Paul managed to get a pass and Bliss was able to talk Farmer Garland into letting her off at the same time.

Actually Tom Garland always gave in to her. "Can't refuse such a pretty lass anything," he'd tease with a grin.

During the day Bliss and Paul took long walks along the seafront and over the cliffs. At night they clung to each other in the bed that was small for Paul even when he was alone.

"I've something to tell you," he said a couple of weeks before Christmas....

Bliss, suddenly transported from the forties to the nineties, shifted on the wooden slats of the bench, opened her eyes and considered walking to the bus stop. Her traitorous brain had brought her back to the quarrel again. Simon Flynn's fault. There was something about that man. Ever since he'd arrived, doors to the past she had padlocked securely years ago kept falling open.

But she didn't want to leave the bench yet. The sun's warmth felt good on her face and on her arthritic hands and knees. The tightness in her chest had lessened. The splash of the waves hitting the rocks was soothing, almost hypnotic. Her eyes slipped shut again....

Paul's voice had an apologetic note to it. This was not going to be good news. He sat up against the headboard. After glancing at his solemn face, Bliss sat up next to him, covering her upper body with the sheet.

"Honey, I don't know how to tell you this," he'd started, and her heart had begun beating erratically. He'd found another woman. He was being sent back to the States. He'd volunteered for a dangerous secret mission and was going to die.

"I can't be here for Christmas," he said, looking sad.

At first she'd felt relief. Her imaginings were worse than the real thing. But then she felt a disappointment so deep she was almost nauseated.

"But you said you'd come. You must come!"

He put an arm around her shoulders. Usually she would sink back against it automatically, but this time she kept herself rigid. "You promised."

"My crew has a mission that'll keep us up north through the holidays."

"What kind of mission?" She knew she sounded sulky, rather than interested, but she couldn't help it. The disappointment was too great.

"Hush-hush, I'm afraid."

"Is it dangerous?" she said, alarmed all over again.

"Not at all. I just can't talk about it."

Men always said that when they didn't want to get into explanations. The war was very convenient for them. Bliss's cousin Josie had told her that. Josie's soldier husband had used that excuse a couple of times, and then she'd found out he was seeing a nurse in Plymouth.

Paul tried to kiss her, but she turned her face away. "I made such plans," she told him. "I wanted you to see what an old-fashioned English Christmas was like. Mum and I have been scrounging ration coupons for weeks. Farmer Garland promised me a little tree, and I thought we'd sing Christmas carols round the neighbors. I was going to make Christmas pudding and mincemeat pies, and Mum dug out an old box of Christmas crackers in the shop, the kind made of crin-

kly paper and you pull them open and get a prize and a
paper hat.'

She sounded like a sniveling infant and she didn't
care—though she did have the sense to stop short before confessing she'd daydreamed he might give her a
ring for Christmas. "I even told Farmer Garland my
mum was ailing so he'd give me extra time off," she
persisted, feeling more and more aggrieved, pulling her
knees up to her chin and holding them tightly.

"Oh, now, Bliss honey," Paul said, "you shouldn't
have done that. You shouldn't lie to get out of your duty
when there's a war on."

She couldn't believe he was criticizing her behavior on
top of letting her down so badly.

She glared at him. "That's a bloody self-righteous
thing to say."

"'I could not love thee, dear, so much, lov'd I not
honor more,'" he quoted, and she softened immediately. Was he finally, *finally* saying he loved her? For
that she'd forgive him anything, even the loss of the
Christmas she'd so carefully planned.

She turned toward him eagerly, then froze. He'd
paled terribly under his tan. The area around his eyes
had darkened.

"What's wrong?" she demanded.

He shook his head, looking stunned. "I shouldn't
have said that. That's one of my wife's favorite quotes.
I shouldn't have used that here, in bed, with you. I was
determined all along to keep my American life and my
English life separate."

The earth spun erratically on its axis. The room tilted,
righted itself, tilted again. For a couple of minutes, Bliss
was sure she was going to be sick. Her father's voice

thundered in her ears, "The woman taken in adultery."

But it wasn't her adultery. It wasn't. It wasn't.

"Goddammit," Paul said. "I should have known that would slip out sometime."

She stared at him. "Why didn't you tell me?" Her voice was a choked whisper. "You don't even wear a wedding ring."

He glanced down at his left hand, his mouth twisting. "That wasn't intended to deceive, honey. When you work around aircraft, a ring's a hazard. I knew a guy who lost his finger..." His voice trailed away.

The sky was falling and she couldn't bear it. "I trusted you, Paul. How could you betray me like this?" Weeping, she flung herself facedown on the mattress.

"Bliss, darling Bliss." He stroked her bare back. "I'm not betraying you, honey. If anything, I've betrayed Jane and Libby. And I wouldn't even say *that's* so, considering Jane and I have a sort of agreement."

She stopped crying. Cold-eyed, she pulled herself to her knees and looked at him. His expression was filled with shame.

"Jane and Libby?" she echoed.

He nodded. "My wife and daughter."

"You have a daughter."

"She's only a year old. I haven't seen much of her. I didn't get too many leaves at home before I came over here. Didn't really ask for them. Jane and I aren't all that fond of each other, to tell the truth. We get along, but that's about all."

Bliss took a deep breath, climbed off the bed and put on her dressing gown, suddenly self-conscious, for the first time, about her nakedness. It was difficult to quarrel seriously with someone when you were both in the nude, and this was definitely serious. Bliss might deride her father and his piousness to her friends, but she'd been exposed to his Bible lessons since birth and they'd left their mark.

Paul's thoughts must have been running along similar lines, for he, too, pulled on what he called a bathrobe. Taking her arm, he urged her to the settee and sat down beside her. "I married Jane almost two years ago," he said in a flat voice. "Hell, I was twenty-three years old, the Japanese had invaded Pearl Harbor, the end of the known world had come. I thought I could die anytime."

He laughed harshly. "I guess my father thought so, too. He went on and on about me getting married, having an heir. And there was his candidate ready to hand. Jane, his partner's daughter. Marriage to her would make everything hunky-dory. Jane was pretty and presentable, she knew how to behave and so on. She was forever playing golf, so I figured she'd pretty well leave me alone. Which she did."

"What kind of a marriage is that?" Bliss demanded. "You're not supposed to marry to leave each other alone."

His expression was earnest. "It's no kind of marriage—that's what I'm trying to tell you. That's why I *didn't* tell you. It doesn't matter. Jane doesn't care what I do."

"But..." Shaking her head, Bliss fell silent. He couldn't seem to understand that she never would have gone to bed with a married man, had recently begun to hope she could marry him herself.

"Jane and I never did as well together as you and me," he continued. "Jane isn't, well, she's not all that interested in sex. She did want to have a baby, though.

Her father was putting as much pressure on her as mine was on me. They've been pals for years and years."

He sighed deeply. "For a while there it looked fairly hopeless. She just wasn't getting pregnant."

"So that's how you knew about your sperm count," Bliss said, feeling more and more hopeless as he went on.

He nodded. "I never did tell my father it was my fault she wasn't having a baby. So we started watching her monthly schedule, aiming for the best days. Not much fun there, that's for sure. But just as we were ready to give up altogether, she got pregnant. The result was a girl. Libby. Dad was pretty annoyed at first, having ordered a grandson, but Libby burped at him a couple of times and he fell for her. She's quite a charmer. She's—"

"I don't want to hear about your baby," Bliss said through clenched jaws. "I think you'd better go."

"You don't mean that." He stood up and gazed down at her, looking so absolutely astonished and so handsome she wanted to fling her arms around him and tell him of course she didn't mean it. He had sixteen precious hours left on his pass, and they could spend it as they always spent it—together, talking, loving.

But her father's voice spoke in her ear again, and she hardened her heart and shouted at Paul, "I certainly do mean it. I want you to go now. And never come back. I don't ever want to see you again. It's over. Over. Over..."

"Have you seen my bucket?" a young voice asked.

Bliss opened her eyes to see a rosy-cheeked boy of about five standing at her knee, looking very worried. He was dressed in jeans and a puffy red anorak, his blond curls ruffled by the slight breeze that had come up.

"Bucket," she repeated, feeling dreadfully disoriented. Had she fallen asleep?

"My bucket and spade," he said firmly. "I left them here under this seat when I went to the lav."

"I haven't seen them," Bliss said.

His face crumpled as if he was about to cry, but then a voice hailed him, and he and Bliss both turned to see a very young woman, evidently his mother, standing by the next bench, holding a small spade and colorful plastic pail aloft.

The child ran to her, instantly happy again.

Bliss felt stiff. She'd been sitting far too long and the sun had gone behind a patch of cloud.

It was just as well the youngster had interrupted her. She had no business reliving the past. What possible good could it do? She was glad the little boy had come along before she could get to the really bad part—that awful Christmas without Paul, without even a card from him. The terrible New Year's when she'd thought for a while she wanted to die. Then the long lonely worrying time until the end of February when Paul had come back unexpectedly and she'd had to tell him she was pregnant.

CHAPTER FIFTEEN

THE RESTAURANT in the High Street, the same one pictured on the postcard Paul had given Libby, was called The Tea Pot. It met with Simon's complete approval. He liked the copper kettles and the antique teapots of various shapes and sizes that lined the shelves high on the paneled walls. He liked that the tables were sensibly square and roomy, the tablecloths white, starched and immaculate, and the chairs comfortable. There was no nonsense with candles or tiny lanterns; the lighting was overhead and bright enough to see what you were eating and who else was there. Best of all, the plants— and there were many—were all real.

To make him even more content, the very young black waitress brought them a basket filled with hot garlic bread the minute they sat down.

Obviously fearful of intimacy, Rebecca had decided they should meet in a restaurant, rather than at the cottage. Simon had chosen this particular restaurant because he was curious about it, because Paul might have visited it and because it was pretty—he hoped the atmosphere might soften Rebecca's attitude.

So far it wasn't working. She'd gone back to her original persona, businesslike, no-nonsense, wearing the plain white blouse and black skirt she'd worked in all day, her hair pinned back with an unyielding barrette. Behind the oval spectacles, her amber eyes looked withdrawn, remote. The message was clear: do not touch.

On the other side of the restaurant, a young couple in their early twenties were finishing their meal off with dessert, hers a chocolate mousse by the look of it, his some kind of custard. As Simon glanced their way, the young man held a spoonful of his dessert toward the young woman and she sucked it off the spoon without taking her gaze from his face, her hand touching his to help guide it. Then she returned the favor. The smile on her face was lazy, sensual.

Looking at them, Simon felt a yearning that was truly painful. At the same moment, he realized Rebecca was also watching the pair. Her expression quite possibly mirrored his.

Their eyes met. "Shall we order?" Rebecca said briskly, averting her gaze.

Simon sighed and picked up his menu. It was short but interesting. "What's the fish of the day?" he asked the waitress when she promptly came over.

"Got a nice bit o' sole, fresh off the boat," she told him with an attractive musical accent that brought the calabash trees and coral beaches of the Caribbean into the room.

"Sold," he said.

The waitress had a lovely smile. He was in need of smiles today.

Rebecca decided on something called cottage pie. They both ordered tea. What else could they do, considering the name of the place?

While they awaited their orders, they indulged in meaningless small talk, about the weather, which was sunny, the restaurant, which was crowded, the High Street, likewise.

The food arrived just as Simon decided he couldn't stand another second of this stilted exchange. For a minute he stared down at his plate in shock. He'd expected a filet, not a whole sole. The flatfish was so large it covered the entire plate. The accompanying vegetables had to be served on a separate dish.

His face must have been a study. Rebecca laughed, which did the usual wonderful things for her face and filled her amber eyes with light. Something strong and vital tugged at Simon's heart.

"That's better," he said.

A slight flush stained her high cheekbones. "I'm sorry, Simon. I know I'm being grotty. I'm still in shock."

He nodded agreement to that. He'd felt like an invalid since yesterday morning, someone bent and fragile who ought to be sitting in a chair with a blanket over his knees.

He looked back at his plate. There was nothing to do but dig into the fish and see what happened, he decided. Certainly it smelled great.

Tender and moist with just a slight tang of lemon and pepper, the first forkful made him feel convalescence was possible, after all. "This is the best thing I've ever eaten in my entire life," he told the waitress when she came to refill the teapot. "Is there any chance I can take the chef home with me?"

She grinned. "I'll have to ask him—he has a mind of his own, you know, being a man. But I must tell you, he's my husband and he's perfectly happy in Penmorton. He likes best to cook fish."

"Well, if he ever wants a change, tell him to bring you to Seattle, Washington. We have some pretty good fish there too, but people don't always cook it properly.

They tend to slather it in butter and wrap it in foil and overbake it on a barbecue until it's as dry as stale bread. He could teach the Pacific Northwest a thing or two."

"I'll be sure to tell him," she promised.

The friendly exchange made him feel even better, until he noticed Rebecca was looking at him quizzically. "What?" he asked.

A trace of pink edged her cheekbones again. "I'm not sure I... Well, it just occurred to me... I remembered you saying you had difficulty connecting with people, and I wonder why you thought that. You seem to get on well with everyone." She bit her lip. "With the possible exception of Gran. Mrs. Stubbins, Mr. MacDonald, the waitress just now, you seem very..."

"Easy?" Simon laughed shortly. "I have no problem with short-term relationships, Rebecca. It's the long-term stuff I can't handle. I never seem to get beyond one-night stands."

He grimaced as she flinched. "That didn't come out right. I was speaking figuratively."

"It's all right, Simon," she said softly. "I know what you meant. I think." The little frown he always watched for worried itself into place. "Perhaps you just haven't taken enough time in the past to let things develop." She closed her eyes momentarily, then opened them again. They looked misty. "Meaningful relationships don't happen in a matter of hours or days," she said slowly, sounding as if she might be trying to convince herself, as well as Simon. "It takes weeks, months, years even."

He nodded. "You're probably right. That's another thing I'm chronically short of, time."

Smiling sympathetically, but also looking as if she really wanted to cry, Rebecca began eating her savory meat-and-potato mixture in her usual dainty way, fork in her left hand, knife in her right. Simon was quite sure he'd never be able to manage the method, but he certainly admired the gracefulness of it.

"Have you decided yet when you're going back to Seattle?" she asked between bites.

Did that mean she'd just as soon he left now? What was the point of his working at raising his spirits if she was going to knock him back down with a thud? "I'll go back when I get Grandfather Paul's mystery completely solved," he said firmly, then resumed eating his wonderful fish.

"That may not be possible," Rebecca said.

"Then you'll have a lodger for a long time to come."

"Simon!"

"I mean it. This thing isn't just a mystery any longer, it's an obsession. I'm not going home until I've cleared it all up."

She set her knife and fork down at a precise angle across her plate as though she'd lost her appetite. Simon hadn't started out with much appetite himself, but he wasn't going to waste one bite of this amazing sole.

"You don't have business to attend to?" she asked.

"Probably, but my partners can take care of anything that can't wait."

He was astonished to hear himself say such a thing. A month ago he could not have imagined staying away from Seattle this long—away from his office, his meetings, his computer with all its charts and tables, his E-mail and fax machine, his pager and his cellular phone.

He wasn't sure if it was crossing the Atlantic that had presented him with a whole new perspective on life, or if he'd have experienced the same result had he merely taken a vacation in California or Las Vegas. Maybe it was just the Cornish air.

"It'll probably sound stupid to you, but I have this strong feeling that I have to make sense of my grandfather's life before I can do anything about my own," he said slowly. He wasn't at all accustomed to talking about his feelings, but Rebecca seemed to bring things out of him.

"My life hasn't been that great lately," he went on. "I got into some kind of rut where the only thing I did was work. Grandfather Paul was like that. My father's like that, too, if you can accept that golfing for a living is work, which it really is. Neither of them have ever found time for more than a token home life. They'd show up for meals, use the bedroom for a night or two, then rush back to their treadmills."

He hesitated, looking down at his plate. "I found myself doing the same. If I went out at all, it was just to a bar. Not that I ever drank more than a couple of beers, but I'd tell myself I was relaxing, even while I was thinking about the latest problem at work."

Her gaze was fixed on his face. This was a woman who listened without interrupting. What a rare gift that was, in female or male. When he was around her, words tumbled out of him so readily he felt like a walking thesaurus.

He shook his head abruptly. "I'm sorry. I seem to be in a cathartic mode." He tried a smile, but it didn't quite come off. "It's a good thing there isn't a couch handy."

The expression he'd come to associate with her more than any other was showing now—it held compassion, caring, concern. For him. Very gently she placed her hand over his where it lay clenched on the tablecloth. Electricity zapped an urgent message along his veins and arteries, but he forced himself to stay in place and not allow his hand to turn over and grip hers. She might reject him, and he couldn't stand the thought.

"I'm so afraid of turning into a loveless man like my grandfather," he blurted. "I have this recurring dream where I'm a cardboard cutout with a large hole in its center. I would say that's a pretty definite indication that I feel I'm missing something."

Even as he told her this, he realized he hadn't had the dream since coming to England, since meeting her.

Her eyes glistened with moisture. For one wonderful wild moment, he thought she was going to lean across the table and kiss him. Instead, after pressing his hand lightly one more time, she sat back, straightened her spine and nodded briskly. "I've remembered a relative of Gran's," she said, pushing her plate to one side. "Her cousin Josie. The daughter of her father's brother."

"You're willing to go on with it," he said, relieved.

She nodded again. "I'll do what I can, Simon. Now that I know how much it means to you..." Her voice trailed off, then came back stronger. "I vaguely remember meeting Josie when I was little. She had really bright red hair. She was a bit eccentric, but quite nice. A Mary Poppins sort of person, very cheery and bright, but inclined to do strange things. She liked to take star baths."

Simon raised his eyebrows.

"You lie out on the grass or the beach naked under the stars."

"Sounds like a great idea."

His flippancy was a mistake. The color on her cheekbones flared brighter. Okay, no more suggestive remarks. She was obviously genuinely disturbed by this cousin thing.

"Josie told me she and Gran used to be great friends when they were young. They often went to the cinema together. Gran absolutely loved going to the pictures."

Simon shook his head. "Judging by the way Mrs. Stubbins talked, she was a movie nut too. I probably go to the movies once, maybe twice in any given year. Of course I'm not much to go by, since I do very little that could fall under the heading of recreation."

Again Rebecca gave him that melting look of compassion. He sighed. "Talkies were pretty new when Gran was in her teens, remember," Rebecca pointed out. "Films were still a phenomenon. Color had just been introduced. The star system was going strong, and movie stars were people of mythic proportions. Now we're all so blasé. We've watched countless hours of television, witnessed formerly unimaginable special effects on screen. It's all old hat to us. But it was new and glorious then."

Rebecca fell silent and appeared to be sorting something out in her mind. The small wrinkle in her forehead appeared on cue. "I looked through a package of old photos I turned up in the attic while Gran was on her morning walk," she said at last. "I came across Josie's wedding photograph. That's what reminded me of her. She was very pretty, though a bit toothy. She married a soldier. Luckily both their names were on the back of the picture, so I have her married name, which I'd forgotten. Chickering. Everyone called her husband Chick, I remember, including Josie. He played the drums in a military band."

"Do you have any idea where Josie is now?" Simon asked.

"Not exactly." Rebecca looked more comfortable with this more neutral subject. "When I met Josie, she was just visiting Cornwall. She was going back to Edinburgh the next day. As I recall, her husband had been stationed in Scotland after the war—he was regular army—and when he retired they stayed there. I remember asking her why she didn't wear a kilt.''

"How far is Edinburgh, five, six hundred miles?"

"Something like that, but we don't have to go that far. I remembered something else. Some years ago a woman came to the shop and introduced herself as a friend of Josie's. She told Gran that Josie was back in Cornwall. It took me several minutes to remember if she'd mentioned the town, then I recalled thinking about pirates and wishing I could visit Josie on the chance I might see a couple.''

"Penzance?" Simon guessed. At her nod, he continued, "That's great, then. All we have to do is look up..."

She was shaking her head. "I've already tried telephone information. I was told her phone had been disconnected. I wasn't able to find out why.''

Simon sighed, partly from frustration, partly because he'd finished his fish and was sorry the experience was over. Pouring more tea for both of them, he considered the problem. "How old would Josie be?"

"She was older than Gran by a few years. She'd be eighty or so, I guess.''

"She could have died.''

"Yes.''

"Could you ask your grandmother casually if she knows what happened to Josie?''

Rebecca mulled over that idea for several minutes, and he was able to watch the process once more—the grave expression, the puckering of her normally smooth brow. There was a great sadness building in him, alongside the yearning generated earlier by the loving young couple. It was as if he'd given up hope of ever being close to Rebecca again. Was it really over? Why did it hurt so much? He'd always just drifted in and out of relationships before. What made this time so difficult? The fact that it wasn't his idea to end it, or the fact that it was tied in somehow with his grandfather's experience?

Rebecca looked negative. "Gran's already suspicious," she said. "She kept on at me yesterday and again today wanting to know what was wrong, what was worrying me." She looked at Simon directly, pain showing so clearly in her eyes that his jaw clenched in sympathy. This separation was all so unnecessary! If he'd had the sense to think through his stupid theory and realize the absurd consequences of it, he'd have kept his big mouth shut until he had a lot more information.

"Gran's already sure you have something to do with the problem," Rebecca went on. "If I mention Josie, I'm afraid she'll start putting two and two together and making a dozen. She's very shrewd, especially when she thinks people are hiding things from her. I remember when my last boyfriend and I had a parting of the ways...."

He didn't like thinking about her with another man, he realized. Which was odd, considering he'd never held to a double standard. Once people were grown-up they were bound to have had experience. He wouldn't expect a nineties' woman to sit around waiting for the one perfect man to come along and give her life meaning. He wasn't really feeling pangs of jealousy, he assured himself. It was just that he didn't want to picture her with someone else because he wanted her to be with him. *Always.*

Always? The word shocked him. That particular word had never before entered his mind in connection with a woman. It was an alien concept, a terrifying concept, and his mind scurried away from it like a frightened mouse.

He realized that Rebecca was still talking and gave her his full attention.

"I didn't want Gran to realize that the reason Todd had given up on me was that he felt he came a poor second to Gran." She sighed. "I needn't have bothered trying to hide it. Gran had wormed it all out of me within forty-eight hours. I'm not good at keeping secrets. I tend to blurt things out without thinking."

Her eyes seemed hollow with despair. She was biting her lower lip. He wanted to make all the hurt go away. He wanted to kiss her. He wanted to take her back to the cottage and make mad, passionate love to her. All night. All the next day.

Instead, he brought the conversation back to the subject. "Can you think of any other place Josie might have gone, any other connections? If she's still alive, that is."

Rebecca hesitated, worrying her lower lip again. She was going to drive him totally insane if she kept doing that. "It did occur to me she might be in hospital or a nursing home."

"In Penzance?"

Oh, he did love the way the skin between her brows puckered when she thought things over. "That would be a place to start, I suppose."

"Okay," he said briskly, looking around for the waitress. "I'll handle the telephone search tomorrow.

Clytie will let me use her office, I'm sure, so you won't have to worry about your grandmother overhearing."

She looked startled.

"Clytie and I are becoming good friends," he said.

"Like us," she said sadly.

HE BEGAN his reacquaintance with Cornwall's telephone operators the next morning at the Smugglers' Inn. As he'd expected, Clytie had no problem with his using the phone. "No need," she said, when he offered to pay. "I'll take it out of your 'ide." She smiled wickedly, both hands puffing up the sleeves of the dress that was her choice today. "And very nice 'ide it is too, love."

He went through three operators, telling each one he wanted the numbers of every hospital and nursing home or old people's home in Penzance. No, he didn't know the individual names. No, he had no idea what streets they might be on. Finally he found an operator with a honey-mellow voice who was prepared to be helpful. After a minute or two she rattled off several numbers. He thanked her and started methodically going through them one by one.

Just as lost objects are always in the last place you look, so was Josie a resident in the last place on his list, a convalescent home called Villa d'Este.

"*Jocelyn* Chickering, do you mean?" asked the precise British voice on the other end of the line.

"Well, we call her Josie," Simon said.

"*We* call her Mrs. Chickering." The woman had a pseudogenteel accent Simon found grating.

"Is she all right? I mean, is it okay for us to visit? My friend is her cousin, well, second or third or something removed, but definitely related."

"We *always* encourage visitors, Mr. Flynn, whether the person in question is a relation or not. The mental health of our patients is extremely important to us."

He felt duly chastised.

THEIR FRIDAY EXCURSIONS were becoming commonplace. Calling in her friend Doreen Oliver again, Rebecca informed Simon she'd be ready to leave at nine o'clock.

"You're always on at me to go out more," she reminded Gran as she brushed out her hair.

Gran had, as usual, expressed her disapproval. Her bright brown eyes examined her granddaughter's face in the dressing-table mirror. "I never suggested you should go out with a tourist," she said dryly. "Especially an *American* tourist."

Without moving her gaze even a little, she added, "Seems as though you've become inseparable, you and Mr. Flynn. Shall I start calling you Tweedledum and Tweedledee?"

"Simon and I are just friends, Gran," Rebecca said briskly, knowing it didn't sound true, even though it was now. Perhaps a little wishful thinking had entered into her voice and turned it slightly plaintive.

"Why Penzance, then?" Gran wanted to know.

Rebecca said the first thing that came into her head. "There are some rare bookstores on the Causeway-head."

Well, that wasn't a lie.

"Simon Flynn has an interest in rare books, does he?" Gran asked.

"Oh what a tangled web we weave when first we practice to deceive," Rebecca quoted silently.

Hastily, without answering—she would not, could not, tell an outright lie to her grandmother—Rebecca pulled her hair through a black ribbon rosette, settling it in at the nape of her neck. Kissing Gran's lined cheek, she headed for the door. *I will not feel guilty, I will not feel guilty,* she chanted in her mind as she went down the stairs and through the shop to the front door.

CHAPTER SIXTEEN

THE ROAD from Penmorton joined the A30 a few miles
outside town, and they were able to make good time to
Penzance. The harbor town was at the end of the area
known as the Cornish Riviera.

On the way, Rebecca told Simon that the famous pi-
rates of Penzance that Gilbert and Sullivan had written
about were not entirely fictional. At various times in its
history the town had been raided by pirates from the
Barbary Coast, partly destroyed by troops under Oliver
Cromwell's command, burned to the ground by the
Spaniards in 1595 and bombed by the Germans in
World War II.

"In spite of all that, it's survived very nicely," she
told him. "It's a major tourist center, famous for its
subtropical vegetation, and it's usually the first place in
England where flowers bloom in the spring."

They stopped briefly to admire St. Michael's Mount,
which was topped by a castle—partly medieval, partly
seventeenth century—that rose dramatically out of the
sea. "It can be reached by a causeway at low tide, but
the tide's in now, so the castle's inaccessible," Rebecca
said. "That's where Jack the giant-killer did his good
deed for the day."

She'd be talking about the weather again next, Rebecca thought. Was it obvious to Simon that she was
straining for something neutral to talk about? She

glanced at his face. He was looking straight ahead, concentrating on his driving, his mouth and hands tight, his eyes sad. Yes, it was obvious.

The Villa d'Este was in the center of town behind a street that featured several antique stores. Rebecca had always wanted to browse through them but had never had the time.

The approach to the convalescent home was through a narrow cobbled alley. Several elderly ladies were seated in the large window that overlooked the alley. They waved vigorously as the Peugeot carefully nosed its way in. Rebecca waved back. Probably, Rebecca thought sympathetically, her and Simon's arrival was the most exciting event of the day.

Josie Chickering became flustered the minute they entered her room. "I didn't expect you until half past the hour," she cried, pulling with one hand at the old-fashioned steel curlers in her amazingly red hair. Her other hand clutched the elaborate handle of a stout, wooden walking stick. "I don't even have my teeth in or my clothes on," she added unnecessarily.

She was wearing a sagging chenille dressing gown. "Don't get your knickers in a twist," her bedridden roommate advised in a raspy voice. "How often do you get a couple of beautiful young people come to see you? Just be glad they bothered." She glared at Simon. "Not one of my sons comes to see me. Not one. Been here two months, I have. After all I did for them. Grandchildren, you say? They don't care, either, rotten lot."

"Oh, shut up, Mabel," Josie said.

"We'll wait in the lounge," Rebecca said hastily.

"Sorry we butted in," Simon said. "Lady at the front desk told us to come on up. We should have called first."

"You're a Yank," Josie said with a wide grin, evidently forgetting the absent false teeth. "Lovely, lovely. I've always been partial to Yanks. Almost ran off with one during the war. Very handsome, he was. Ernie somebody. Part Seminole Indian, he told me. Wonderful cheekbones. But I didn't quite have the courage. It all worked out, though. My husband Chick and I turned into a regular Darby and Joan. That's inseparable companions, usually elderly," she added for Simon's benefit.

She made a shooing motion toward them. "Here I am being a chatterbox. Away with you. I shan't be a tick, I promise."

"Definitely worth waiting for," Simon said gallantly as he shook Josie's hand twenty minutes later.

The flaming red hair was obviously bottle-fed, Rebecca thought as Josie twinkled up at Simon, but all the same, Josie looked quite pretty with her curls fluffed out and her teeth in and makeup on. Shorter than Bliss and almost as thin, she wore dark trousers and a blue blouse with a cascade of ruffles down the front. In her room she'd looked every year of her age, but now she could pass for sixty. She had difficulty walking, though, and leaned heavily on the walking stick.

Sitting down with a grunt next to Rebecca, Josie set the stick alongside, took hold of Rebecca's hands and squeezed them tightly. She smelled of talcum powder. Her hands were soft. "Little Rebecca," she said. "How nicely you've grown up. I always knew you'd be a smashing-looking woman and here you are. You cannot imagine how happy I am to see you, pet."

Her eyes, the blue-green of a tropical sea, looked suspiciously shiny. Rebecca felt her own puddling up.

Putting both her arms around the older woman, she hugged her warmly.

Taking her glasses off, Rebecca cleaned them with a tissue from her handbag. "I didn't know where you were, Aunt Josie," she said. "You didn't come back after that last time, when I was ten or so, and I lost track of you. A few years ago, someone told me you were in Penzance, but I'd completely forgotten—until just recently, when I had a need to find you. I wish I'd sought you out before—I've wished for a long time I had more family."

"You had a *need* to see me?" Josie echoed. Her eyes filled again. "I was afraid of this. You've come to tell me Bliss is dead."

"No, no." Rebecca hugged her again to reassure her. "Gran's in good health. Well, you know, she has arthritis and a heart condition, but day to day, she's keeping quite well."

Josie let out a long sigh. "Well, that's a relief. It was the first thing I thought of when I got the message from her nibs that you were coming to see me."

"Her nibs?" Simon queried, pulling up a chair and sitting opposite.

Josie laughed. "George Bernard Shaw said the Americans and English were two peoples divided by a common language," she said. "Can't argue with that, can we?" Her smile was a lot more attractive now that it had some teeth in it. Rebecca remembered describing Josie to Simon as rather toothy. She'd made sure since she'd been in her teens that Bliss kept her annual dental appointment. Perhaps no one had reminded Josie. Josie hadn't had children, Rebecca remembered.

"Her nibs," Josie said to Simon, "is her ladyship, the Queen Bee, the stingy old grinch who runs this place."

"Does she answer the phone?"

"She does indeed. Did you have a go-round with her? She sounds like she has a mouthful of silver spoons."

"Right," Simon said, smiling.

Josie smiled back, then patted Rebecca's hand. "Now, my dear, tell your old auntie what this need of yours is."

"I'd like to know first why you and Gran don't have anything to do with each other anymore," Rebecca said, not wanting to plunge straight in, almost afraid of what she might learn.

"Well, pet, that's a very good question and one I used to ask Bliss years ago. I don't think she ever gave me a definite answer." She broke off as tea arrived in the hands of a very young woman with a beaming face who called Josie dear and love and asked after her health in the most patronizing voice Rebecca had ever heard. She hated it when young people treated old people as if they were mentally deficient.

Josie rolled her eyes as the girl left, showing her reaction was the same as Rebecca's. "I'll be Mum, shall I?" she said brightly, pouring the tea.

After serving them their cups and passing round a plate of digestive biscuits, she looked from Simon to Rebecca and back again. "I'm not sure how much I should say in front of your young man," she said to Rebecca.

"He's not my young man," Rebecca said quickly, and saw Simon's dark eyebrows slant upward in a frown.

"I'm only the lodger," he said to Josie, who looked understandably puzzled.

Simon gazed steadily at Rebecca and said, "I think we have to tell her just who I am."

After a moment Rebecca nodded.

Simon leaned toward Josie, looking very intense. Watching him made Rebecca's heart contract with yearning. "Does the name Paul Carmichael mean anything to you?" he asked. "I'm his grandson."

Josie's reaction was almost the same as Winifred Stubbins's. "You don't look anything like him."

Once again Simon explained his father's Irish genes.

Josie's eyes widened. "I never would've guessed you were a relation of Paul's, but now that I look at you more closely, I can see you favor him round the eyes. His were that same blue, like pieces of summer sky. But then, you'd know that."

Lifting her cup, she took several dainty sips, then set the cup back in its saucer, smoothed the ruffles on her blouse and sat back on the sofa. "Yes, I knew Paul. I was with Bliss when she met him."

She went on to tell them about the party in London she and Bliss had attended, how Paul had come over to talk to Bliss and ask her where she'd gotten her suntan. "You could see the sparks between them from the start," she said. "Bliss's eyes never left his face all that night, or after, come to that. Wherever they were, her face would turn toward him, like a flower searching for the sun. That first night they danced, they talked, they looked at each other. Oh, it was lovely to see them. Romantic. Bliss looked more beautiful that night than I'd ever seen her before or since. She had on a sort of gold dress, and Paul was in uniform. They made a lovely couple."

"They fell in love?" Rebecca asked, her voice soft.

"Oh, my, yes. There was never any doubt of that. Though according to Bliss, Paul never talked about love. But he was absolutely besotted, make no mistake.

I saw them together several times after that first meeting. Paul was getting some treatment for an injured shoulder in hospital at Plymouth. Something to do with a machine gun coming off its mount and hitting him. He was in Plymouth for a month at least, getting a ride into Penmorton every day. Then he had to go back to his base somewhere south of Norwich, but he still came down to Penmorton every chance he had. Bliss would get off from her land-army job. The farmer she worked for fancied her, she said. He'd let her do anything she wanted."

Josie drank some more tea, her gaze unfocused. It seemed to Rebecca that the old woman had forgotten they were there, she was so caught up in her memories. "They couldn't stand not to be together," she said. "I'll never forget the way they looked at each other. They had that special glow lovers get, like they invented the whole idea of sex. Lovely they were, very passionate looks at each other the whole time, just like the pictures. Ingrid Bergman and Humphrey Bogart in *Casablanca*—that's who they put me in mind of. Not that they resembled those two, but they had that kind of intensity or whatever you want to call it."

"They were definitely lovers?" Simon asked. "You know that for a fact?"

"God bless you, yes," Josie said with an arch look at him. "Couldn't get enough of each other. Not that it was only sex. They cared for each other, that was obvious. But sex was a big part of it. They had at it anywhere they could find. One time in my parents' house in Looe—they'd come over to spend a day, and Mum and I went to the cinema. They said they'd already seen the picture. But then when we got there, we were told the projector had broken down, so we went back home.''

She laughed heartily. "There they were, starkers, in front of the fireplace. November it was, I think. I can see them still. Right on the hearth rug. My mum was that shocked she almost had a stroke. She was going to tell Bliss's dad, but I talked her out of that, sharpish. Later Bliss told me they'd also made love in the old huer's house and the pillboxes on the promenade, and that cottage next to your house. Not to mention the public air-raid shelters down the bottom of Robin Hill.''

"Pillboxes?'' Rebecca queried.

"They were some sort of defense posts,'' Josie explained. "Gun emplacements was the official title. Though by the time Bliss and Paul were using them, there weren't any guns in them. Not very comfortable, Bliss said. Concrete. They'd lay out jumpers and jackets for softness.''

"So she confided in you quite a lot, then,'' Rebecca said, surprised to hear Bliss had ever been that open with anyone.

Josie nodded, her lined face crinkling into a naughty smile. "I'm sparing you the details, pet, but that doesn't mean I don't know 'em. We always told each other everything, Bliss and I. We were about as close as two girls can get. Until—''

She broke off abruptly.

"Until what?'' Simon said urgently, refusing to let her suddenly clam up the way Mrs. Stubbins had.

Josie frowned, then shrugged. "Well, I expect you know anyway, and it was all a long time ago, so where's the harm. I was going to say we were close until Bliss got pregnant.''

There was a complete and utter silence. Somewhere in the building a man laughed. An old man by the sound of it, Rebecca thought, for the laughter was feeble. Someone was hammering on the floor above them. Someone else was pushing a wheeled cart or wheel-chair that had need of some lubrication on one of its wheels.

"You didn't know," Josie said, looking stricken.

Rebecca took her hand and squeezed it. "It's all right, Aunt Josie. We'd guessed. Or at least Simon did."

"Paul told you?" Josie asked him.

He shook his head. "I knew nothing about Bliss until after Grandfather Paul died."

"Paul's dead," Josie said heavily.

Simon nodded.

"Well, I'm not one to speak ill of the dead, Mr. Flynn, but your grandfather was not at all kind to my friend Bliss when he found out she was pregnant. Went missing right away, he did. Same old story, isn't it, when you come right down to it. Boy meets girl, boy gets girl pregnant, boy vanishes."

She made a sound of disgust. "There he went, Paul Carmichael, rushing back to his base with his tail between his legs. Bliss's mum tried to ring him up to give him a piece of her mind and got told he wasn't there. But he'd said all along he wasn't leaving until the end of May or the beginning of June 1944, and this was only March."

She shook her head. "It was a terrible thing. Bliss's dad almost went bonkers when he found out. He was the rector, as I expect you know, but he was always one slice short of a cut loaf. Uncle John Edward was all for dashing up to the base and bashing Paul's head in for what he called 'soiling' his daughter. He didn't do it, of course. He was always more talk than action, that one. Next thing anybody knew, he wanted Bliss to say it was rape, so he could have Paul up on charges.''

She laughed shortly. "Nobody in Penmorton would have believed it was rape, not after seeing those two together, clutching each other as they walked, mooning over each other all the time. There was a lot of gossip in Penmorton, as you might expect. Rector's daughter was supposed to behave like Caesar's wife—above suspicion. As in rectitude. Nowadays, film stars and such brag about having their babies without marrying the father, but back then an illegitimate baby was considered a dreadful sin. People *knew* who the father was, of course, and that he hadn't wanted to marry Bliss. She was so humiliated, poor thing. I can only suppose that's why she married Foster—to stop the gossip.''

Rebecca swallowed hard. "Then it's true. Foster wasn't my grandfather.''

"Only by marriage,'' Josie confirmed. She looked a little embarrassed. "I'm not sure I should be telling you all this. I've an idea Bliss hasn't told you very much at all, has she?''

Rebecca shook her head. "Nothing,'' she said. "She's never wanted to talk about anything that happened during the war. She says she can't remember it.''

Josie's penciled eyebrows rose almost to her hairline. "Do you believe that?''

"I do if that's what Gran wants me to believe. But I do want to know the truth, Aunt Josie. It's important to me. I think in the long run it might be important to Gran that I know. Being secretive, she's closed off a part of herself from everyone, including me. And you. Evidently she's shut herself off from anyone who knew about Paul and her. I'm beginning to think she was afraid someone would talk, first to my dad, I suppose, then to me. I really think she'd be happier if she could get it all out in the open.''

Josie patted her hand again. "You're a good girl, you are, Rebecca." She poured herself another cup of tea and offered more to Simon and Rebecca, who both refused. "Well, the whole truth is Paul Carmichael got Bliss pregnant, and when he found out, he scarpered. End of story.''

Her eyes watered. "Bliss...poor, dear Bliss never did recover from it all. She'd loved Paul so much. After he went away it was like the light, the glow that had been inside her just switched off. She was never the same. Bitter, terribly bitter. And she directed it against herself, rather than Paul. 'I was such a fool,' she'd say over and over. I used to come into Penmorton when I was down from Scotland to see my mum and dad, but after a while I stopped because I obviously reminded Bliss of what she'd had and lost. She as good as told me she'd rather not see me.''

Josie looked accusingly at Simon. "Paul never wrote her, not once. He just went away and left Bliss to cope with the scandal and the baby.''

"Paul was never happy again, either, according to my mother," Simon said. "Just before he died..." Simon hesitated, seemed about to say something, then changed his mind. "He kept a photograph of Bliss and a postcard of Penmorton until he died. He gave them to my mother shortly before his death. We hadn't known anything about Bliss until then. My mother was... intensely curious. She wasn't able to come to England, so she asked me to come in her place.''

"Did Gran know Paul was married?" Rebecca asked.

"Not at first," Josie said. "I'm not sure when he told her, but I think it was when she said she was pregnant. See, I wasn't round her much at that time..."

She laughed a little self-consciously, then waved a hand dismissively in front of her and said, "Well, the truth is I was having a bit of an affair myself. A naval officer who... Well, that's neither here nor there. It was wartime, remember. England was a very dangerous place to be. About the time Paul was here the tide had begun turning in Europe, but there was still a chance we could any of us get killed at any minute. Bombs, land mines. Right after D day Hitler started sending over those flying bombs. A hundred a day in the first fortnight. Sixteen hundred people killed in that same period, loads injured. It was like the blitz all over again."

She hesitated, looking momentarily confused. "Damned if I can remember what my point was," she said with a rueful laugh. "Nothing unusual about that. I'm getting so absentminded I'd forget my head if it was loose."

"You were telling us about your naval officer," Simon said, and she flashed him a grateful glance.

"Well, there he was and here I was and his wife was somewhere else, and I'd just found out my husband was visiting some tart when I thought he was off on a secret mission. Well, you know how redheads are. Had to get my own back, didn't I?"

She gave Simon a saucy grin. "It was right after my naval officer left town I met my Seminole friend. So you might say I was keeping fairly busy."

She shrugged and stroked her ruffles again, looking quite pleased with herself. "A lot of people had love affairs during the war. We were mostly separated from our spouses through no fault of our own and frightened to death, so we took what comfort we could."

She was silent for a while, apparently lost in thought, then she shook her head and frowned. "I didn't blame Paul for the affair itself, just for going off and not doing anything for Bliss. He had money, she'd told me, but he certainly didn't offer her any that I ever heard of. Not that money was a problem in the Turner family, either, but it was the principle of the thing. He could've at least made Bliss independent of John Edward."

"Were you there when Gran married Foster?" Rebecca asked.

Josie shook her head. "I was in Scotland. Could've knocked me down with a feather when I heard about it. I suppose she'd have married anyone who asked her at that point. Can't really blame her." She sighed deeply. "I never saw a photo of the wedding. I don't even know for sure when it took place. It was well over by the time I heard about it."

She pushed herself awkwardly to her feet. "Speaking of photos," she said vaguely. Grasping her cane, she leaned on it for a minute as though getting her balance. "Broke my hip getting out of the bathtub," she said. "That's what I'm doing in this dump. Soon as I can walk properly, I'll be out of here, back to my horrid little flat with my very peculiar home-help lady. They're both going to look better to me after this. I'll be more careful from now on, believe me. I lay alone in that tub for hours before my neighbor found me—lucky for me she's the nosy sort. Didn't see me go to the shops at the usual time and came snooping round."

She gave Rebecca a narrow-eyed look. "I hope you're taking your calcium supplements." Her face cleared. "Well, of course you are, you with your health shop."

Rebecca nodded and smiled, and Josie left the room with a promise to return in a few minutes.

Rebecca and Simon sat in silence for a while, then Rebecca sighed. "So it seems Paul Carmichael really was my grandfather, too."

"It looks that way," Simon agreed. "I don't see why that has to make a difference to us, though."

"But it does," she said, looking at him directly, her eyes sad.

If Simon had been going to argue, Josie's return with a photograph album prevented it. "I had my nosy neighbor bring this in when I heard you were coming," she said to Rebecca. "I had an idea it wouldn't be just a social visit."

She put on a pair of glasses, opened the album and patted the sofa beside her for Simon to join her and Rebecca.

One picture showed Bliss and Paul sitting on the bench in the courtyard behind the house and shop. Another showed Bliss and Paul, in their respective uniforms, walking on the promenade.

"That was taken by one of those candid photographers who used to stand around on the seafront and take pictures first and ask if you wanted them after," Josie commented.

In the next shot, Bliss was wearing a full-skirted dress and high heels, and Paul was in a suit and shirt and tie. Both were laughing, looking into each other's eyes.

Simon studied the picture of his grandfather laughing for a long time. Bliss looked beautiful, Rebecca thought.

Next came Bliss and Paul in front of the Cock and Fox pub, then one on the cliffs, another in front of the huer's house, still another outside the shop. They were wearing civilian clothes. Casual clothes, though not as casual as the way people dress in the nineties. A sports coat and slacks for Paul, cardigan and a pleated skirt for Bliss. They were usually gazing at each other, not paying any attention to the camera, arms linked.

"Bliss threw this album into the dustbin after Paul slung his hook," Josie said as she turned another page. She looked brightly at Simon. "After Paul went missing," she explained. "I saw it sticking up above some other things when I went to get rid of some fish bones. I rescued it, thinking some day Bliss's baby would want to see pictures of his daddy. I never told Bliss. And then I moved round quite a bit and forgot about it. My husband and I had put some of our belongings in storage, taken some to Scotland, left some with my mum and dad. It wasn't until Chick died six years ago that I went through it all and sorted it out."

She paused for a minute, looking sad, probably thinking of her husband, Rebecca decided. Then she briskly turned another page. "I was moving into my flat and didn't have a lot of room. So then I had to look at everything I'd ever owned, and there was the album. I didn't think it would be right to throw it out, but Travis was dead and I'd lost touch with Bliss. It seemed as if it would be a bit uncomfortable to show up again after all that time had passed. So I did what I usually do when I don't know what to do—nothing." She sighed. "It's a shame when people drift apart, isn't it?"

She fell silent for a few moments, then sighed again. "Well, it's too late now to think of how I could've done things differently, isn't it? The truth is Bliss hurt my feelings badly. She made it very clear that I wasn't welcome in her life anymore, so I stayed away. I should've realized she was just striking out because she was hurt. We all do that. It's human nature.''

Another heavy sigh, then she went on turning pages until she reached the end of the photographs, about a third of the way through the album. Then she closed the album and put it in Rebecca's hands.

"There now, it's yours, pet, and you and your young man can decide how to split the pictures up, seeing as how Paul was granddad to both of you.''

Obviously realizing the implications of that, she gasped, then put her hand over her mouth as though to stop any more words from escaping. "Oh, my goodness, I see why you say he isn't your young man,'' she said to Rebecca. "If Paul was Travis's dad that makes you two cousins, doesn't it? First cousins.''

"We're not sure what the exact relationship would be,'' Simon said. "It's not as if we shared both grandparents.''

Josie looked doubtful, then glanced from Simon to Rebecca and shook her head dolefully. "I'm thinking this is not a relationship you're glad to know about. You have that look about you, too, you know. The look I mentioned in connection with Bliss and Paul. The glow. It's all round you, especially when you look at each other. When you first came into my room, I thought, Well, now, that's nice that Rebecca has found a young man to love, isn't it? But I was wrong, wasn't I?''

Rebecca swallowed against a severe constriction in her throat. "Yes, you were wrong,'' she murmured.

CHAPTER SEVENTEEN

THEY ATE LUNCH with Josie in the restaurant at the Villa d'Este. Painted in institutional green, with bare tabletops and metal chairs, it had all the ambience of a hospital cafeteria. Even Josie's cheeriness wasn't able to overcome the depressing atmosphere. As soon as they finished eating, Rebecca suggested they return to Penmorton.

The afternoon sun shone on sheep-dotted meadows, plowed fields, the ubiquitous stone walls with their covering of foliage. After half an hour or so, during which he was obviously doing a lot of thinking, Simon asked, "Do you remember when your father's birthday was?"

"Of course I do," Rebecca said. "It was September first. We always had a cake and a little party on birthdays when Mum and Dad were alive. Gran and I have kept up the custom, though it seems a bit sad when there's just the two of us."

"So that means Bliss conceived around the end of the previous year?"

"I suppose so. What are you getting at?"

"I'm not sure. I keep looking for a flaw somewhere. A wrong date or something. Anything."

"You're not going to find any flaw, Simon. I can't imagine Josie would lie about something this important."

"She might not lie, but she could be mistaken. She admitted she wasn't around much at that time. So all she had to go on was hearsay." He glanced at Rebecca sideways. "Do you know what year your father was born?"

"Well, of course I..." She frowned. "No, I'm not really sure. I always thought he was born about the end of the war in Europe, but that can't be right, because that would be May 1945. He was definitely born in September."

"What if that was September 1945? That would be around the end of the war with Japan. But September 1945 would be more than a year after Paul left England."

"Well, that can't be right then, either, can it?"

"It could be if Josie was confused."

"But she said there was a scandal, and Mr. Cornwood said there was a scandal."

"So maybe Bliss had an affair with Foster after Paul left," Simon suggested. "Maybe she was lonely, so she went out with him and then got pregnant and had to marry him. Josie could have confused the two relationships. It might have been Foster that John Edward was angry with. Winifred Stubbins said they argued all the time."

Rebecca looked at Simon. His face was grave. The five-o'clock shadow that always showed up at one o'clock was back. In her mind she could feel its roughness against her fingers. She also missed the hovering smile that had seemed so much a part of him. "I think you're grasping at straws, Simon."

"It should be easy enough to check. Surely you have a birth certificate for your father."

Rebecca had no memory of ever seeing one, but a thought occurred to her that might be helpful. "There's a photograph around somewhere of me as an infant in a very fancy christening gown, all lace and embroidery," she said. "I asked Mum about it once, and she said the gown was originally Gran's and that Dad was christened in it, too. If he was christened, then..."

"Would you like to bet your great-grandfather Turner officiated at your father's christening?"

"The records would be at his church," she concluded. "We could ask to see them. I'd rather do that than ask Gran."

"Did you know John Edward Turner?" Simon asked.

She nodded. "He used to give me money to memorize Bible verses. You'd be amazed how many I can quote even now. I don't know if I was a mercenary little thing or just terrified of my great-grandfather. He was sort of odd, full of himself, a real religious fanatic. I didn't see much of him. My father didn't like him, and I suspect it was mutual. Now I think I understand that more than I ever did. Dad was the child conceived in sin. John Edward wouldn't have been able to see past that."

She was silent for a moment, thinking of how that must have upset Gran. "I don't believe finding a record of my father's birth will change anything, Simon."

"It's worth a try," he insisted. "If that doesn't answer all questions, we can go back and talk to Mrs. Stubbins. Once she knows we've found out about the baby, she might be willing to tell us all she knows, don't you think?"

"Why is this so important to you, Simon?" Rebecca asked. "True, I'm not willing to, well, go along with what we were doing before, but that would have ended, anyway. Sooner or later you have to go back to America."

"It matters," Simon said. He looked as if he wanted to say more, but he stopped himself.

"All right," Rebecca said, feeling suddenly very tired, unable to go on arguing. "Gran's therapy session got put off until Monday at her therapist's request. Which means I don't have to rush home. We'll stop at the church on the way."

PINK ROSES GREW on a trellis around the front door of the small church. In a wide strip of soil at the side, impatiens, poppies, lupins, snapdragons and other flowers Simon couldn't name created a riot of color against the staid gray stone of the church wall.

The present rector was elderly and a little deaf. After greeting Rebecca, he accepted without question the story that Simon was interested in his family's genealogy and would like to examine the parish records for 1943 to 1945.

The rector very kindly allowed them to use his office, brought the three ledgers to them from the archives, propped the first one on a dictionary stand, then excused himself to show a small group of tourists around the church.

Starting at the beginning of 1943, they read each entry for the entire year, then moved on to the second ledger. The wedding of Foster Penberthy and Bliss Turner was recorded on Saturday, August 12, 1944 in the firm, heavy, but perfectly legible hand of John Edward Turner.

Simon's stomach tied itself in a knot. Rebecca let out a long, heartfelt sigh. Simon wanted to put his arm around her. Surely even a cousin could express affection, support. *Face it, Flynn,* he told himself, *your feelings for this woman are anything but cousinly. You can't be trusted to touch her without wanting to go further.*

Carefully they turned pages until they reached Friday, September 1944. Travis Penberthy. Born to Foster and Bliss Penberthy. All right and proper, names matching up.

They both stared at the entry for several minutes. Then Simon murmured, "Josie said it was March when Bliss told Paul she was pregnant, and he took off to his base and wouldn't answer phone calls."

"She got pregnant a couple of weeks before the Christmas holidays," Rebecca said.

"Looks that way."

They read to the end of that book, went through the 1945 book because it was there, then put all three books tidily on the rector's desk and left, stopping to thank the rector on the way out.

In the car Rebecca said, "No wonder Gran didn't have any photographs of her wedding. It took place less than three weeks before my dad was born." She paused. "I can't understand why she married Foster if he was already a drinker."

"Possibly she thought she'd be better off with any husband than no husband, considering the times," Simon suggested. "Maybe it seemed like the best way to avoid problems for Travis."

She nodded without looking convinced. "I also wonder why Foster married *her.* I suppose we'll never know that, either."

"That's a question I'd like to have answered," Simon said. "Foster's role in all this is definitely murky."

"You want Foster to be the villain, don't you?"

His gaze met hers. "Don't you?"

Behind her amber eyes, a brief struggle took place. Finally she managed a wistful smile. "I don't know. He was my granddad. Not much of one, but when I was a child, I thought family was supposed to be loved, so I loved him, even though he often smelled and talked funny."

Simon put an arm around her shoulders, inhaled the delicate lavender scent that was always with her. "I'm sorry, Rebecca. The truth is I was hoping we'd find out Josie's memory was mistaken. Not just for Paul's sake, but because I don't want to be your cousin. I even had the thought that we might find out the original baby had died and Travis was Foster's son, after all. But the dates tend to point pretty strongly to Paul."

He kissed her lightly on the cheek and felt her stiffen. He was making her uncomfortable. Very casually he removed his arm. "No wonder Paul was so miserable the rest of his life. He must have been eaten up with guilt. Deservedly so. If he really did love Bliss, how could he run away and leave her like that?"

Rebecca turned her head to look at him. Her eyes behind the lenses were soft as molten gold. She was always compassionate, this woman. "I'm sorry, too, Simon. I don't have any answers. I just wish..." The telltale pink stained her cheekbones.

"I can't tell Bliss that Paul loved her all along," Simon said harshly. "It would be a mockery, considering the way Paul acted."

He sighed. "My poor mother is a dedicated romantic. She'll find it hard to accept that her father was such a rat. I'm not sure I can accept it myself. The Paul I knew wasn't the type you warm to, but he had a code he lived by in business. He was always very honorable. His word was as good as his bond, that kind of thing. In fact, he was so honest he..."

He frowned and thought about that for a couple of minutes. "You know," he said slowly, "we only have Josie's word that Paul took off without doing anything for Bliss and the baby. I just can't believe he would do that. Maybe it wasn't his idea to leave. Maybe when Bliss found out he was married, she wouldn't have anything further to do with him."

"The church records—" Rebecca began.

"The church records show that Bliss married Foster in August and gave birth to Travis in September. Period. Josie admitted herself she wasn't around at the time. Maybe Bliss *wanted* Paul to leave."

Rebecca shook her head. "The only person who knows what really happened is Gran, and now that I know the story I'm even less inclined to bring it up with her. She had to live through that whole terrible episode. She obviously married a man she didn't love after losing the man she did love. And after all that, after the child of that love had grown up and become a wonderful man, a devoted son she absolutely adored, he was taken from her, too. How can I possibly stir up those dreadful memories?"

"Winifred Stubbins knew more than she was willing to tell," Simon said pointedly.

Rebecca smiled tiredly. "If we talk to Mrs. Stubbins again and she confirms Josie's story, will you give it up and go back to America and get on with your life?"

"You're anxious to get rid of me?"

"I think it would be best under the circumstances if you were to leave, yes." Her voice was low and she wouldn't look at him.

"I'll see what Winifred has to say before I make any promises," Simon said as he started the car. "When can you get away again?"

Rebecca sighed. "On Sunday, I suppose. I could be ready about half-past ten. I usually drive Gran to the seafront after breakfast on Sunday mornings. She likes to walk along the promenade. We could go to Tintagel after that." She glanced at him, then looked away. "No sight-seeing this time, though."

Simon didn't answer. He couldn't answer through the sudden tightness in his throat. Her words had brought such a strong memory of that wonderful afternoon they'd taken shelter at the Queen Guinevere Hotel. Could he hope for another storm to force Rebecca back into his arms?

How could she talk so glibly about him going back to America and getting on with his life? What kind of life was it going to be without her in it?

The thought shocked him so the car swerved a little as he pulled out into traffic, but the shock wasn't as great as it might have been a month ago, or even yesterday. Slowly, gradually, his mind had come to accept words like always and forever in connection with Rebecca. The truth was, much as he wanted to find out exactly what had happened between Bliss and Paul, much as he knew it was time for him to report back to business, the bottom line of the quest had changed.

He didn't want to leave Rebecca Penberthy, and he wasn't going to until he'd proved without a doubt that they were indeed cousins.

HE SET HIS WRISTWATCH alarm for 7:00 a.m. so he could enjoy a leisurely breakfast, something he'd never seemed to have time for but had come to appreciate since arriving in Cornwall. As usual he was ready to go too soon, showered, shampooed and shaved, dressed in a black T-shirt and jeans, his few dishes washed, bed neatly made. Jogging to the corner, he bought a *Western Morning News* at the newsagent's and jogged back again, digging out a black sweatshirt to wear, having discovered it was quite chilly outside.

At 9:45 he was skimming through an article about the renaissance of Glasgow when someone pounded the door knocker. He looked up to see Rebecca standing outside the French doors.

He flung them open, surprised that she had knocked so demandingly. She was dressed for the trip in her jeans and a heavy Aran sweater of creamy wool. Her long, black hair was neatly tied back. She hadn't worn it loose since Simon had so stupidly passed on his theory about Paul and Bliss.

"You're early," he started to say, but then he noticed that her face was flushed, as though she'd been running. Behind her glasses, her amber eyes looked stunned. "What's wrong?" he asked.

"She's here," she said in an agitated voice, one hand gesturing vaguely. "She just arrived. Without any warning. Just like that."

Puzzled, Simon took hold of Rebecca's arm, eased her into the cottage and closed the doors.

"Mrs. Stubbins. Winifred Stubbins," she said in answer to his raised eyebrows. "Evidently one of her grandsons had to go to Plymouth on an errand, so she had him bring her here in his lorry. They were waiting for Gran and me when we came back from our walk. The boy just left. Winifred's going to spend the morning with Gran. Whoever would have thought she'd make the journey, after all? What if she tells Gran we visited her in Tintagel? What if she tells her *why* we went?''

Simon would not have expected that his first response to the situation would be relief, but that was what he felt. The jig was up, the cat out of the bag, the truth would have to be told.

"It's probably for the best, Rebecca," he said calmly. "Sooner or later we were going to have to talk to Bliss about Paul."

"No, we weren't," she said. "If anything is to be said to Gran, I'm the one who should say it, and as carefully and tactfully as possible and only under favorable conditions."

"Did Mrs. Stubbins see you?" Simon asked.

Rebecca frowned. She pulled off her glasses and agitatedly began to clean them with a tissue. "Well, of course she saw me. I was with Gran when she arrived." She took a deep breath and put her glasses back on. "I couldn't believe my eyes when she climbed out of that lorry."

"Did Bliss hear her greet you? What exactly did Mrs. Stubbins say?"

"She winked at me," Rebecca said. "She asked if Bliss Penberthy still lived here." Her eyes widened. "Oh, that's right, she *didn't* greet me by name. She must have been pretending she didn't know who I was."

"What happened next?" Simon asked.

Her forehead puckered. "I was so shocked I'm not sure I even remember. Oh, yes, Gran came round from behind me and Mrs. Stubbins told her who she was—it was obvious Gran hadn't recognized her. Gran got real stiff at first, but Mrs. Stubbins flung her arms round her and hugged her really hard, and Gran sort of melted and patted her and said she was glad to see her. She looked it, too, though she got very tearful. Then Gran told Winifred who I was, and Winifred acted as if she was meeting me for the first time.''

Rebecca thought for a moment, then nodded as if to confirm the truth of what she'd said. "I must have been too shaken to realize she was behaving like a stranger.'' She frowned again. "So then she asked Gran if she could visit until noon. Gran said that was fine, and they sent the grandson off and went upstairs. I muttered something about getting milk from the shop for their tea, but I came over here, instead. What are we going to do?''

"There isn't anything we can do,'' Simon said reasonably. "I'm not sure we need to do anything, anyway. From what you say, it sounds as if Mrs. Stubbins isn't going to tell Bliss we went to see her.''

He put his hands on her shoulders and smiled down into her anxious face. "Don't worry, okay? If she does decide to tell all, we'll go to work on damage control.''

"So you don't think she will talk?''

"Judging by the way she greeted you, I'd say not.''

She gave a sigh that was obviously generated by relief. Then she looked up at him from under her eyelashes in a way that was unintentionally sexual and made his fingers tighten their hold as heat pulsed through him.

"Will you come upstairs with me?'' she asked. "I can't handle this alone. I'm so nervous I'm liable to blurt out the full story myself and that wouldn't do anyone any good.''

"If you want me to come, I'll come, of course,'' he said soothingly.

She looked a little less frantic, but still vulnerable—and infinitely appealing. What he really wanted to do was to put his arms around her and hold her very close and kiss away that little worry wrinkle. And then he wanted to ease her across the room and into his bed.

But he was committed to act in a cousinly way. With great care he removed his hands.

IT WAS HIS FIRST VISIT to the private quarters of the Penberthy house. He liked the living room on sight. A large, sunny room, it had a slightly worn, lived-in look, with three squashy soft armchairs and two flower-covered love seats bracketing the fireplace. Filled bookshelves also flanked the fireplace, hardcovers mixed with paperbacks in random fashion, the kind of arrangement that meant the books were there to read, not to decorate.

There were several casement windows. An old Persian carpet, its jewel colors muted with age, covered the wood floor, and some excellent watercolors hung on the one windowless wall. The overall impression was of comfort and cleanliness and warmth.

"I ran into Simon, so I brought him up to meet your friend, Gran," Rebecca said, striving for a light tone that didn't quite come off, in Simon's opinion. She'd remembered to pick up a small bottle of milk from the shop and held it up ostentatiously.

Bliss, sitting very straight on one of the sofas, gave Simon her usual dragon-lady look. Her bright brown eyes flashed a question at Rebecca's face, but Rebecca pretended not to notice. Simon could read the question very clearly—*Why on earth would you bring this outsider into this private reunion?*

Winifred, dressed as before in a roomy smock, dark green this time, her frizzy gray-and-white curls just as unruly, greeted him as if he was a complete stranger.

Actually she overdid the surprise at hearing he was an American, and Rebecca began to look distinctly uncomfortable, as though she was having a crisis of conscience over the deceitful situation.

"How long are you here for, Mr. Flynn?" Winifred asked in an arch voice that shouldn't have fooled anyone.

Bliss looked at him questioningly, her head with its neatly pinned up gray hair held stiffly to one side. "Yes, Mr. Flynn," she asked. "How long *are* you planning to stay?"

"Not much longer," he said ambiguously, which appeared to cheer Bliss up tremendously.

Luckily Winifred decided the social amenities had been taken care of and started talking to Bliss about their school days. Soon they were chatting very amicably about field hockey and something called rounders, which he gathered was some basic form of baseball.

As was usual in this country, on any occasion, or even without one, tea was served. Rebecca did the honors, while the older women chatted on. She also provided a toasted tea cake, which was an oversize currant bun cut in wedges. Winifred ate most of the cake fairly quickly and Rebecca went off to toast another one.

Preceding every other sentence with "Do you remember?" Winifred and Bliss worked steadily through their school years, touching on Mr. Medlicott briefly and jokingly. They talked about the day war was declared, but left the rest of the war alone, except for getting quite lively on the subject of Winston Churchill, whom Winifred had thought was wonderful and Bliss hadn't.

The friendly argument brought some color to Bliss's elegantly gaunt cheeks, so that she looked better than

Simon had seen her so far. She seemed sad when Winifred's grandson showed up early and Winifred prepared to leave.

"So, are we friends again?" Winifred asked straight out, enveloping Bliss in another hug.

"I'd like that, Fairy," Bliss said simply. She placed a thin hand against Winifred's plump cheek and patted it gently. "It's good of you to forgive me."

"Wasn't you needed forgiving," Winifred said stoutly. "If you ask me, it was that damn—" She broke off as Bliss's eyes widened in obvious alarm. "That damn war," she finished lamely. "Will you come and see me?" she asked.

Bliss smiled. She was looking tired, Simon thought, but all in all fairly pleased to have seen her old friend. "I expect Rebecca would drive me sometime. Where are you living now? I can't come to see you if I don't have your address."

Winifred looked worried, as well she might. Possibly playing for time, she took her time putting on the coat Rebecca was holding for her. Then she sighed, took her business card out of her handbag and handed it to Bliss.

Bliss studied it, her face closing. "That's a nice place, Tintagel," she said after a silence that seemed to rattle against the walls. "I'll look forward to seeing it again."

The two women parted affectionately. At least his quest had accomplished one good thing, Simon thought. It had brought two old friends together again. He escorted Winifred down the stairs, which took considerable time, with much heavy leaning on the banister.

"Did I give it away, letting Bliss know I live in Tintagel?" she asked as they went through the shop. "I didn't know what else I could do, seeing she asked."

"You had to tell her," Simon agreed. "I think she did put two and two together. I'm sure she remembered Rebecca and I went to Tintagel last Monday." He sighed. "Don't worry about it, Mrs. Stubbins. I've an idea we're going to have to level with Mrs. Penberthy pretty soon."

Mrs. Stubbins had stopped to rest against the shop counter.

"Rebecca and I had planned to come and see you today," he added. "We wanted to ask you some more questions."

She frowned. "Rebecca looked frightened when she saw me. Was she afraid I'd tell on you both?"

Simon nodded. "She worries about her grandmother's heart condition."

"I've found even damaged hearts can usually stand up to things better than one might expect," Winifred said. "What sort of questions?" she asked with a sharp look.

Simon heard a sound behind him and glanced over his shoulder to see Rebecca coming into the shop. When he was sure she was alone, he turned back. "We went to see Josie Chickering yesterday," he said. "Bliss's cousin. Did you know her?"

"Well, of course," Winifred said. "She and Bliss were thick as thieves at one time. But I haven't seen her for years, as long a time as it's been since I saw Bliss." She frowned. "She was older than us."

"She's eighty now," Rebecca said, joining them. "She broke her hip a while ago, so she's in a convalescent home, the Villa d'Este in Penzance. She says she'll be going back to her own flat as soon as her hip's better. She has home help."

"Poor thing, having to rely on someone hired," Winifred said. "She never did have children, then? I've been blessed with my lot. Wonderful they are. Their kids, too, ever so good all of them. Always popping in to check up on me. One or the other always wanting me to live with them, but I won't do that unless it's absolutely necessary. I like it quiet. And I want to work with the little doggies as long as I can."

She frowned at Simon. "You said you had more questions. I take it Josie told you more than I did."

He nodded and she sighed. "Very well, then, but I don't think it's a good idea to talk here."

"Gran's taking a nap, but I agree with you," Rebecca said. "Perhaps we could follow you home..."

"Well, I have to have my lunch now," Winifred said, patting her ample middle.

"We could meet you wherever you like," Simon said at once.

"I always did like The Tea Pot in the High Street," the old woman said with a wink. Then her face sobered. "Mind you, I don't want to queer things with Bliss now that we've buried the hatchet. So I'm not promising anything. Is that understood?"

"Understood," Simon said with a sigh.

CHAPTER EIGHTEEN

THE TEA POT WAS as packed for lunch as it had been for dinner, but at Simon's murmured request, the waitress led them to a corner table that was protected from the rest by a large ficus tree. Winifred was happy with the roomy and armless chairs.

"I sent Jason off to the Cock and Fox for his lunch," she told them as they helped her off with her coat and got her settled. "He was just as happy to be on his own. He's a nice boy, but restless if he's not the center of attention. A little spoiled, you might say. Too good-looking, that's his trouble."

She beamed at Rebecca. "I'm happy to have made up with Bliss. Should have done it years ago. It always seemed like too much effort to come all this way, but Jason's lorry wasn't too uncomfortable. I quite enjoyed the ride."

"Gran was pleased to see you, too," Rebecca said. She glanced at Simon apologetically. "I told her we were meeting Mrs. Stubbins for lunch. I just can't keep on deceiving her. She was feeling a bit tired, said she wanted to lie down awhile."

Rebecca considered for a moment if she should tell Simon and Winifred her suspicions, then decided she would. "I think myself she wasn't so much tired as that she suspects some subterfuge and wants to be alone to think about it. I have an idea she'll soon be asking us questions."

"Which means we need to be prepared," Simon said, then paused so they could give the waitress their order. This involved quite a serious and lengthy discussion where Winifred was concerned. She finally settled on a prawn-cocktail starter, followed by a double order of Irish stew with a basket of rolls, plus an apple dumpling for the sweet. Rebecca felt less and less hungry as the list went on. She didn't dare look at Simon as she ordered a small salad and he asked for the same.

When the waitress finally left, Winifred started munching the hot garlic bread while Simon filled her in on everything Josie had told them. Rebecca added a few words when it seemed necessary.

"That Josie always was a chatterbox," Winifred said when they and the basket of bread were finished.

Rebecca pushed her glasses up on her nose. "Did she tell us the truth?" she asked. "I don't mean to say I think she was lying, but she said she wasn't in Penmorton much at that time, so we wondered if she might be mistaken..."

Winifred was already shaking her mass of frizzy curls. "I'm sorry, love, Josie wasn't mistaken, not in any of it. It was exactly like that. Bliss came to see me right after Paul went away. I lived on Clara Avenue in Penmorton then, with my mum and dad. I can see Bliss now, sitting all huddled up in my mum's rocking chair, sobbing her heart out because she was pregnant and didn't know what to do."

Her plump face was set in unaccustomed lines of strain. She seemed to Rebecca to have almost forgotten where she was, so engrossed was she in remembering her friend.

"I asked her if she'd told Paul," she went on. "She cried so hard she couldn't even talk for the longest time, then she said yes, she'd told him, and he'd gone back to his base straightaway and wasn't ever going to return."

Her mouth tightened. "I said a few choice words, I don't mind telling you. Now, I didn't know he was already married. That never came up. I don't know if Bliss ever knew, either."

"According to Josie, Paul told her he was married when she said she was pregnant."

"Well, then, poor thing, I suppose she didn't want to tell me in case she looked stupid not to have asked him before that."

Simon sighed. "It sure looks as if you and Josie heard the same story. I guess we'll have to accept it."

"I always liked Josie," Winifred said, evidently not hearing the heaviness in Simon's voice. Rebecca had heard it—and felt a heaviness of her own that seemed to weigh down the back of her neck and shoulders so much it was hard to sit upright. She'd thought Simon's hopes of finding some error in the story were unfounded, but evidently some part of her had wanted to believe.

"Josie was always a positive sort of person," Winifred noted. "Lots of fun." Her eyebrows climbed. "She certainly did like men, though."

"So she told us," Rebecca said, trying to rise above the depression that was threatening to settle around her like a dark cloud. "But she said she and her husband had a happy marriage, after all."

Winifred's face smoothed out as she beamed again. "Well then, she was as fortunate as me. I take it she's a widow, too? Perhaps I'll get Jason to take me to see *her* one of these days."

The waitress arrived with a loaded tray, and they were all silent while she served them, except to tell her thank-you. Winifred polished off her prawn cocktail in nothing flat, then buttered a roll and tucked into her Irish stew about the time Rebecca and Simon started in on their salads.

After a couple of minutes, Winifred looked from one to the other of them and said, "All right, then, what gaps do you want me to fill in?"

"Any you can think of," Simon said.

"We especially wondered if you knew why Gran married Foster Penberthy," Rebecca said. "I realize she probably wanted to make the baby, my dad, legitimate, but if he was a drinker already, I can't understand why she chose *him.*"

For a while, Winifred steadily spooned up her Irish stew. Rebecca thought she was probably going to refuse to answer or else say she didn't know. But then, quite suddenly, the old woman put down her spoon and looked Rebecca in the eye. Her own gray eyes were moist.

"Here it is, then," she said. "The unvarnished truth. That marriage was all John Edward's idea. The rector. He was the one insisted she had to get married. He offered Foster a share in the business, the shop, if he'd marry her, and Foster took him up on it. John Edward didn't care that Foster was a ne'er do well and a heavy drinker, did he? He just wanted someone else's name for that baby. Anyone's except his. Bliss agreed, because she wanted to take the stigma of illegitimacy off the baby. Travis. And it worked. As time went on, people forgot Foster wasn't Travis's real dad. I don't think Travis ever knew he wasn't."

She sighed loudly. "I tried to talk Bliss out of it. My mum was willing to take her in. Baby, too. But Bliss was stubborn and independent, and after holding out for several months, she'd come round to thinking that having Foster's name would be better for the baby. Her dad wasn't one to take no for an answer, anyway. If she hadn't done what he told her, he'd have made her life miserable, which it probably was, anyway, living with Foster. Her mum told me it wasn't much of a ceremony. John Edward did it himself at six in the morning when no one else was up and about. He brought in two army mates who weren't local boys to be witnesses."

She made a face. "I suppose John Edward didn't want anyone to see Bliss getting married because she was about eight months gone by the time she agreed. Or else they thought Foster was most likely to be sober that time of the day. But that wasn't the end of Bliss's troubles by a long shot. Travis was a breech baby. She almost died before they got him turned around. Afterward the doctor said she couldn't have any more children."

She glanced at Rebecca. "She must have been heartbroken when your dad and mum were killed. By then I hadn't seen her for years, of course, but I read about it in the paper. I wrote her, but she never wrote back."

Rebecca nodded, afraid to speak in case the tears that always threatened when she thought of her parents spilled over.

Winifred reached across and patted her hand. "Foster was a dead loss as a husband, but at least he mostly stayed out of Bliss's way. And I just know, from being a grandma myself, she's very lucky to have you."

Rebecca nodded again as Winifred smiled mistily and went back to her stew. Both Rebecca and Simon had given up on their salads some time ago. There didn't seem much to say now, but they managed to make small talk until Winifred was finished with her meal and her grandson arrived in his lorry.

"I think I'm beginning to hate Paul Carmichael," Rebecca said fervently as Simon maneuvered the Peugeot through the midday traffic on the High Street.

"Well, he was never an easy man to love, but he had a lot of good points," Simon said. "He wasn't much older than Bliss, remember, two years maybe, which would make him twenty-five when they met. He was probably too scared of his own father to do anything as drastic as divorce Jane. The old man ruled with an iron hand, from all reports. My mom was terrified of him, and she's not a lady who scares easily."

Rebecca felt, rather than saw, him glance at her. She could understand everything he was saying in theory, but in practice she couldn't accept any excuses for Paul Carmichael.

"He ruined Gran's life," she said flatly.

Simon sighed. "Yes, I suppose he did."

They were driving up Robin Hill now. Rebecca could see the shop just ahead. She was going to have to go in there and face her grandmother and tell her she had learned her secret. And not by accident, but by seeking it out.

"Seems to me," Simon continued as he parked the car in the alley behind the cottage, "the best way to make up for unhappiness in the past is to try to be very happy in the present. Is the cousin thing really all-important?"

Worried, her stomach tied in knots at the thought of telling her grandmother everything, afraid that no matter how gently she broke it to her Bliss might get worked up and risk a heart attack, Rebecca wasn't able at the moment to consider anybody else's feelings.

"I suppose your idea of happiness in the present is having sex," she said harshly.

She regretted the words the minute they were out of her mouth, but it was too late. Simon's normally healthy-looking face blanched. He got out of the car without a word and strode rapidly away.

She was determined not to cry. Blinking hard, her hands clenched tightly together, she concentrated on breathing in and out. It was several minutes before she felt composed enough to go on into the house.

Bliss was nowhere to be seen. At first thankful that she wasn't upstairs, thinking she was probably down in the courtyard tending her garden, Rebecca splashed cold water on her face and eyes. But then when she came out of the bathroom and looked out her bedroom window, she saw that Bliss *wasn't* there among the herbs and flowers.

She ran down the stairs. The shop was empty. Could Bliss have gone over to the cottage to question Simon?

For the second time that day she banged the cottage knocker in a panic. Simon's surprise when he opened up told her Bliss wasn't there, but she asked, anyway.

"She's not in the house? Could she have gone for another walk?" he asked.

Rebecca clutched the doorjamb, feeling weak in the knees all of a sudden. Of course that must be the explanation. But still... "It doesn't feel right, her going off like this when we already took our morning stroll. And she didn't leave a note. She's usually very thoughtful that way. We both try to let each other know where we are at all times. She knows I worry about her."

He went over to the wardrobe and pulled out his jacket. A breeze had come up and it was a little chillier than before, though Rebecca felt warm enough in her heavy Aran jumper. "We could take my car and look for her," he suggested as he pulled on the jacket and fastened the zipper. "Where does she usually walk?"

"Just in this general area, not too far away usually. She doesn't like to go down Robin Hill because then she has to come up again, and that's too much work for her heart." She started backing out of the doorway. "I'll go. You needn't bother."

He looked hurt. "I'm as concerned as you are, Rebecca."

She sighed. "I'm sorry, Simon. I'm out of my mind with worry and it's affected my manners. Of course you can come with me, but I'll drive. I need to be doing something constructive."

Her little Ford was middle-aged, but well maintained. She spent almost an hour driving every possible street she thought Bliss might be walking, but without success. Wondering if they could have missed her, she pulled in behind the cottage on the next pass and raced back through the house and shop.

"Is there any special place she might have gone? Some place that has meaning for her?" Simon asked when she returned, looking so disconsolate he wanted to hold her.

She fastened her seat belt, biting her lower lip, the little frown puckering her forehead. "She's been known to take the bus to the churchyard," she said after a minute or two, suddenly looking hopeful. "She likes to take flowers to my mum and dad once in a while. And she did mention yesterday she had some marigolds in bloom.''

The churchyard was visible from the street. Being Sunday afternoon, there were several people there, arranging fresh flowers, tidying the graves. Bliss was nowhere in sight. Just to be sure, Rebecca checked inside the church, though she'd heard Bliss say many times she'd never again go inside the place where her father had preached so bombastically.

She shook her head when she returned to the car. She was beginning to get really worried now. Then she remembered the one other place Bliss might be. Starting the car, she glanced at Simon. ''Every now and then she catches the bus from the corner down to the seafront. She likes to walk on the promenade. She hasn't mentioned it for a while, but it's a possibility.''

They saw her from some distance away. She was sitting on a bench, her posture as perfect as always, looking out at the English Channel. At first relieved, Rebecca began worrying again almost at once. The breeze was stronger on the waterfront. It didn't seem to Rebecca that the cardigan Bliss had put on over her thin jumper and skirt was warm enough.

''I've been frightened to death,'' she said as she sat down next to the older woman. ''What on earth did you think you were doing going off like that without leaving a note?''

Bliss gave her a wan smile. Her eyes had a faraway look that disturbed Rebecca. ''I'm sorry, love. I didn't think. I just wanted to be by myself for a while.''

She glanced up at Simon, then away. ''It was a shock seeing Fairy,'' she murmured. ''I can't get over how much she looks like her aunt Toss. We used to make jokes about her aunt Toss—children can be so cruel. I wonder if Fairy remembers how cruel we were. I hope not. I hope nobody's cruel to her. She has such a kind heart, Fairy. Always did have.''

Rebecca looked worriedly up at Simon. Bliss seemed to be rambling. "Let's go home, Gran," Rebecca said, taking her hand.

Bliss shook her head. "I'd just as soon sit here for a bit, love. It's nice here. I've always liked it. The sea has great therapeutic powers. Someone I used to know said that. I've always remembered it." Her head to one side, she added very quietly, "I thought I'd forgotten, but I hadn't. Not ever." There was a break in her voice that moved Rebecca close to tears.

Sitting down on her other side, Simon took off his jacket and placed it around Bliss's shoulders. Rebecca wasn't sure how she'd take to that, but to her surprise, her grandmother didn't shrug it off or make a nasty comment about someone taking liberties. Instead, she put her hand to the collar and held it closed and glanced at Simon almost shyly.

"We need to talk, Bliss," Rebecca said.

"Not today," Bliss said gently, still with that far-away look in her eyes. "Fairy's visit was enough for one day. I've been thinking about things ever since she got here. There are so many things to think about once you open the door. Things come tumbling out higgledy-piggledy. I think my mind is tired."

"We should go home, then. Let you rest."

Bliss smiled at her in a vague way that worried Rebecca even more, but she sounded sensible enough when she spoke again. "I'm all right, love. I've got my tablets with me if I need them."

"How about a cup of tea somewhere?" Simon suggested. "I understand tea is good for everything."

He was trying to cheer Bliss up, bless him. He looked at Bliss, smiling that lovely smile Rebecca hadn't seen in a while.

Bliss shook her head, gazing beyond Simon at the channel. Rebecca was becoming seriously concerned. Bliss wasn't behaving like herself at all.

"A beer, then," Simon said, still game but apparently desperate. "How about I buy us all a beer at the Smugglers' Inn."

"I haven't drunk a beer in ages," Bliss said, looking surprisingly taken with the idea.

Simon jumped up and put his hand down to her. "Shall we, then?"

And to Rebecca's complete surprise, Bliss put her hand in his and let him help her to her feet.

THE PUB HAD quite a crowd. The middle-aged woman who'd played the piano when Simon first visited the pub was there again. A darts tournament was going on at the other side. Simon caught sight of Corny Cornwood waiting his turn, his cap bill tilted up a fraction, feathered darts clutched in his left hand, beer mug in his right. His beautiful dog was sitting on his haunches to one side of the line of men, his eyes alert.

Simon settled Rebecca and her grandmother in a corner on the same side as the piano, as far from the darts teams as they could get, then went up to the bar to order, afraid of what might trip off Clytie's tongue if she came to serve them.

He'd done well to worry. The first thing she said, after giving him her usual wide smile, was "What's this, then, my darlin'? You're courting the granny, as well as the daughter? Don't you think Mrs. Penberthy's a bit old for yer?"

"As long as I can't have you, it doesn't much matter," he told her with a phony leer.

"And what makes yer think yer can't 'ave me?" she said saucily, looking very pleased. She was wearing her African outfit again today and her hair was a strange shade of orange with streaks of hot pink.

"Mrs. Penberthy's not too well," Simon said after ordering a Guinness and two half-pints of mild and bitter. "We thought it might do her good to get out for a change."

He figured that if Clytie accepted this story, she'd be less likely to come out with something outrageous in Bliss's presence.

On an impulse, while Clytie was drawing the beer, he wandered over to the pianist. "How are you with World War II songs?" he asked.

"Go on," she said with a smirk. "You aren't old enough for that lot."

"My grandmother used to sing to me," he said, which was only half a lie. His Irish grandmother *had* sung to him, but only Irish songs. She wanted him to appreciate his heritage, she'd said.

The pianist's eyes misted sentimentally, and then she glanced meaningfully at the empty beer mug on the piano top. Simon got the message. When Clytie returned he gave her his credit card and told her to slake the pianist's thirst for as long as he was in the pub. He was rewarded for his generosity by "Roll out the Barrel," being pounded out as he joined Rebecca and her grandmother. The song wasn't quite what he'd had in mind.

Bliss had taken off his jacket and placed it carefully over the back of his chair. It was warm in the pub and also noisy. Not such a good idea to come, perhaps. Although Bliss was looking perceptibly brighter, as if she might even be enjoying the convivial atmosphere.

"Cheers!" Rebecca said, lifting her mug. They all clinked glasses, Bliss with a faint smile on her patrician features. Rebecca nodded at Simon as though to thank him for suggesting the pub. He nodded back and decided just to relax and enjoy being here with her.

The pianist started in on "Pistol Packin' Mama," which he supposed was the right vintage, though still not the sort of tune to create the atmosphere he'd hoped for.

"I'm hungry," Bliss announced.

Rebecca looked shocked. "You didn't have any lunch?"

She shook her head. "Fairy ate all the tea cake," she said dolefully.

Rebecca and Simon exchanged glances. Was Bliss actually making a joke? "That salad didn't do a whole lot for me," he admitted.

Rebecca laughed, which worked its usual magic on her face, filling her amber eyes with light. "Mrs. Stubbins ate so much at The Tea Pot we lost our appetites," she told her grandmother. "They do pretty good sandwiches here," she added.

"We've a nice bit of fresh crab," Clytie told Simon when he went to the bar. "I could do you some crab rolls."

That sounded good to him. Living in Seattle, he ate a lot of crab and all kinds of shellfish. After checking with Bliss and Rebecca, he returned to the bar to place the order. On the way back to the table, he stopped by the piano. The woman was rollicking through "I've Got a Gal in Kalamazoo."

"Could you try something a little more laid-back?" he asked her.

She looked at him blankly.

"Something quieter, more romantic?"

She saluted him with her mug. "Anything you want, governor."

The crab rolls were delicious. Bliss ate with seemingly good appetite. Rebecca wanted only half of hers, so Simon finished it for her. "The sea air," he said.

Bliss's lips were moving slightly as though she was mouthing the lyrics to the tune now being played. Simon listened. "I don't recognize that one," he said.

"'The White Cliffs of Dover,'" Bliss said. The faraway expression was back in her eyes.

"I'll Walk Alone" followed. That was more like it, Simon thought. Bliss was visibly melting, might actually be enjoying herself.

"Travis used to like that song," she said softly when it was done and the pianist took a short break to get her beer mug refilled. "He had a nice tenor voice, sang all the time. Do you remember?" she asked Rebecca.

Rebecca nodded and put her hand over Bliss's on the table. "I haven't forgotten anything about him, nor Mum, either."

"Sometimes it's best to forget," Bliss said.

Rebecca and Simon exchanged glances again.

The darts tournament, it seemed, was over. The players were starting to leave, calling cheerio and goodbye to Clytie. Simon couldn't remember what time the pubs closed, but he thought it was sometime in the afternoon, then they opened again in the evening. The three of them should probably leave soon.

Rebecca was still holding her grandmother's hand. Both women's eyes were moist. The expression on Rebecca's face was the one Simon was always moved by, the one that showed how very much she cared.

"I miss Travis," Bliss said.

Rebecca swallowed. "Me, too."

The pianist started playing again. This time the tune was instantly recognizable to Simon. It had been featured in the movie *Sleepless in Seattle*, which he'd watched on video not long before he left for England.

He was searching his mind for the title when he realized that Bliss was now humming along. He gave Rebecca a startled glance. She was staring at her grandmother's face in apparent amazement.

After a couple of minutes, Bliss began putting words to the music. Her voice was thin but quite charming, definitely on key, which was more than Simon could ever manage.

"I didn't realize that song belonged to World War II," he said when the pianist switched to something else.

Bliss still had a faraway look in her eyes. *"Casablanca,"* she said. "The film came out in 1942. Dooley Wilson sang, 'As Time Goes By,' in it. It was very popular."

She stopped speaking abruptly. "I think we should go home now," she said. "I'm very tired."

"Do you need your tablets?" Rebecca asked.

Bliss shook her head. "Just a nap. I'll be fine once I have a nap." She looked at Simon suddenly, more directly than she'd looked at him that day. "You remind me of somebody," she said abruptly.

He was taken aback and glanced at Rebecca for guidance. She shook her head. "Mrs. Stubbins said I reminded her of Clark Gable," he said. "But I don't think that's really so, do you?"

She seemed to have lost interest. She stood, picking up her handbag.

There weren't going to be any more revelations today evidently. Simon wasn't sure whether or not he wanted to hear any more tomorrow. He wanted things between him and Rebecca to get better, rather than worse, and that didn't seem to be the way they were going.

CHAPTER NINETEEN

HE BEGAN ITCHING soon after he went to bed. He was so sleepy that for a while he just scratched himself unconsciously, but gradually he realized it wasn't normal to feel quite this itchy. Even his toes felt itchy.

Still only half-awake, he sat up and switched on the bedside lamp. He could see nothing except some faint pink areas on his shoulders and feet where he'd scratched himself. He switched off the light and tried to compose himself for sleep again, but the itch only worsened.

After a few minutes he turned on the light and took another look. Now he could see a few faint welts on his shoulders and arms. There were even a couple under the hair on his chest. When he kicked the covers off, he could see a few more on his legs and feet.

Alarmed, he got out of bed and went over to the dresser, twisting his body in an attempt to see his back. There, too, he could see a couple of raised ridges. And on his buttocks.

He was getting itchier. He searched the medicine cabinet in the bathroom, but found only toothpaste, a box of Band-Aids, a bottle of aspirin. In the bathroom mirror he saw a weal forming on his face.

What the hell was this? He'd never had anything like it. Could it be poison oak or ivy? He didn't even know if they grew in England. Besides, he hadn't been in any woods lately. Nor had he been around an animal where he might have picked up fleas. Not that these things looked like fleabites, anyway.

His sweatshirt? Sometimes clothing caused irritation. But the sweatshirt he'd worn today was cotton, and it wasn't new. It had been laundered. He'd worn it on the plane coming to England and hadn't had a problem with it then. And a problem with a sweatshirt would hardly affect his toes and rear end.

The itching was becoming more and more intense. It was almost impossible not to scratch, but he sensed it would not be a good idea.

He could think of only one thing to do. Pulling on a pair of boxer shorts, he headed for the door and stumbled across the courtyard, stubbing his toes on the bricks, bumping into Bliss's tubs of herbs, cursing under his breath at people who didn't use floodlights in their yards.

He pounded on the back door of the house and hoped he'd awaken Rebecca and not Bliss. A moment later Rebecca's voice called out from above, and he looked up to see her head faintly silhouetted against the starry sky.

"I'm sick. Something's wrong with me," he called up, and noticed that his voice suddenly sounded hoarse.

Rebecca descended in no time and hustled him back across the courtyard to the cottage. With her sure hand on his elbow he didn't bump into anything this time.

"I've got lumps all over me," he told her as she propelled him through the doorway. "I'm itching like crazy."

"In the bathroom," she said calmly. She took a tissue from a box on the windowsill and polished her glasses thoroughly, then looked him over from head to toe, touching him lightly here and there. "Urticaria," she said. "Hives. You're having an allergic reaction, probably to the crab."

"The crab? There was something wrong with the crab? I've been poisoned?"

"If you'd been poisoned you'd be vomiting and having diarrhea. You haven't, have you?"

"Not yet." His voice was even hoarser now, and he put his hand to his throat. "I'm losing my voice. My throat's closing up."

"It's all right, Simon," Rebecca said soothingly. "I think you're going to live."

"You think?" He realized she was teasing him. "This is no time to make jokes," he said grumpily. "I can't stand this itching."

"Well, we can do something about that," Rebecca said. Bending over the tub, she pushed in the plug and turned on the faucets. "Don't scratch," she ordered, and left.

The itching immediately became even more urgent, but he managed to keep his hands off his body until she returned carrying a box of baking soda, which she proceeded to empty into the tub.

"Take off your shorts and get in," she told him as she swished the water around.

He didn't argue. If there was any chance of putting the fire out, he'd dive in headfirst.

The cool water did soothe him a little, though it also made him shiver. He splashed some on his face and head; there were even a couple of welts on his scalp.

Rebecca knelt next to the tub and began sloshing a washcloth full of water over the parts of him that weren't submerged. She was wearing a nightgown of fine white cotton, he noticed. It was modest, but also fairly revealing in the bright light of the bathroom.

"You must be feeling better," she said dryly. He realized she'd caught him looking at her breasts.

"One or two degrees," he said, leaning back in the tub and smiling at her. "I'm still itching, but it feels as if it's all under the surface now. What was wrong with the crab, do you suppose? How come you and Bliss didn't have a reaction?"

"There was probably nothing wrong with the crab," she said. "You can develop a food allergy at any time, even if it's a food you've eaten for years. You may find you're allergic to shellfish now, and lobster, as well as crab. It often happens that way."

"But I live in Seattle," he moaned. "The stuff grows on beaches. Shrimp, clams, oysters. I love all of them. Are you sure that's what's wrong with me?"

She smiled brightly. "Well, it's that or someone put a curse on you, in which case we'll need to find a bullock's heart and stick pins into it until the ill-wisher takes off the curse."

She stood up. "Sorry, but you'll have to approach such foods very carefully until you find out how extensive the allergy is."

"You're not leaving me?" he asked as she turned away.

She shook her head. "I'm going to get some lotion from the shop. And some antihistamine tablets. Stay put until I get back."

"But it's cold in here," he complained.

"Hot water would make you itch more."

He muttered under his breath about people he'd thought would have more sympathy for someone who was suffering, then realized it hadn't even occurred to him to worry about her seeing him naked.

Of course he'd been more concerned with the itching than modesty, but still, even though she'd seen him naked before, he'd have thought it might cross his mind to be mildly embarrassed by this situation. Instead, he'd felt as comfortable as if they'd been married for years.

Married.

"You can get out and dry yourself now," Rebecca said from the adjoining room. "You'll still want to scratch, but I'm going to put some lotion on you and you'll be fine then."

When he emerged she handed him a glass of water and a couple of pills to take. A few minutes later he was lying facedown on the bed, Rebecca leaning over him. "Here now," she said softly, as if to a child, and dabbed something on his shoulder that felt like ice.

"Cold," he complained, squirming.

She tapped his shoulder lightly and kept on dabbing. "I believe there's a cure for a rash I've heard about that involves a live chicken, but I'm not sure if I'm supposed to hang it from the rafters or round your neck, so I'm reluctant to try it. This is the only alternative."

How could he not laugh? "I get the message. Quit complaining."

"That would be nice."

He turned his head sideways on the pillow so he could look up at her. She hadn't put on a robe over her nightgown. Did that mean she was as comfortable with him as he was with her? If he kept looking at her he wasn't going to be comfortable for long. Already he could feel some stirring of interest in certain areas.

"I'm sorry Rebecca," he said. "I've never had anything like this before. It scared me."

"It'll pass."

"When?"

"Two or three days probably."

"You're not serious."

"I'm always serious about medical matters, Simon."

Which would have sounded fine if he hadn't heard laughter in her voice. "You can turn over and I'll baste the other side," she said, the chuckle even more evident.

"I think you're enjoying this," he said as he rolled over.

"Men are always amusing when they're sick," she said. "They think they're dying if they have the merest sniffle, so if they..."

Her voice trailed away.

She was looking down at him, a flush staining her cheeks. "I'm very responsive to touch," he said as she recommenced dabbing lotion on his right leg.

"So I see."

Her voice was stern, but her eyelashes had a tremor to them that gave her inner laughter away. Blessed relief was following in the wake of her dabbing motions, all the way up his legs and now on his abdomen and chest. As the itch lessened, desire increased. There was no way to hide the fact. Not that he wanted to.

He waited until she'd treated every hive, then reached for her left wrist and kissed the back of her hand. "Thank you," he said with heartfelt sincerity.

"Better?" she asked.

"Much."

He tugged lightly on the captive wrist, hoping to unbalance her, but she stood firm. Setting down the cotton pad and bottle of lotion on his nightstand, she screwed the bottle cap on, then sniffed the fingers of her right hand. "I smell medicinal," she said.

"So do I."

"I need to wash my hands, Simon."

"No, you don't."

He was still holding her wrist. So far, she hadn't attempted to pull away.

Very gently she touched his throat. "Can you swallow all right?"

He tried. "No problem. I guess the pills took effect. My voice seems okay, too."

She nodded. "You should be able to sleep now."

"I doubt it," he said.

Her eyes met his. "Simon," she said. He wasn't sure if it was a sigh or an entreaty. Either way it reverberated through him.

"Take your glasses off, Rebecca," he ordered, and she did, laying them carefully on the nightstand. He tugged again on her wrist, and this time she leaned over him and kissed him very gently on the mouth. At once he put his arms around her and rolled with her so that she ended up on the bed beside him, her legs entangled in her nightgown and trapped between his.

"Please," she whispered.

"Please yes, or please no?" he asked, leaning over her and looking down into her face.

Her eyes filled with their special light. "I don't know."

"Would it help if I told you that I love you?" he asked very gently.

He wasn't sure which of them was more surprised by that question, but the minute it was out of his mouth he knew it was the truth. He smiled. "That's been coming on me ever since I met you," he murmured. "It passed through some scary thoughts like 'always' and 'forever' to get here, but here it is."

She seemed stunned. "If this was an old movie," he continued, "this would be the part where the knight asks his lady for her hand, and body, in marriage. Will you marry me, Rebecca?"

Now she seemed more paralyzed than stunned, openmouthed in a most attractive way, her lips just barely parted. He wasn't sure, but he thought she might have stopped breathing. It seemed a good opportunity to kiss her and he did so, touching his tongue to her lower lip and just sort of easing it inside so that he could taste her sweetness. She didn't smell medicinal at all. She smelled of lavender, which seemed to go directly to his head and other areas like an aphrodisiac.

He eased the nightgown up over her hips and breasts, and lifted the soft-as-gossamer garment gently over her head. Then he tossed it aside and brushed her lips again with his own.

She still seemed to be in a somnolent state. Yet her mouth responded hungrily to every movement of his, and her hands stroked him and gripped him.

She was dreaming, she thought. She had to be dreaming. Though she'd suspected in Tintagel that she was beginning to feel strongly about Simon Flynn and had thought after making love to him in this very bed the same day that the strong feelings just might represent the happy-ever-after sort of state, circumstances had changed.

It had been pretty well established that they were blood-related, hadn't it?

She couldn't see his face clearly. His head was between her and the lamplight, a shadowy oval with a light-filled aura. His mouth was moving on hers more demandingly now, and it seemed impossible to refuse to give all he was asking for and maybe even demand a little something herself.

So what had she been thinking about? Oh, yes. That they were maybe related. Well, it wasn't so close a relationship that what they were doing together was unthinkable, was it?

While she was thinking, his mouth had traveled down over her throat to her right breast. His cheek and chin felt rough against the tender skin, but not unpleasantly so. His tongue was teasing the nipple on that side erect. The slight tugging motion sent her blood singing sweetly, wildly, through her veins.

Her hands cradled his head, holding it tightly to her, her body arching to give him easy access to her breast or any other part of her he wanted to explore.

But there was still the fact that his grandfather, who was evidently *her* grandfather, had ruined her grandmother's life. All of that was true.

Yet somehow, in this dream state, where his large, very competent hands were moving over her body, and his wonderfully firm mouth was working its own special magic on her left breast now, it didn't seem important.

Come to think of it, it didn't make any more sense for her to blame Simon for Paul's wrongdoing than it did to blame herself, if he was her grandfather, too.

Did that sound logical? It all seemed too complicated to think about. It was much easier to simply let her body relax under his and feel him smile against her breast. She could imagine that smile, the smile that always hovered, playing around his mouth, playing over her body, blessing every part of her with warmth and love.

Love.

He'd said he loved her.

"Rebecca," he murmured now.

She knew instinctively that he was ready for her now. It was time to stop thinking, to let her mind cloud over. As her arms guided him over her, she closed her eyes against the lamplight and imagined clouds penetrating each part of her brain. Bright clouds they were, edged with the hot red of passion, billowing and growing.

She arched against him to let him know she was ready, too.

His mouth covered hers as he entered her, so that her gasp of excitement entered him. His mouth continued to move on hers as his body rose and fell and thrust forward. She moved with him, now together, now apart, as though their lovemaking had been choreographed and mapped out on a paper that only he and she had seen.

Slowly, gradually, and yet far too quickly, the sweet pressure of orgasm built inside her and filled her. Moaning deep in her throat, she did not want to breathe for fear of letting the pressure go too soon, while at the same time she longed for its release. His hands lifted her, his mouth coaxed her, and as the orgasm finally reverberated throughout her entire body, she felt his body arch with his own release.

"So that's what it's supposed to be like," he muttered against her throat a long time later.

Had she slept? She wasn't sure. She did know she had floated in another dimension for some time, not thinking, just being.

He'd sounded sleepy. Carefully she eased out from under him until she was lying next to him. His right arm lay across her middle. She stroked it lightly. Still bumpy.

"I don't itch anymore," he murmured.

But he would again soon, she knew. With all that activity, most of the lotion she'd applied had probably been wiped off. She eased out of bed, found a fresh cotton pad and began dabbing lotion all over him again. That playful smile of his showed up again, but he didn't open his eyes.

"'Oh Woman! in our hours of ease,/Uncertain, coy, and hard to please,'" he muttered. Then his brow furrowed. "Walter Scott. Must be the Cornish air making me quote all the old stuff. Can't remember the rest. Dee dah dee dah, something something. Oh, yeah. 'When pain and anguish wring the brow,/A ministering angel thou!'"

His eyelids cracked open, showing that vivid blue. His mouth curved lazily.

"Very good," she said, and went on dabbing.

His eyes closed and his chest rose and fell evenly.

When she finished, she draped the sheet over him, but left the blanket off. It was better that he stay cool. With any luck this would be a mild attack and he'd feel better in the morning.

Picking up her nightgown, she went into the bathroom and took a shower. Simon was right—the water pressure had improved since he worked on the nozzle. He was a very handy male to have around. In fact, it was difficult to imagine him *not* being around.

She wrapped a towel around her hair, then another around her toga-style, which reminded her of Tintagel. With a sigh she wiped the steam from the mirror with a flannel, fetched her glasses and put them on.

Her face was very flushed, probably from being abraded by Simon's perpetual five-o'clock shadow.

Her eyes looked shiny, also questioning.

Questioning what?

He loved her, he said.

Did she love him?

Yes.

Did she want to marry him?

Yes.

Could she marry him?

No.

Not just because of the blood tie.

Gran suspected. Come the morning, she'd have to be told the truth—that Simon Flynn was Paul Carmichael's grandson. She was going to know that the two of them had conspired behind her back to dig out her secrets.

In so doing they'd fallen in love and at the same time discovered barriers to that love.

So Gran must be told all but the last part, because the last part would make her remember all the pain she'd suffered because of Paul Carmichael.

Then Simon Flynn could take the story home to his mother and satisfy her curiosity, and Rebecca would stay here in Cornwall and care for Gran for the rest of her life.

That was the way of it. And there was no changing it.

Still gazing at herself in the mirror, Rebecca saw that behind her glasses, her eyes had lost their questioning look. And their shine.

CHAPTER TWENTY

"HI, MOM," Simon said across the Atlantic cable.

"It's about time you called me again." He'd known Libby would be exasperated with him. "First you tell me not to call the Penberthys' house, then you leave me in limbo."

Yes, she added in response to his questions, her ribs were healing just fine, though she still couldn't lie down flat or breathe without pain, mostly because of the damaged cartilage. "The doctors keep shooting novocaine under my ribs with a syringe that looks like a bicycle pump," she informed him. "But never mind all that. What's happening over there?"

"Well, there's been some action," Simon told her, then passed on what he and Rebecca had learned from Josie and their second interview with Winifred Stubbins.

"Where are you calling from?" Libby asked when he was done.

"The Penberthys' hallway."

"I thought you couldn't do that without Bliss listening in."

"I waited until they went out for the evening. Bliss had a therapy session in Plymouth—her Friday appointment was canceled. She has arthritis."

"It's the only telephone in town?"

Trust his mother to stick to what she considered the point. "I can't go out. I'm a mess—hives all over," he confessed. "I suddenly became allergic to crab."

"Your grandmother Flynn was allergic to shellfish," his mother said without offering any sympathy.

"That makes me feel a lot better."

"What aren't you telling me, Simon?" she asked abruptly.

"I'm in love, Mom." He hadn't intended to say anything about Rebecca, but the words seemed to burst from his mouth of their own accord.

"With who?"

"Whom."

"Don't mess with me, Simon Flynn."

"I'm in love with Rebecca, Mom."

"Rebecca Penberthy? Bliss's granddaughter? The one you called the girl?"

"I've asked her to marry me. You'll like her. I know you will."

Silence echoed along the line for several seconds. "Hello, Mom?" he said gently after a while.

"What did Rebecca say?" Libby asked, sounding faint.

"She hasn't said anything yet. Things got a little...confusing."

"Well, you can't marry her," Libby said firmly.

Once again Simon found himself taking the receiver from his ear and staring at it. Was this the same woman who'd been nagging him to get married for at least eight years?

"It's against the law," she was saying when the receiver was back to his ear.

"Whose law?"

"Washington State law. She's your cousin, Simon. We determined that last time we talked. Don't you remember Gordy Fremont? He wanted to marry his cousin Amanda and found out he couldn't. They had to move somewhere."

"You're not serious."

"I am, absolutely. Their attorney told them."

"Rebecca and I only have one grandparent in common."

Libby was silent, for almost a full minute this time. Then she said very solemnly, "I don't think that makes any difference, darling. Do you want me to look into it?"

"Who's going to know we're cousins?" Simon demanded.

"Rebecca."

Damn. Typically, his mother had sensed the weak part in this whole arrangement. Rebecca still didn't feel right about it. Why else had she avoided conversation all day? She'd come over a few times to dab lotion on the itchy areas he couldn't reach, but had told him firmly each time that she didn't have time to talk or to dally, the shop was busy, Gran needed her to do something, she had to cook dinner, they were going out... She hadn't made eye contact with him once.

"I've got to go, Mom," Simon said, wishing he hadn't called. It was depressing enough to have to sit around not scratching all day without having to face facts. Just for once, he didn't want to face facts the way he'd been brought up to do. He wanted to grab Rebecca and run.

"WHAT'S WRONG, love?" Bliss asked in the tender voice she reserved for Rebecca alone.

Rebecca attempted a smile and failed abysmally. Gran had caught her staring out the kitchen window at the night-dark buildings across the street, tea towel in hand, tears running down her face. Rebecca had no idea how long she'd been standing there in her nightie, looking out, seeing nothing.

"I've told you three times the tea is steeped and ready," Gran said quietly. "You look as though you need it. Come and sit down, and let's talk about whatever it is."

Rebecca took off her glasses and patted her face with a paper tissue, blew her nose a couple of times, then hung the towel over the edge of the sink and took a seat at the round table where her grandmother had set up the tea things. They usually had a cup of camomile tea and a plain biscuit or two before going to bed. Often they sat awhile and talked over things that had happened that day. It was a tradition they both enjoyed.

"I'm sorry, Gran," Rebecca said as she poured the tea. "I was just thinking."

"Well, whatever you were thinking wasn't pleasant, judging by those tears. And I didn't see any onions in your hands. What's wrong? Did my therapist tell you I'm going to die?"

"Gran!" Startled, Rebecca jiggled the teapot enough to splash liquid onto the polished oak table. Hastily she reached for a paper napkin and wiped it dry. "The only thing the therapist said to me was that you're doing much better with your exercises," she said. "You were there when she said so. What a thing for you to say!"

Gran chuckled softly. "Woke you up, didn't I?" She tipped her head to one side. "You still haven't answered my first question. What brought on the tears?"

Rebecca sighed. "It's not anything I want to talk about. It's something I have to work out for myself."

"Something to do with Simon Flynn, I'll be bound."

Rebecca opened her mouth to deny it, but nothing came out.

"He's your lover, is he?"

Rebecca stared openmouthed at her grandmother for a moment, then nodded helplessly, blinking hard to hold back a fresh onslaught. She never could lie when Gran asked a question straight out. She never should have let things get this far. "I don't want to talk about it, all right?" she said miserably, and picked up her teacup.

"All right. You sit still while I talk," Bliss said. "First of all, I'm not an idiot. I've seen the way he looks at you and the way you look at him. I'm not so old I've forgotten what those kinds of glances mean. What I want to know is what's happened in the last few days? And don't tell me nothing has, because you've changed. From waltzing round all starry-eyed in the furry dance, you've gone to letting out long sighs and staring out of windows and crying. You hardly slept all last night."

"I told you about Simon's allergic reaction to the crab. I had to treat him several times."

"You came home at two in the morning and kept walking back and forth in your bedroom. I'm not deaf, Rebecca. I'm seventy-five years old and I sleep lightly. I know when you're not sleeping. So what happened? Did you have an argument? Did he treat you badly?"

Rebecca shook her head. Bliss's bright brown eyes were boring into hers, demanding a proper answer. Just as she'd feared would happen all along, the words came tumbling out. "He says he loves me. He's asked me to marry him."

She saw the telltale movement of Bliss's hand toward her heart. "What did you tell him?" Bliss asked.

"I haven't told him anything. He knows it's not possible for us to marry."

The tightness in Bliss's face gave way to relief. "So you don't love him."

Rebecca burst into tears again.

Hauling off her glasses, she reached for the tea towel, the only thing handy, and buried her face in it. "I don't know what's the matter with me," she said, her voice trembling. "I never cry. You know I never cry. It must be that time of the month."

She heard Bliss's chair move and felt Bliss's hand touching her head lightly, awkwardly stroking her hair, already loosened for the night.

"You do love him."

Rebecca nodded.

Bliss's chair scraped again as she sat down. Heavily. Rebecca hurriedly wiped her eyes and squinted at her. Bliss's lined face was pale, pinched with fatigue and perhaps something more. "Do you need your tablets?" she asked, suddenly alarmed.

Her grandmother shook her head. "Perhaps a glass of water."

Rebecca stood up and filled a glass. "Are you in pain?"

"No, it's just that silly old tightness."

"We'd better get you to bed."

Bliss shook her head, took another sip of water and set the glass down. Her color was better now. "Sit down, Rebecca," she said firmly.

Rebecca sat and put her glasses back on.

Bliss reached across the table and took hold of Rebecca's hands and held them tightly. "You have to tell me the truth, love. I didn't think I wanted to hear it, but I keep worrying and worrying about what's going on. Far better I should know the truth."

Once again she was looking very directly at Rebecca. "You and Simon Flynn visited Tintagel a week ago. Fairy Stubbins lives in Tintagel. All of a sudden, after fifty years, Fairy decides to visit me. Isn't that an amazing coincidence?"

Rebecca stared helplessly at her.

"I told you before—I'm not daft, love. I know how to add two and two." She took a shaky breath. Her lower lip trembled and pain showed deep in her eyes. Rebecca wanted to stop her from saying whatever it was that was affecting her so much.

"Gran—"

Bliss's mouth tightened over the tremor, stopping it. "I want to know—" she swallowed hard "—how exactly is Simon Flynn related to Paul Carmichael?"

Rebecca was too stunned to speak for a minute. "How did you know?" she managed at last.

Bliss's mouth twitched slightly at one corner but didn't quite form a smile. "Well, Paul's eyes were that same blue. But lots of people have blue eyes. It wasn't until we were in the pub that I suddenly noticed Mr. Flynn had eyebrows like Paul's. The way they slant."

Rebecca nodded. "Mrs. Stubbins noticed that, too, but only after she knew." She took a deep breath. "Paul was Simon's grandfather."

"Was?"

"He died. Paul died a couple of months ago."

Bliss closed her eyes.

"I'm sorry, Gran."

Bliss held up a hand as if pleading for silence. Rebecca waited.

Finally Bliss opened her eyes again. They looked darker. "Paul had a little girl. Libby," she whispered.

"Simon's mother."

"Simon came here looking for me?"

"Yes."

"Why? To tell me Paul was dead? Paul died for me more than fifty years ago."

Rebecca swallowed. "I'll have to let Simon tell you his purpose, Gran."

"Very well." She hesitated again, obviously organizing her thoughts. "So then you both talked to Fairy. Anyone else? You made more than one sight-seeing trip." She emphasized the word "sight-seeing."

Rebecca winced. "We went to see Josie Chickering."

"You did?" Bliss's whole face softened. "I tried to track Josie down a year or so ago. I suddenly felt lonely for her. I couldn't find her anywhere."

"She's got a flat in Penzance. Right now she's in a convalescent home, though, because she broke her hip. It's getting better. She said she'd be going home soon."

Bliss was still pale, but there was a faint smile on her face. "I'll go see her. Perhaps you'd drive me. Is she still cheeky?"

"Very. We liked her, Simon and I."

"Simon and you." She let go of Rebecca's hands and began massaging her own as if they pained her, which they usually did.

"D'you want me to heat up some paraffin?" Rebecca offered.

Bliss shook her head, then looked at Rebecca again. "Josie and Fairy told you all about Paul and me?"

Rebecca nodded.

"They told you the baby was Paul's."

"Yes."

"So you've worked out that you and Simon are related and that's why you're so upset, because you really do want to marry him."

"That's not the only reason I can't marry him, Gran," Rebecca protested. "After the way his grandfather treated you... And besides, you know how I love Penmorton. I could never go live in a strange country."

"You'd love it." Abruptly Bliss stood up and turned away, heading for the door.

"Gran—"

"I'm all right. I just have to go and think about this for a while." She didn't turn around. "I want you to do something for me, Rebecca."

"Anything, Gran." Her voice was hoarse, she realized, probably because of all the tears she had yet to shed.

"I want you to tell Simon Flynn that I want to talk to him. But not until he's well. When do you think that will be?"

"By tomorrow evening, I should think."

"Very well. Invite him to dinner. There's a good roasting chicken in the freezer. Put it in the fridge to thaw, will you? I'll do that mushroom gravy you like so much. By the time Mr. Flynn comes, I'll have thought everything through and will know how much to tell him."

"I don't understand, Gran."

"You don't have to. Not yet." She took a couple of steps toward the door, then stopped. "What would you like to have happen in this situation?"

Rebecca sat up very straight. "I think it would be best if Simon went back home so that you and I could go on with our lives just the way we did before."

"You wouldn't miss him?"

Rebecca closed her eyes and immediately felt as if she was standing on the edge of an abyss. Stretching to infinity, it lay at her feet, waiting for her to fall into its dark, bottomless depths.

Taking a deep breath, she opened her eyes and tried to inject a firm note into her voice. "I'd get over it," she lied.

As soon as she heard Bliss's bedroom door close, she folded her arms on the table, laid her head on top of them and let the tears come the way they'd been wanting to all day.

CHAPTER TWENTY-ONE

BLISS HAD DRESSED in her prettiest blouse, the rose pink one that reflected color to her complexion. It had a bow at the neck that she'd managed to tie herself, though not without pain, Rebecca was willing to bet. With it she wore her good tweed skirt, stockings and low-heeled shoes.

"You look very nice, Gran," Rebecca told her, straightening up after basting the chicken.

"You, too, love. I've always liked that dress. It's just the right shade of yellow. Don't you think you should wear an apron to protect it?"

Rebecca turned down the heat under the potatoes. "I'm being careful." She sat down at the kitchen table, took her glasses off and wiped the steam from them with a tissue.

"Mr. Flynn is coming?" Bliss asked, pulling out a chair so she could join Rebecca.

"He'll be here any minute." Rebecca hesitated. "Could you bring yourself to call him Simon?"

"I'll think about it."

Bliss's voice was very steady, but had an underlying tension.

Rebecca decided it might lighten the atmosphere if she told her about the telephone call she'd received that day. "Josie rang me an hour ago," she said.

Bliss looked wistful. "I'd like to have spoken to her."

"You were bathing. She said Fairy had been to see her and was disgusted with the place Josie was staying in. The food wasn't fit for pigs, she said."

Bliss shook her head and smiled. "Fairy always did speak her mind."

"Anyway, the upshot is, Fairy wants Josie to come and stay with her in Tintagel for a while. Try it out. If they get along all right, she'd like Josie to stay with her for good. They could take care of each other, she thought."

Bliss shook her head again. "Well, that's one good thing to come of all this, I suppose. If it works."

"Do you think it will?"

"I wouldn't be surprised." Bliss looked down at her clasped hands. "Perhaps I'll ask if there's room for me. That would be something now, wouldn't it, the three of us together—"

"Gran!" Rebecca was indignant. "Have you been worrying that I'll accept Simon's proposal and go off to Seattle with him? It's not going to happen. I've told you that. I'm going to be right here with you. Always."

Bliss gave her a loving look, but there was a sadness under it that made Rebecca wonder again exactly what her grandmother had in mind for this evening. She'd thought of little else all day while she waited on customers and wrapped packages of tea or herbs and engaged in conversations. She and Simon knew everything that had happened in 1943, and they knew what it meant. Hearing it all over again wasn't going to make any difference.

Rebecca had seen him for only a few minutes that day, during her lunch break. She'd wanted to make sure he was recovering from his allergy attack and to let him

know Bliss knew what they'd been up to and wanted to
talk to him this evening.

"I doubt she's going to end up thinking any more
highly of me," he'd said gloomily.

As though her thoughts had conjured him up, she
heard a knock on the lower door.

She flew down the stairs, opened the door. He'd put
on a white shirt and tie, gray pants and a lightweight
black jacket. His hair had a damp sheen and was neatly
combed. He looked very smart, very attractive. Too
attractive. The back hallway had suddenly run out of
air.

"No more weals?" she asked. His face certainly
looked clear.

"Only a couple on my backside," he said.

"Oh." Their eyes met. His wry smile was very much
in evidence. "Dinner's just about ready," she said
breathlessly. "Please, whatever Gran asks you, answer
her honestly. It's time."

Turning away, she started up the stairs before he had
a chance to touch or kiss her. If he did that, she'd never
make it through the evening, she felt sure.

The chicken was done to a turn. Gran's mushroom
gravy was wonderful, the potatoes and green vegetables perfectly cooked. It was the first time the three of
them had shared a full meal, Rebecca realized. And
probably the last.

Bliss seemed content to eat and talk about Penmorton's history. But just when Rebecca was about to burst
from tension, which she could also sense in Simon, her
grandmother put her knife and fork neatly side by side
on her plate and dabbed her mouth with her napkin.

"I'd like to know what made you decide to come to Penmorton, Mr. Flynn," she said, then glanced at Rebecca and made an amendment. "Simon."

Simon nodded, then sat silently for a couple of moments. "It began after my grandfather, Paul Carmichael, died," he said slowly. "He was a difficult man to know. He tended to keep his feelings to himself. Sometimes I wondered if he had any. He was never demonstrative, always distant. My mother said it was as if somewhere along the way he'd lost some essential part of himself and hadn't been able to find it again. She also said he'd never quite caught on to what family life was supposed to be."

Bliss put a hand to her throat.

"Are you all right, Gran?" Rebecca asked softly.

She nodded, but her eyes were moist. "Please go on," she said.

Simon told her about the photograph and postcard of Penmorton Paul had shown his mother, then explained about the accident that had prevented Libby from coming to find Bliss herself.

"Why on earth would either of you want to find me?" Bliss murmured.

Simon hesitated, then said, "Mom felt she'd never really known her father," which Rebecca knew wasn't the whole reason. According to what Simon had told her earlier, he'd traveled to England hoping to find some missing part of himself.

He went on to explain how Libby had persuaded him to come in her place and how he'd found out where Bliss lived.

"Why didn't you tell me who you were?" Bliss asked.

Rebecca touched her arm. "That was my fault, Gran. I'd told Simon about your heart condition and warned him you mustn't be exposed to stress."

"I hate being coddled," Bliss said.

"We decided we'd try to find out exactly what had happened between you and Paul, so we could make an educated decision on whether it would upset you to know who Simon was," Rebecca went on.

"And you decided it would upset me too much?"

"Until you came out with it, yes."

Bliss shook her head, then looked at Simon. "It pains me to know Paul was so unhappy," she says. "Especially as it was my fault."

"How can you say that?" Rebecca protested. "He didn't even tell you he was married, did he? And then when you told him you were pregnant, he just went off back to his base and never got in touch with you again."

"That's all quite true...except for the last part," Bliss said. The faraway look was back in her eyes. "Paul did ring me before he went back to America. He wanted to be sure I was all right."

"Oh, certainly," Rebecca said bitterly. "That was really kind of him."

"Yes, it was," Bliss said. She looked at Simon again. "As I understand it, you've been told all about my affair with your grandfather and the fact that I was pregnant when he left. Is that correct?"

Simon nodded. He was very solemn. Deep in his eyes, pain flickered. For Bliss? His grandfather? Himself? There was no way Rebecca could tell, but she responded to his pain, laying her hand over his on the table. At once he turned his hand over and clasped hers tightly, but he didn't look at her.

"We had this terrible argument," Bliss said, her gaze turned inward. "Paul visited me in the middle of December. He had an unexpected three-day pass. I was so happy—until he told me he wouldn't be coming for Christmas. Then I was angry. I'd been planning the holiday for ever such a long time, and I'd even lied to the farmer I worked for, telling him my mum was ill and needed me home for the holiday. Paul said I shouldn't have lied, it wasn't honorable, and then he let it slip that he was married and had a little girl."

Her face crumpled, and Rebecca was afraid for a minute that she was going to cry, but then she passed a hand over her face and went on with her story. "I was such a proper little thing, for all I'd been so daring as to have an affair. I'd never have let Paul lay a hand on me if I'd known he was married. No matter that I loved him practically from the beginning. My dad...well, let's just say he'd left his mark on me with all his ranting. It was a sin to lie with a married man. Ignorance of the facts would not have been an acceptable excuse."

She shuddered slightly. "I didn't know there was a worse sin to come."

"Gran, you don't have to—"

Her eyes flashed. "Yes, I do, Rebecca. I have to say all of it. It was fine to keep it secret when it wasn't hurting anyone except me, but now the lies have affected you."

She managed a half smile that was so wistful Rebecca's heart contracted. "I love you more than anyone in the world, Rebecca," Bliss continued. "I can't bear for you to be unhappy."

"But you don't have to tell me if you don't want—" Simon gripped Rebecca's hand. She subsided. "I'm sorry, Gran. It's up to you how much you tell us, of course."

Bliss nodded. "When Paul told me he was married, I sent him away. I told him I never wanted to see him again. I told myself I'd never loved him. I hated him. He'd deceived me. He'd made me commit adultery. He'd led me into sin. I kept telling myself over and over that I was angry. Not upset, not hurt, not broken-hearted, but angry, angry, angry."

She was gripping her hands together very tightly. Rebecca was afraid she was hurting herself, but didn't want to interrupt again.

"I couldn't make myself come home for Christmas after that. My mum was upset, but I couldn't help that. I told her I had a job to do, that there was a war on. Oh, I was very righteous. So I went back to the farm and told Tom Garland my mum had recovered and I worked all through Christmas and the following week, worked and worked as if the hounds of hell were after me."

She gave a miserable-sounding laugh. "I never worked so hard in my life, before or since. I pulled out so many tomato vines from the greenhouses my hands were orange for weeks. Then I broke all my fingernails working on Tom Garland's ancient tractor. It didn't even have a steering wheel, just a couple of levers . . ."

She looked wistfully at Rebecca. "I think I'd like a cup of tea, love, if you don't mind."

Rebecca jumped up and put the kettle on. When she sat down again, Bliss said, "None of this is really important anymore, except that I haven't thought about that time all these years, didn't *let* myself think about it. But I have to explain to you what my feelings were, so you'll see why—"

The kettle whistle interrupted her. She waited until the tea was made and the cups in place before going on. "I was running around that farm like a chicken with its head cut off," she said. "I was everywhere at once, working day and night. In between I kept thinking that Paul might have been killed by now and nobody would have told me. I shouldn't be mad at someone who might be dead. But all the time I was so very angry, and I think perhaps a little insane. I hope I was. It might explain—"

Again she broke off, poured milk into all three cups, then lifted the tea cozy and poured the tea. After a few sips, she seemed ready to go on. "On New Year's Eve I was working in the barn, mucking out, still furious. Just before midnight, Tom Garland came out to see why I was clattering round and invited me in for a glass of cider to toast the new year. The other land-army girls had all gone home for the holidays—he'd given everyone the time off. He was like that. Very kind. His wife had gone to stay with her mother, did I mention that? *Her* mother really was ill. So there we were, the two of us. Alone. He'd always fancied me. And we had a glass of cider. And then another. And he asked me what I was so angry about and I started crying and he...comforted me."

She lifted her teacup and finished what was in it, then poured more.

It was a minute before Rebecca realized exactly what Bliss had implied. She'd been caught up in the story, had been able to visualize Bliss taking out her anger on the straw in the barn, the older farmer coming in, inviting her for a drink.

"You made... You and the farmer? Tom Garland?" Rebecca squeaked. She swallowed hard, forcing her voice down to its normal register. "You and Tom Garland went to bed together?"

Bliss sighed. Remembered sorrow had dulled her usually bright eyes. Her face was gaunt, bleak. "Isn't that the stupidest thing you've ever heard? For someone to get so angry with a man who hadn't told her he was married, then let another man she *knew* was married take her to his bed."

"Then you mean . . ." Simon didn't finish.

Bliss laughed, but there was no mirth in it. "I was always very regular. I'd had my period just before Paul came in the middle of December. So when it didn't come by the middle of January, I knew."

Her lower lip trembled and she couldn't seem to go on.

"You were pregnant," Rebecca said, still not quite recovered from the shock, but wanting to help. "And you didn't know if the father was Paul Carmichael or Tom Garland."

Bliss nodded dejectedly, then sipped more tea. Simon hadn't touched his, Rebecca noticed. He was still holding her hand. She took hold of Bliss's hand with her free one. Bliss didn't look up, didn't seem to *want* to look up. "I didn't know what to do," she said. "By the middle of February, I knew for certain I was going to have a baby. I didn't think I was ever going to see Paul again. I certainly wasn't going to tell Tom Garland I was pregnant. I came home to Penmorton and pretended I was sick. Actually it wasn't a pretense. I was ashamed, heartsick, desperate."

She let out a long, painful sigh. "At the end of February Paul turned up without warning. I was in the shop helping my mum. He came rushing at me, telling me he was sorry, he'd missed me, couldn't stay away. Later on, when I could get away, he told me he'd had to come back to explain that his marriage hadn't been at all happy from the start, that it had been arranged by his father..."

She glanced apologetically at Simon.

"I know about that," he said. "He was telling the truth—Mom told me the same thing. Her grandfather wanted Paul to marry his partner's daughter so the business would stay in the family."

"He said he never would have gone back on his marriage vows if he'd loved his wife or she'd loved him, but he also said he couldn't get out of the marriage because his father would never forgive him and would probably cut him off. He thought if he explained, it would be all right, and we could just go on as before until the time came for him to return to America."

Neither Rebecca nor Simon said anything when Bliss paused. It was obviously getting more and more difficult for her to go on. Her eyes were hollow with remembered grief. "I told him I was pregnant," she said flatly. "I told him what had happened New Year's Eve. I told him why it had happened, how it *had* happened and how sorry I was that it had happened."

She closed her eyes, and a tear crept out from under her eyelid and slid slowly down her thin cheek. Rebecca got up and brought a box of tissues to the table. She put one in her grandmother's hand.

Bliss nodded her thanks and wiped her eyes. "Paul had told me..." she started, then swallowed and coughed slightly. When she started over, her voice was stronger. "Paul had told me earlier that we didn't need to use any kind of contraceptive because he had a low sperm count. But he hadn't told me that he'd had an operation after his little girl was born. Apparently it was his wife who'd wanted a child, and he'd agreed to have just one. As soon as she—Libby—was born, he had an operation so he couldn't have any more children. He said he'd regretted it since, but at the time he'd thought of it as a way of getting back at his father, who'd practically ordered him to have sons.''

"My father wasn't Paul's baby," Rebecca said slowly.

"There was no way he could have been," Bliss said.

"But Mrs. Stubbins, Josie, they—"

"Paul went away," Bliss said, leaning forward. "After he told me he couldn't have fathered the child, he went away. Why would he stay? After the dreadful thing I'd done."

"He hadn't exactly—"

Bliss held up her hand. "It was fifty years ago, love. It doesn't matter who did what. Paul lied to me by omission. I betrayed him. The blame could be spread equally. But it doesn't matter now. The important thing is that you know for certain that Paul was *not* the father of my child. As for why Fairy and Josie told you he was, they thought they were telling you the truth. *I* told everyone Paul was the father. What else could I do? He was gone, so it wasn't going to hurt him. Why say it was Tom Garland's child? I certainly didn't want to break up his marriage. He really was just a kind man who wanted to comfort me. Besides I didn't love him. I didn't want to marry him. So, yes, I said it was Paul's child and I pretended I hated Americans. I did such a good job of lying to everyone that I couldn't bear to face them again, so I just cut myself off. I almost convinced *myself* that Travis was Paul's child, as if I could rewrite history by pretending."

"Your father made you marry Foster Penberthy," Rebecca said.

"Yes, well, it was Dad's idea, and I fought it for a while, but then I gave in. I knew it would make my life a lot easier if I did what he wanted. And I thought it would be best for the baby. I didn't care about anyone *but* the baby by then. I never loved Foster, but I was as good a wife to him as I could be under the circumstances. On the day I married him, I told myself the past was dead. I was Bliss Penberthy, wife of Foster Penberthy, and anything that happened to me before that day had no meaning for me."

She closed her eyes, shaking her head, her face bleak. "You can't do it. You can't wipe out the past. It's there in your mind waiting to step forward. All it takes is the sight of waves breaking on the shore or the sound of a certain song or the taste of a particular food."

Opening her eyes, she glanced at Simon. "Or the slant of a young man's eyebrows." She smiled faintly. "Rebecca asked me why I wasn't nicer to you," she said. "At the time, I didn't really know. I just sensed you were a threat to the peace of mind I'd fought to keep for fifty years. I think subconsciously I recognized small likenesses to Paul."

Rebecca looked at Simon, then whispered, "So Tom Garland was my father's father."

"We're not related." Simon touched her face with such gentleness she was moved almost to tears. "You're not any kind of cousin to me."

She shook her head, her eyes prickling with unshed tears. For her grandmother, this time, not herself.

Leaving her seat, she knelt beside Bliss and put her arms around her waist. "I'm so sorry you've had such an awful life, Gran," she said.

Bliss stroked her hair. "It wasn't all bad, love. Your father was a great comfort to me. As for Tom Garland, well, he gave me a son to love, who in his turn gave me you. He was a very nice man, Tom Garland. Travis and you inherited his kindness, I like to think. Tom had no children of his own.''

She swallowed. ''He had the loveliest golden brown eyes,'' she murmured, then sat up in her usual straight-backed way. ''Well, that's all of it. I brought a lot of it on myself and now that I've admitted that to myself and you, perhaps I'll be able to forgive myself. And Paul. We were young and stupid.''

''There's something I haven't told you,'' Simon said.

Bliss laughed shortly. ''Well, if there's ever a time for confession, it's now.''

''Just before my grandfather Paul died, he gave your photograph and the postcard of Penmorton to my mother.''

She frowned. ''Yes, you told me that, but I don't—''

''He said something to her. She told me there were tears in his eyes and his voice was anguished.'' Simon frowned, the better to remember the exact words. ''He said, 'If I hadn't been so stupid, if I hadn't left Bliss behind in Penmorton, I might have been a happy man. I loved her. I just didn't know how important love was.' My mom asked him if Bliss was the woman in the photograph and he said yes, then he added, 'Tell her I loved her.' That's why she wanted to find you—to tell you that. That's why she wanted me to come in her place.''

Bliss's eyes swam with tears. ''He really said that?'' she whispered.

Simon nodded. ''Those were his last words.''

Her face, in spite of the tears, was suddenly radiant. Simon wondered how he could ever have thought of her as a dragon lady. At this minute he saw her as she had appeared in the photograph his grandfather had given his mother, saw her as his grandfather had seen her—young, vulnerable, filled with hope and optimism, glowing with life. And love.

Getting up from his chair, Simon knelt on her other side and put his arms around her, his hands touching Rebecca, whose face was also alight.

"Well, if we aren't the soppy ones," Bliss said after a moment. "Up with you both," she said, patting them indiscriminately. "I'm away to my room to rest."

She looked up at Simon as he helped her to her feet. "And to remember," she added.

He watched her approach the door, then realized he couldn't let her leave yet. "Wait a minute, Mrs. Penberthy. Bliss," he said. "I've an important question to put to you."

She turned around.

"How would you feel about living in the United States?"

She smiled through the last traces of her tears. "Is this a proposal, Simon?"

"It is," he assured her. He went to her and took her hands in his. "I'm about to propose to your granddaughter again, and I've an idea her answer this time would be that she can't go away to Seattle and leave you. So I want it made clear that I know this and that you're part of the deal."

Her eyes, bright again, searched his face. "How would your mother feel about me being there?"

"She'd think it was all her idea and take full credit for finally roping in a daughter-in-law *and* a new friend."

"What about your grandmother? Jane Carmichael?"

"She has a condo in Phoenix, Arizona, so she's not in Seattle often. Besides, she doesn't worry about anything except tee time. That's t-e-e," he spelled.

Bliss laughed. "I'm thinking I might like Seattle," she said, then she took her hands from his. "And I'm thinking you'd better ask my granddaughter how she feels about all this before you buy any airplane tickets."

Simon smiled as he watched her leave the room. The dragon lady had turned into a gallant lady right in front of his eyes.

He swiveled around and saw that Rebecca was standing, waiting, her cheeks slightly flushed, her eyes full of light behind her glasses.

"I love you, Rebecca Penberthy," he said as he took her in his arms.

"And I love you, Simon Flynn," she said gravely.

He kissed her luscious mouth and smiled against it. "I'm getting itchy," he said. "I think I need another treatment."

"I think I know where your itch is," she teased.

He kissed her again. "Will you marry me, Rebecca?" he asked solemnly. "I can't make another Penmorton in Seattle for you, but there's probably room for another health shop."

"Now *there's* an offer I can't refuse," she said. "In any case, as long as you've verbally kidnapped my gran, I don't see that I have any choice. So, yes, Simon Flynn, I will marry you."

He leaned his head back and looked directly into her face. "You told me when we first met that you had no desire to leave Penmorton."

Her mouth curved. "I lied. I just didn't think I'd ever be able to leave, so I kept telling myself I didn't want to.

I will miss this house, my shop, the town, but I've never really believed a place is as important as the person you're with. I suppose I was just waiting for a knight to come along and carry me off on his white charger—or an airplane.''

The kiss lasted a long while this time. When they finally pulled apart, he took her hand and gestured at the door. ''I think this is the part in the movie where the very perfect noble knight throws his lady over his saddle and gallops off to Camelot.''

''I don't much like the idea of being thrown over a saddle,'' she said, straight-faced.

''Well, then, can I talk you into accompanying me to my castle and giving me a treatment?''

She raised an eyebrow. ''You may have to take your clothes off.''

She thought she would never tire of watching that smile of his dance around his mouth and into his eyes. ''I'll try to do it in a proper, courtly manner,'' he said.

HARLEQUIN SUPERROMANCE®

WOMEN WHO DARE
They take chances, make changes
and follow their hearts!

Christmas Star
by Roz Denny Fox
Harlequin Superromance #672

Since her childhood, Starr Lederman has always wished on
what her mother called the Christmas star—the first star out
on those December nights just before Christmas. Now her
adopted daughter, SeLi, does the same thing.

But SeLi isn't wishing for toys or video games. She's
out for the serious stuff—a dad for herself. Which
means a husband for Starr. And SeLi's got a man all
picked out. Clay McLeod, rancher.

Clay's not looking for a wife, though. Especially not a woman
as independent and daring as Starr. A woman *he* believes is
having an affair with his brother. His married brother.

But at Christmastime, things have a way of sorting
themselves out....

Available in December, wherever
Harlequin books are sold.

a heartwarming trilogy by *Peg Sutherland*

Meet old friends and new ones on a trip to Sweetbranch, Alabama—where the most unexpected things can happen...

Harlequin Superromance #673 *Double Wedding Ring* (Book 1)

Susan Hovis is suffering from amnesia.

She's also got an overprotective mother and a demanding physiotherapist. Then there's her college-age daughter—and Susan also seems to have a young son she can't really remember. Enter Tag, a man who claims to have been her teenage lover, and the confusion intensifies.

Soon, everything's in place for a Christmas wedding. *But whose?*

> Don't miss *Double Wedding Ring* in December, wherever Harlequin books are sold. And watch for *Addy's Angels* and *Queen of the Dixie Drive-In* (Books 2 and 3 of Peg Sutherland's trilogy) this coming January and February!

3WED-1

HARLEQUIN®

CHRISTMAS ROGUES

is giving you everything you want on your Christmas list this year:

- ✓ -great romance stories
- ✓ -award-winning authors
- ✓ -a FREE gift promotion
- ✓ -an abundance of Christmas cheer

This November, not only can you join ANITA MILLS, PATRICIA POTTER and MIRANDA JARRETT for exciting, heartwarming Christmas stories about roguish men and the women who tame them—but you can also receive a FREE gold-tone necklace. (Details inside all copies of Christmas Rogues.)

CHRISTMAS ROGUES—romance reading at its best—only from HARLEQUIN BOOKS!

Available in November wherever Harlequin books are sold.

HARLEQUIN®
AMERICAN ROMANCE®

"Whether you want him for business...or pleasure, for one month or for one night, we have the husband you've been looking for. When circumstances dictate the need for the appearance of a man in your life, call 1-800-HUSBAND for an uncomplicated, uncompromising solution. Call now. Operators are standing by...."

Pick up the phone—along with five desperate singles—and enter the Harrington Agency, where no one lacks a perfect mate. Only thing is, there's no guarantee this will stay a business arrangement....

For five fun-filled frolics with the mate of your dreams, catch all the 1-800-HUSBAND books:

#596 COUNTERFEIT HUSBAND
by Linda Randall Wisdom in August
#597 HER TWO HUSBANDS
by Mollie Molay in September
#601 THE LAST BRIDESMAID
by Leandra Logan in October
#605 THE COWBOY HIRES A WIFE
by Jenna McKnight in November
#609 THE CHRISTMAS HUSBAND
by Mary Anne Wilson in December

Coming to you only from American Romance!

HFH-1